SEVEN MILES TO SUNDOWN

BOOK YOUR PLACE ON OUR WEBSITE AND MAKE THE READING CONNECTION!

We've created a customized website just for our very special readers, where you can get the inside scoop on everything that's going on with Zebra, Pinnacle and Kensington books.

When you come online, you'll have the exciting opportunity to:

- View covers of upcoming books
- Read sample chapters
- Learn about our future publishing schedule (listed by publication month *and author*)
- Find out when your favorite authors will be visiting a city near you
- Search for and order backlist books from our online catalog
- Check out author bios and background information
- Send e-mail to your favorite authors
- Meet the Kensington staff online
- Join us in weekly chats with authors, readers and other guests
- Get writing guidelines
- AND MUCH MORE!

**Visit our website at
http://www.kensingtonbooks.com**

RICHARD S. WHEELER

SEVEN MILES TO SUNDOWN

PINNACLE BOOKS
Kensington Publishing Corp.
http://www.kensingtonbooks.com

Chapter 1

The town of Rio Blanco had no reason to exist as far as Elwood LaGrange could see. The little adobe town huddled in a dry gulch in western New Mexico Territory, miles from anywhere and serving no purpose. It did not cater to surrounding ranches because there weren't any. A few sourdough prospectors occasionally sought a grubstake from anyone with folding money in his pockets, but only a few.

There was not even a river, which added mystery to the name of the place. There was a sleepy hardware store, a livery barn, three grim cafés, four tired saloons, a dry-goods and grocery emporium, and a scatter of mysterious adobe houses. What people did for a living in Rio Blanco was a vast and impenetrable mystery to LaGrange, although the Mexicans took a living from their gardens of beans and squash and chili peppers, and the scrawny sheep they ran up in the barren hills.

Of course there was the law office of Bixby and Crown, portly gentlemen in black broadcloth suits who frequently dined at the board-and-batten Mint Hotel, even if they had no clients. There was the fieldstone Cimarron Bank on the corner of Casa Grande and Silver Streets, which did no business to speak of because no one had any money, and the scattered establishments of blacksmiths, harness makers, tonsorial parlors, and assay offices. LaGrange could not imagine what these firms lived on, for it was impossible to thrive in a place like Rio Blanco, a town without visible means of support, where dogs slept in the middle of the main street.

There was, also, the white stucco mansion on the nearest rise, a two-story affair with Doric pillars, reminiscent of a Southern plantation home. Elwood knew a beauteous young woman named Guadalupe O'Rourke inhabited the place, but he had rarely seen her. The lamps were extinguished at eight each evening up there. It was whispered she was enduring tragedy.

The only place in the whole town that showed signs of life was the office located above the Cimarron Bank, with gold letters on the pebbled glass door that said MINING PROPERTIES, and beneath it, MALACHI CROMWELL-NAST. Mr. Nast, a gaunt man with chin whiskers and an embarrassed, penitent look, like a Baptist about to receive the full immersion, was rarely visible and LaGrange imagined he spent most of his time in Silver City, where life had some amenities. But there was a lot of traffic in and out of that office.

Since no one was ever on the streets, especially around noon when the sun bore down and a turtle could negotiate Casa Grande Street without the faintest prospect of being run over, Elwood had arrived at a certain conclusion about Rio Blanco: It might blow away whenever a dust devil took it. If Rio Blanco vanished, the world would not be a poorer place.

LaGrange felt at home there because he had no reason to exist either, so he and the town shared the same indifference to the business of living. A modest inheritance guaranteed him a comfortable life, so he would never have to toil for the rest of his days or want for anything or struggle to fulfill any destiny. He had no ambition whatsoever, but he had concealed that reality with some gentleman C's when he studied at Dartmouth, mostly to please his parents, who were now dead and had left him in pleasant circumstances. He was a part owner of the Maine and Nantucket Railroad and a few other delicious properties.

He knew, of course, that the frowning moralists of the world required that he have some serious reason to exist. The world didn't much care for lazy, rich ne'er-do-wells, so he declared himself a lexicographer in pursuit of the new-minted word, and set forth to snare some virgin words like a butterfly collector armed with a net and some stickpins. But that was merely a face-saving front. Obviously, new, improved words would only be found in new, improved places, such as the West, so he had drifted west, content to stare at the hills and yawn after lunch. He had collected a few Western words or phrases, of which his favorite was "stump sucker," a nag that gnaws wooden posts. He had a dozen more on his list, but nothing to equal that colloquial beauty. Maybe that would make him famous: Elwood LaGrange, the man who discovered "stump sucker," a veritable Noah Webster.

He might have no reason to exist, but he did discover ways to entertain himself, the principal one being an unsuspected gift of being slightly obnoxious to others. So there he was in Rio Blanco, a town without purpose, looking for ways to entertain himself, largely by offending as many people as possible. He was especially good at offending others without their knowing it.

But the odd thing about Rio Blanco was that he had great difficulty offending anyone. The citizens of Rio Blanco, about evenly divided between Anglos and Mexicans, did not have an ear for insults, and therefore missed all the offenses that LaGrange heaped over their heads, including calling a few of them stump suckers.

Either that, or the town people had a broad tolerance for odd fellows in tan corduroy jackets, brown plaid knickers, and furry deer-stalker hats. Elwood sported a bushy mustache, which erupted darker brown than his almost-blond hair, which he let grow very long, hoping to offend a cowboy. He often spent his afternoons in the Tia Juana Café, a sourdough prospectors' haunt, notebook before him, listening for new words, but he rarely heard any. Prospectors, as a class, were not gifted with words. Not that it mattered. He might drift on to some other place and sit and listen if he got bored in Rio Blanco.

All of that changed one sleepy spring afternoon. A big brown mule trotted down Casa Grande Street and halted before the Cimarron Bank, its lathered sides heaving, its head drooping. Straddled atop this abused beast was a sourdough prospector of indeterminate age, a man who was plainly in bad straits. In fact, he sagged and slowly toppled to the clay street, sprawled out there in the noonday sun, clutching a grimy white cotton sack.

There being no crisis worthy of the name in Rio Blanco, it took some while for a crowd to gather and stare at the impudent fellow who was halting such traffic as passed down the main street of Rio Blanco. Elwood LaGrange saw all this from the window of the café, and thought the novelty was worth investigating, so he paid his nickel for the coffee he was nursing and meandered into the thoroughfare, blinded by the light of midday New Mexico.

He peered down upon the sourdough, who was clearly in a bad way, his face twisted into a grimace. Around his left thigh was some sort of tourniquet, a belt that had been wound tight with a stick, and below this barrier the leg had ballooned to twice its normal size, bulging the man's britches.

The prospector was gasping for air, and Elwood could see his lungs pumping.

"Bit by a rattler," the man gasped. "Here, look at this!"

He thrust the grimy bag at the nearest spectator, who happened at that moment to be Elwood.

"I found the Lost Doubloon Mine," the man rasped. "Found her, found the gold, and then I got bit backing out of the hole."

Elwood peered into the grubby sack and found it full of milky quartz rock. He feared a rattler might be inside, and dug in gingerly, pulling out a fine specimen of quartz laden with visible native gold that ran in wires and nubbins through the rock.

"The Lost Doubloon! A miracle!" cried an excited clerk with an armband. "Everyone's heard of that!"

"Oh!" said someone, and snatched it from Elwood's paw. Within moments, the grubby sack had been emptied of its contents, and the gathering crowd was studying the gold ore, marveling at its richness.

At that critical moment, the prospector lapsed into a coma.

"Where?" said Malachi Cromwell-Nast, who had descended from his upstairs lair.

The prospector's eyes closed.

"Where, man, where?" asked Nast, kneeling over the prostrate form.

"Vat's your name, fool?" demanded Sergei Gudonov, a revolutionary living in an adobe home on the outskirts of town, seeking gold to start overthrowing governments he despised. Gudonov was the closest thing to a friend that Elwood had.

"I think his name is Hayes," said someone.

"No, it's Stark," said someone else.

"I allus called him Pete," said the livery hostler.

"His name is Villmer," someone said.

"Where, blast it, is the Doubloon Mine?" yelled Nast, bellowing into the prospector's ear from a distance of six inches.

The prospector's sweated mule took offense and kicked Nast in the butt.

There was no sign of life from the prospector. Elias Bloom, the local cabinetmaker and undertaker, assumed the role of physician, there being none in town except for a *curandera* in Mextown that no one trusted, and listened, ear on chest, for signs of life. At last he rose and shook his head.

"Done for," Bloom said. "I guess I'd better plant him. I'll take my pay in the gold."

"Oh, no, you won't," said Nast. "The county will pay."

"Zis has no county here," said Sergei.

Bloom opened the sack and held it out so spectators could return the gold, but a funny thing happened. There was not a piece of quartz in sight. Elwood marveled. Moments before, there had been fifty or so pieces of quartz ore being examined in that crowd, and now there were none.

Nast lifted the prospector up to a sitting position. "Now where did you find the Doubloon?" he roared.

But the prospector had breathed his last.

"Ve haff a fortune and no one knows where," said Sergei. "Maybe I get lucky. Soon I can start a revolution."

"Go fly your flags in Timbuktu," Nast retorted.

Elwood discovered Guadalupe O'Rourke standing at the outer rim of the crowd, and she took his breath away. Glossy jet hair framed a creamy oval face. Two huge lavender eyes peered sweetly upon this sad scene. A tight black silk dress barely concealed a lush figure. In her soft golden hand was one of the missing pieces of ore. She was the sort of woman who turned men into tongue-tied adolescents.

"I'll bury him. And I'll take care of the mule," she breathed, and no one stopped her. She took hold of the reins and started away.

"I'll put him in the livery barn," said the hostler.

She smiled sweetly and shook her head. "You look

after this poor man," she said. "I'll take care of his mule."

Elwood liked her. She was the only civilized person, barring himself of course, in the mob.

"What name do I use?" Bloom asked.

No one knew.

"I'll call him Pete Stark," Bloom said. "That's as good as any. Rest in Peace, Pete Stark, died 1883."

"Ames," said Nast. "Blossom Ames. I know him."

"What is the Lost Doubloon Mine?" demanded a whiskey drummer, affronted by his own lack of knowledge.

"It's why Rio Blanco is here. It's why Rio Blanco's been here over a century," said Nast. "It was lost after a typhoid epidemic, and that's all I'm going to tell you."

Elwood studied several faces, and could pretty well pick the ones who knew the story of the Lost Doubloon Mine. Oddly, he knew the story very well, having heard it while eavesdropping on prospectors in the Tia Juana Café. But Nast had it wrong. Legend was that the whole town had died of the plague, the Black Death, over a century ago. *The plague.* Legend had it that the mine was the richest in the world. If Nast found the mine, he would buy New Mexico, and maybe Texas too. If Sergei ever found it, he could finance enough revolutions to install himself the Holy Byzantine Emperor of Eastern Europe.

Elwood yawned. It had been an amusing noon.

Chapter 2

She had the prospector's mule. She feared the crowd would stop her, but no one did. The mob was transfixed by gold and death and lust for riches. Soon they would start thinking and want the mule, but they wouldn't get it, not if she could help it.

Guadalupe O'Rourke hastened along Casa Grande Street, wishing to distance herself from that crowd. The mule came along easily enough, tired as it was. It was plainly glad to be unburdened of the dying prospector, whatever his name was. She peered back fearfully, afraid someone would notice and take after her, but no one did.

She turned into her lane, which rose steeply to the great home above Rio Blanco. On a plateau behind the manse there was a carriage barn and pens, and she headed there. The mule was the key to everything. If let loose, it might take her to the lost mine. Even if not, she might be able to study its hoofprints and tell them from the thousands of other hoofprints in the area, and maybe with careful searching and matching, she might find her way to the legendary mine.

The clay of Casa Grande Street was covered with hoof and boot prints, all indistinguishable in the dust. No one could possibly trace the prospector's route back to the bonanza. But she could! She studied the mule, finding an ordinary beast without distinction. *Bueno!* She would, if pressed, hand the mob one of her own, close enough to the prospector's mule so that those gold-maddened men would not know.

Madre de Dios! She needed the gold, fast, all of it, before she perished. She reached the crest of her hill, her heart pounding because the rise to the mansion was so steep. Ricardo had wanted it so; had wanted men's hearts to pound by the time they reached his massive front door.

She hurried around the back, opened the gate to the pen, and led the mule through it and into a shadowed stall. There she removed the mule's crude bridle, a halter actually, and searched for a place to hide it. She spotted some planks across beams above, and tossed the prospector's halter there, making sure it was totally out of sight. She swiftly brushed the mule, removing white-caked sweat and all marks of passage. It was a docile animal that let her stroke its pelt and lift its hooves. She lifted each one, studying the shoes for anything unique, any telltale sign that would enable her to pick up the trail. When she got to the off hind shoe, she found what she was looking for; this mule had a slight limp that had worn and rounded the inside of the shoe but not the outside, and gave the hoof a slightly cocked or twisted step. She walked the mule around in the dust, noting the unique print. *Bueno!* A good tracker could find such a thing outside of town. Others would not know what to look for. Not for nothing had she been a horsewoman all her days.

She would start soon. It would take some planning. No doubt every fool in Rio Blanco was right now rushing to his casa to load up some beast of burden with food and a few tools, and hasten into the hills. They would wander for a few days and return without finding the great mine. Such was the fate of fools.

By this very evening there would be a hundred hombres hunting for the newly found mine. By tomorrow evening there would be two hundred. Within a week there would be a thousand, from distant places such as Silver City, all poking and probing every outcrop of rock in every remote and silent corner of western New Mexico. They would bump into one another, shoot one another, steal precious water, poison wells, lame others' animals, lie and steal, for such was the behavior of otherwise civilized mortals when afflicted with the gold madness.

It did not matter. For generations, determined men had hunted for the great and legendary Doubloon Mine and had not found it. They would not find it now, unless that nameless prospector had been unusually foolish and left signs, which she knew had not happened. The vast country stretching across arid country from the Rio Grande to the mountains of Arizona would hold its secret. And she alone had the key, a unique hoofprint. But the key would not last. Wind and rain and sun would demolish tracks. A single spring deluge would wipe out forever any sign left by that mule. The stampede that even now was beginning would obscure the tracks. And then her prize, the shod mule, would have no value at all. She would act swiftly, had to, or she would lose everything. She knew this land better than any of the newcomers. She had traveled it with Ricardo. She would prepare properly and not rush off half-equipped, and come to ruin a few days or weeks later. But above all, she knew the legend. She knew the mine was close, within easy walking distance of Rio Blanco.

Let them all stampede. They would all be back in a few days or weeks, half-starved, destitute, defeated, crazed, mad, desolated. The vast and mysterious arid mountains that rose in most directions would defeat them. Springs were scarce and sometimes the water was poisonous. The silence alone could fever the imagination, drive men mad, terrify even the boldest. The mountains were forbidden land, filled with treacherous chasms, mirages, illusions, brutal heat, parching winds, sudden summer deluges that crashed down and demolished camps or drowned horses. And also the swift deadly arrows of the Apaches.

That huge land took its toll even of the hardiest prospectors. She knew there were scores, maybe hundreds, who had drifted into that dry furnace land, rocky cliffs devoid of vegetation, and never returned.

Yes, she would take much care. She headed for the sunlight streaming through one of the great windows, light that brightened the manse at certain times of the day, and there she examined the nugget. It actually was an ounce or so of quartz, the nubby gold half embedded in a creamy matrix, the gold pure and pocked and twisted in the way it had collected in the rock. She pulled out some tiny rimless spectacles so she could see closer. She didn't know much about geology or mining, but she would be an eager student. She had to be. There were no options left.

Ricardo was missing. For two years she had waited, a lamp in the window. The estate earned nothing. Thousands of hectares of land, several ranchos, none of them earning her a *centavo*. Scores of mining claims, none of them producing. She could not even find the titles to them. What had Ricardo done with all his wealth? She was in debt, or so she was told. She could remedy it only in one way: declaring Ricardo dead and becoming the wife of some man she cared nothing about.

She examined the nugget once more and hid it in the sugar jar in her kitchen. Now she must act swiftly. She was undecided whether to go alone or trust a partner. She would rather go alone. She knew things she didn't want to share with anyone, especially the rude and untrustworthy Anglos who had drifted into Rio Blanco. On the other hand, she was a woman, and sometimes a woman needed a man. . . .

While she was debating all this, she began surveying her house, looking for the things she would need: Out in her sheds were two packsaddles and harnesses, each with panniers. In her kitchen were utensils. In her sheds were mining picks, hammers, chisels, a gold pan, and Ricardo's field kit, with some vials of chemicals. She knew how to use them all. In the shed was a slicker. In the mansion was a bedroll.

She would go alone, and in the dark, and hope to be well outside of town. The dying prospector had come from the east. She would head east. But once out of the Rio Blanco canyon, she would turn north off all roads and trails. At least all modern ones. She and Ricardo had found traces of very old roads, worn into ruts by the passage of lumbering wooden-wheeled narrow carts drawn by burros; transportation that preceded the arrival of all the English-speaking ones.

A knock interrupted her thoughts. She opened to discover Malachi Cromwell-Nast on her veranda, a man she did not want to see.

"*Sí?*"

She guarded the door, did not invite him in, though it was rude of her not to.

He smiled morosely, and tipped his stovepipe hat, obviously aware of her feelings. "It's about your kind offer to care for the man's mule," he said. "I thought it'd be my bounden duty to take care of it, and of course I'll pay for the man's funeral as well. He's a countryman of mine. No need for you to become involved."

"You can have the mule. I don't want him," she said.

His brows rose slightly. "Why, then I'll just take him."

"I only did it because I pitied the poor man. Imagine, reaching this town only to die. It is a sad thing to see life flee from anyone. It hurt me to look at him."

"The mule?"

"Why do you want it?" she asked impulsively, waiting for the lie.

He surprised her. "The mule is not your property. I grubstaked the man, and the mule will help me recover my loss."

"What was his name?"

"Ah . . ." There was the smallest hesitation. "Blossom Ames," he said.

So he was lying after all, she thought. She shrugged coldly. "I will give him to you. And the halter too. But I'm going to pay for the burial. It's the decent thing to do."

He nodded. "I thought you might insist."

She led him around the side of the house and toward the rear slope, where the pens and stables and sheds snugged against a cliff. She grabbed the prospector's halter, walked straight to the one of her own that most resembled the prospector's, and slid it easily over the animal's head, tying it in place. It was a little large, and she hoped Nast didn't notice.

But he did. "Are you sure that's the one?"

She shrugged.

"I want the one."

"Did you see shoes on the prospector's mule?" she asked. He hesitated, and she knew she had him there.

"A brand?"

He shook his head.

"Was it a jenny?"

He smiled slowly, an odd amusement corrugating his morose face. "Mrs. O'Rourke, it was not this one. It was that one there," he said, pointing correctly. "And I will take him. You may put that halter on him."

"Bastante!" she said, so softly she wondered if he heard it. He ignored her.

"You will not take my mule," she snapped.

"It's my mule," he said. "See?" he dug into his breast pocket. "Here are the papers." He handed them to her.

They were not a bill of sale or a title to a mule, but a fifty-fifty grubstake agreement between Malachi Cromwell-Nast and someone, maybe no one, named Blossom Ames.

Chapter 3

Sergei Gudonov studied certain medical texts he had at hand. The dying prospector's gray and shiny leg had grossly swollen; there had been a crude tourniquet above the snakebite. There had been open bleeding around the man's mouth and no doubt massive internal hemorrhage. The man was in shock, with blue lips, shallow breath, and waxen complexion.

Gudonov did some swift calculations: The man had been bitten no sooner than one hour before arriving in Rio Blanco, but most likely around two hours. It depended on the amount of venom the snake had delivered. Even the age of the snake mattered. Yes, two hours would be an excellent compromise. It would have taken the sourdough some minutes to overcome the initial shock, bleed his wound and apply a tourniquet, and find and mount his mule. The mule, not a fast animal, might have managed two or three miles per hour hauling that inert flopping burden up and down steep slopes.

The lost mine was plainly closer to Rio Blanco than most of those idiots imagined. Probably within a three-mile radius, given the prospector's condition, and maybe even less than that. No road from Rio Blanco followed a straight line for more than a few hundred yards, and none was horizontal for more than a few yards. Happily, he put aside his texts and tore his computations to shreds.

Sergei had an enormous head, which bulged out

above his eyes and ears like the cap of a mushroom. He knew he was several hat sizes larger than anyone he had ever met, and therefore had a larger and more excellent brain, and therefore was that much smarter than anyone. This huge and piercing intelligence was now harnessed to the urgent business of overthrowing the Czars. The Romanovs were idiots and so were all their cousins. Russia could better be governed by baboons. The fatuous nobility was utterly corrupt and greedy and oppressive, and spent their time bleeding the serfs of every last ruble. The army was weak and full of rivalry and malice, and large parts of it could easily be bought, a simple transaction intended to fill the coffers of a few swinish imperial officers whose only allegiance was to their purse.

Ha! That's what Sergei was here for. A revolution required cash, lots of it, preferably precious metals rather than treacherous paper. Gold to fill palms and evoke lust. Gold to buy arms. Gold to persuade certain key people to look the other way, do nothing, smile, and shake their heads. Gold to buy pamphlets. Gold. He had puzzled how to get gold, the essential metal that would fuel a revolution, and had concluded there were only two ways: theft or discovery.

Some of his colleagues had taken to theft, which he regarded as stupid and dangerous. Several had been tossed into dungeons and tortured until they blabbed the whole plan. And Sergei's name was among those collected by the Czarist secret police, which is why he was no longer residing along the Volga River, but almost as far away as he could go.

Ah! Better to live obscurely and safely in the New World, pounce like a giant cat on the riches lying everywhere in this virgin hinterland, and then, with the appropriate moment and a few million rubles in hand, buy a revolution. It amused him. Russia could be bought.

He rubbed his hands, as he always did when his rigorous and intelligent ideals were rolled out for examination. He had headed for Rio Blanco precisely because it was the most likely place to find gold. Minerals bloomed in every outcrop of western New Mexico. He had systematically examined the legends and known gold and silver deposits of the American West, and heard about the Lost Doubloon Mine, supposedly near the isolated town of Rio Blanco. It was a credible story: a thriving Mexican gold town a century ago, with a mine nearby that disgorged tons of gold quartz that was shipped to the City of Mexico to line the pockets of the corrupt and rich. And then the sudden epidemic, Black Death, bubonic plague, that had decimated Rio Blanco, and then the blank history, the survivors slumbering in obscurity. Finally, generations later, the Anglos had found a few Mexicans living there for no reason at all except it was where they had always been, tending their gardens, raising a few sheep and goats, fearful of Apaches. The mine? What mine? A blank page. Oh, the Doorway to Hell; yes, they'd heard of that. A strange story about the ancients. Someone had walked into a hole, found gold, but the Devil caught him and everyone had died.

The mine was there! The legend recorded it. So did certain archives in Mexico City. And he had spent months probing the memories of older Mexicans, studying the primitive roads and burro trails, looking for signs of heavy *carretas* hauling ore on their primitive wooden wheels.

And now a major coup! Sergei studied the gold quartz he had pocketed, admiring the flecks and nodes of pure gold in it that were visible under his glass. A simple mill operation to pulverize the quartz and then amalgamate the particles of gold with mercury would suffice handsomely. The great revolution would soon be funded, a cornucopia of gold that would guillotine Czars and Czarinas before cheering multitudes, buy the cartridges that would kill the nobility, one by one, before firing squads, hang the corrupt civil servants by their fat necks, butcher the Czarist police after unmanning them. Ah!

He placed his huge stub-fingered hand across his huge brow, feeling the pulse of intelligence within his skull.

He had focused his enormous intelligence upon geology and mineralogy and mining, plowing through books published in four languages, mastering by sheer booklearning, in a few weeks, what mining engineers and prospectors and mine supervisors required a lifetime to master. He had been a surgeon's mate among the Orenberg Cossacks, mastering medicine until he privately knew he was better at it than the corrupt and stupid doctors he worked with. That was how he knew about the bite of pit vipers such as the Western American rattlesnakes. He knew that the venom destroyed blood vessels until the victim bled to death within.

The Cossack physicians dabbled with tinctures and sawed limbs and played chess; Sergei devoured German texts and followed the experiments of Pasteur and Lister. But Mother Russia did not value intelligence or competence, quite the contrary: Any man who showed signs of superiority endangered himself, and was likely to end up in a dungeon or plowing tundra in Siberia. Ah! It would be so good to create a nation that valued wisdom and intelligence! He would like to govern it; he had the native gifts that would be required, especially a willingness to hang the stupid.

But all that was for the future. Right now he must see to several things: He must spread the word that the prospector was eight or ten hours away when bitten, and so draw all the gold-rush fools out into a diaspora far from Rio Blanco. How naive these Americans were. They would believe anything, especially from a brusque foreigner. And then he must began a quiet, systematic search of the rugged countryside east of Rio Blanco, the most likely area.

Of course, some idiot might happen upon a pile of the mule's spoor at the mine entrance and claim the prize before Gudonov found it. Luck was always a possibility. Gudonov sighed. He would do what he had to do, eliminate the lucky. The fate of one mortal was nothing compared to the fate of a nation yearning to be freed from its oppressor. So, what did it matter? One life was nothing, just dust. But the vector of his thoughts bothered him. Could there not be a revolution built on principle?

But luck had not led anyone to the Lost Doubloon for a century. He smiled, knowing what he would do next. He would improve his own luck. He whirled out into the city with giant, muscular strides. In the yellow clay streets of Rio Blanco he spotted all the signs of a gold rush; men were crowded around the hardware store, stuffing pans and picks and shovels into their kits. He saw no women at all, but there were few enough in town, and almost none of them Anglos. Knots of men exchanged ideas. Go here, go there, Stark or whatever his name was had come down from the east; look for spoor, fresh spoor would tell the tale. Gudonov smiled. Within hours, the whole area would be littered with fresh mule and horse manure.

He joined one of the knots of men. "I tell you," he said in his stiff English, "I tell you, this man vass at least twenty hours dying. That long it takes for the leg to swell up. He rode most of a day and night, yes?"

"How do you know?" asked a sourdough with an untrimmed beard.

"Vass I a surgeon's mate in the Russian cavalry?"

"You think he rode that long?"

"Maybe longer. Who dies from a rattlesnake at once, unless the fangs cut a blood vessel? This man was struck in the muscle of the calf. Too bad he didn't get here sooner. One could get help, get someone to suck the wound, draw the venom. But he had a long way to go."

Men nodded wisely. That was all that was needed. Gudonov repeated his theory here and there. Within a few days, most of the prospectors would be a dozen miles away. Not a soul refuted or questioned his wisdom. He knew his theory would spread from man to man to man. Not many gold-seekers were secretive. Most traveled in packs.

He returned, contentedly, to his adobe home, watching half-a-dozen more gold-seekers head out of town, most on foot and tugging a burdened burro or mule. He would have to see to his own kit, but he planned on leaving at midnight and was in no rush. There would be some moonlight to guide him.

He wished he had some topographic maps, but all he would have was his own memory and some notes from his own all-too-casual previous explorations of the hills near Rio Blanco. Most of the rises were naked igneous rock with a little cactus or greasewood in the creases. He could not imagine how a mine might be concealed where everything was visible, the air was transparent, the sunlight glared and probed into every crevice and corner.

Still, this was not just rough country; it was brutal. Not enough rain had fallen over aeons to smooth it down, erode its harshness. It exuded a sinister and secretive quality, as if it held dark secrets too terrible for mere mortals to contemplate. There were no real ranches; the scrub vegetation supported little but an occasional goat.

Sergei packed methodically. He was an army man, used to the field, knowing exactly what would keep him alive, healthy, and comfortable. He would respect the murderous sun, take a small canvas shelter against wind and rain, and the hatchet, mining hammer, horn spoon, and pick and shovel that would be essential. He added a blowpipe and charcoal briquettes and a tiny iron mortar and pestle. He pulled from a drawer the Smith and Wesson Russian it amused him to own, and a box of cartridges. He added a pair of thick Hudson's Bay blankets and a canvas sleeping sack. He carefully wrapped a syringe and some potassium permanganate crystals that, dissolved in water, could swiftly be injected in the event of a rattlesnake bite.

That left food. He needed very little because he intended to stay within a day's walk of town, for he was persuaded the Lost Doubloon was no more than two days' walk from Rio Blanco and that was why the ancient town existed. Two one-gallon canteens. Some frijoles, always filling. Self-rising flour, salt and sugar and coffee. A small silver vial of vodka he took pains to import from Albuquerque at great cost for comfort and recreation and antiseptic.

He waited until dusk and headed for the livery barn where he boarded an unruly bronc, as the Americans called these native mustangs, and two feisty, sure-footed little burros that could carry fifty pounds each in a packsaddle.

But the livery barn was empty. Not an animal in it. The hostler had vanished. Gudonov grunted and wished he had been swifter. Every four-footed beast in the place had been commandeered, with or without the consent of the owner. Annoyed, he lashed at himself for not using the brain he was possessed of.

But then he smiled. He knew where he might find a pair of fine animals, unless those too had been stolen, which he doubted. He waited for full concealing dark, leisurely sipping vodka in his kitchen, liking the bright intensity of the stars, and then climbed the hill toward Mrs. O'Rourke's darkened manse.

Chapter 4

Guadalupe O'Rourke fumed. Malachi Cromwell-Nast had taken the mule, and she didn't doubt that he had employed a ruse. He was incapable of an honest act. He got what he wanted. He would see for himself that the dead prospector's mule had a peculiar twist to his off hind foot, and it made a distinctive print, and that would give him the advantage he sought. He would soon be out prowling the slopes with all those other gold-mad prospectors aching for fortunes, but hunting for the odd print while the rest studied anonymous rocky slopes.

But she wasn't defeated! She had studied that hoof and the print it made in the tan dust of her stock pen. Indeed, she could walk out there now and see it, that lopsided print, deeper and wider on the outer edge. That print in the dust had burned its way into her mind and she knew she would never forget it. Nast might have the mule, but not all the advantage.

She didn't know exactly what to do, but she knew that within hours she would be off with all the rest, scouring the rocky ribs of land for the Lost Doubloon. She had never done such a thing, but what did it matter? She had need!

How often she had seen Ricardo load up a mule or two and head away. The thought of Ricardo stabbed her as it always did. She was not truly a widow, though

in her heart she feared she was. Richard O'Rourke
had vanished two years ago. No bones were found.
His mules never returned. The equipment he took
with him had vanished with him.

His livelihood was filled with mysteries, and
Guadalupe could not even say for sure just what he
did. He had simply told her he was a trader, but she
knew there was more to it. He was a gunrunner who
regularly delivered arms to revolutionaries in
Sonora. He was older than she by twenty years. He
was rich. He was commanding. He was an hombre!
He had acquired a fortune by mysterious means,
which he never revealed to her, though they were
closer than it was possible for two mortals to be. She
knew he was protecting her with his silence.

She sighed, letting the pain of remembrance well
through her. She could not stop or slow or mute it. A
wash of pain, like an arroyo roaring with water after
a summer's storm, would flood her heart, and then
she would have to sit quietly and wait for the present
time to return to her.

They had met at a *baile* in Hermosillo, the dusty capital of revolution-torn Sonora, where her father had an
estancia that stretched almost to Bahia Kino. And what
an evening that was. She, barely nineteen, raven-haired,
creamy of flesh, small and lithe and lush and ready. He,
an Irish Mexican, graying at the temples, with red-gold
hair, hazel eyes that caught and bored into her until she
felt she had no secrets at all. That night was volcanic.
Lightning from a distant storm over the mountains
flickered. He didn't wait to be introduced, but caught
her elbow and steered her out to the quiet of the veranda. He spoke to her in fluent Spanish.

"I am Richard O'Rourke. I found out your name. It
is Guadalupe. I saw you and loved you. All my days I
have waited for you. I wish to marry you."

She was speechless.

It was the things she did not say that June night that made the night so memorable.

She did not say, "But Señor, we have barely met."

She did not say, "I am flattered, but this is hasty."

She did not say, "I don't even know you. You are an utter stranger."

Instead she said, "Oh, *sí, mi corazon.*"

He said, *"Mañana."*

She did not say, "We must wait!"

She did not say, "But we must get my parents' permission."

She did not say, "Propose to my parents and we will wait a year."

Instead, she nodded and touched his cheek. He kissed her, his lips soft and gentle on her, not burning at all, not brimming with desire, but his very touch made her give way, like a dam breaking under a flood. She had never felt such a feeling.

He said, "A magistrate will do it."

She simply nodded, her mind awhirl, the touch of him so gentle and perfect that she felt she had entered heaven.

And so it was. He was there at the whitewashed adobe rancho the very next morning. He did not ask her to elope with him. Instead, he asked to meet her parents in the shadowed parlor.

The stranger with the red-gold hair stood before her parents, introduced himself in perfect Spanish, took Guadalupe's hand, and asked for their blessings. He did not ask permission; he asked for their blessing.

"And when?" asked her father.

"Come with us to the magistrate," Ricardo said.

"Ah, Dios!"

Her mother smiled.

They were married in a civil ceremony within the hour.

Later, a friend of Guadalupe's teased her a little. "It

was the animal in you that caused this thing," she said, a little enviously.

"No," replied Guadalupe. "I looked into his eyes and I saw paradise."

She smiled at the memory. Not that the animal in her had been ignored. Heaven forgive the madness of her passion. It had been a perfect marriage, though one thing remained unanswered: She didn't entirely know what he did, or how he earned such a substantial living. But what did it matter? She knew only Ricardo, and Ricardo knew only her.

He brought her to this place in the United States, smiling. "It is safer here," he said.

She found herself the mistress of a great house perched atop a hill overlooking a sleepy town. A strange place, but one with grand views. From the west windows she could look out upon noble blue mountains, their tops white in the winter, their upper slopes black with pines. In every direction the town was hemmed by yellow and tan slopes, arid and harsh, a tumble of naked rock. Below was a splash of green, where several wells nurtured trees and fields and gardens that shocked the eye with their verdant color. It was a good place to be, a place to raise sons and daughters. Someday she would conceive . . . when Ricardo returned.

If he returned.

Pray God, before everything was taken from her. The servants were gone. Amidst many tears, she had let them go. She could no longer pay them. Now she was alone, and not even old Alphonso was there to look after her needs or fill the wood boxes or draw water. *Dios!* How would she pay for that prospector's burial? She had volunteered to do it, without thinking.

She would find that gold. The story had fascinated her. The fabulous Doubloon Mine was the reason this town existed. When she closed her eyes, she could feel that mine calling to her, drawing her. She thought she could almost close her eyes and be drawn, step by step, to the hidden entrance. Somewhere, not far away, a fortune slumbered. A dangerous fortune. The mine exuded darkness.

She would find the mine. Ricardo always had pack-saddles and panniers and mules and tack on hand. He needed all these things for his business, whatever it was. He transported things destined for secret places, guns and maybe valuables too. Perhaps even refugees or spies or desperados who needed to cross a border. Often he was gone a week, sometimes two. He would kiss her, smile, and tell her when he might be expected, and he always returned. Until he didn't return.

She remembered shakily the anguish that stretched into days and weeks and months.

Now she would go find the gold. She stepped outside, heading through the familiar dark to the large shed, and found a packsaddle with panniers. It would do. She began collecting what she would need. She had never prospected, never camped alone, never filed a claim or built marker cairns. But all this she would do if she must. She gathered rough clothes. She intended to travel as a man and thereby be less conspicuous. Her jet hair would lift into a bun and slide into a hat. She wished she might go with someone; she could name a dozen men in Rio Blanco who would gladly accompany her. But then she would have to share the mine. No, every instinct told her to go alone; the gold called, it summoned, it sang a song, and she would listen to that song.

By the light of a single coal-oil lamp, she began her preparations. How often she had watched Ricardo do this! Clothing, *sí*. A blanket, *sí*. A canteen, *sí*. A pot, cup, kitchen knife, spoon, tin plate and cup, *sí*. Pinto beans, tins of tomatoes, rice, hard rolls, coffee, sugar, salt, *sí*.

She grew aware of a presence, subtle and unfathomable. Someone was around the casa. She had experienced this a few times, and headed at once for the chest where Ricardo kept his arms. He always had arms, good modern ones that used cartridges and repeated. She selected a shining black Colt revolver she kept loaded with .32-caliber shells.

Yes, someone was about. Someone more felt than seen. She returned to the kitchen and doused the coal-oil lamp so that her eyes would become accustomed to the deep night. When at last the night grew plain to her, she quietly opened the door upon the back patio, which overlooked the pens and sheds.

The mules were stirring. She felt the tread of their hoofs through the slippers she wore, and heard them snuffle and grunt. Then she understood. Someone was stealing them! She hastened into the darkness, aching for the sight of the thief. The mules were hurrying through the gate now, hurrying out into the night, driven from their pen by someone. Some damned prospector whose lust for gold exceeded his honor!

Whoever it was did not see her. She hurried toward the pen, wanting a target. She had never shot at a human being, but would not hesitate now. Whoever was here was no friend of hers. She spotted him at last, or at least a black hat sliding through the night, just behind the mules he was herding before him.

She debated whether to yell. No, that would achieve nothing. A shot in the air might. She lifted her revolver and fired. The noise shocked the night.

"Alto!" she cried. *Halt!*

The thief ducked, his hat no longer rising over the back of the mules. She could see nothing. She heard slaps; the mules broke into a trot. She thought she saw the hombre, leveled her revolver, and fired. It bucked hard in her hand, shocking her wrist. She lowered it, shot again, and again, and again, and again.

A mule shrieked. None stopped. Neither did the thief.

Chapter 5

Guadalupe's finger yanked the trigger again and again, but there was only a click as the hammer landed on empty brass.

"Hijo de puta!" she yelled, and then took off after the retreating mules. She could still hear them, clopping steadily through town.

She waved her empty revolver at the sound, itching to shoot whoever stole Ricardo's mules. She would follow; she would find the *cabrón,* the he-goat, the *ladrón,* the thief. She strode hotly, feeling her heart pound, but the trotting mules gained ground, and then she heard nothing. Someone had pushed them into a yard.

She kept on, patrolling Casa Grande Street, her senses alive. Then she sensed a creature before her, and found a mule, limping.

It was Ricardo's. She knew it at once and pushed back a flood of grief. Her bullet had hurt it.

"Oh, Paco, Paco," she said.

The mule muttered.

It was standing; it could hobble.

She stared, horrified, at the suffering animal.

"Come with me, poor thing," she said.

It did, limping painfully beside her, willing itself to return to the great casa on the hill.

"Ah, Dios," she sighed.

It followed her all the way to the corral, slowly, hobbling steadily.

At the house she found a match, lit a coal-oil lamp, and headed for the pen. She found the poor animal standing stiff-legged, its head low. She swiftly discovered a gash where her bullet had plowed a trench across a stifle. Some blood soaked his flank.

"Ah, Dios," she cried.

There was little she could do. She might try some salve if the mule would stand still and not kick. But that would take two or three people. She put out hay and oats and made sure the water trough was full.

Ricardo always had mules, and sometimes burros too. He would take several of them with him on his trading trips, and kept them all in good condition, extravagantly grained and watered and curried. This one, Paco, was one of his better ones, young and strong and faithful.

She returned to the casa, plucked up the revolver from the kitchen table, ejected the brass cartridges, and reloaded from the pasteboard box of shells Ricardo kept in the drawer. Now let some *ladrón* come!

Tomorrow at dawn, she would slip out and station herself on the east edge of town, and intercept the one who stole her mules. It would be someone lusting for gold. She would sit behind a boulder and wait, and when the he-goat came, she would shove the revolver under his nose, and then watch his eyes widen!

Ah, Ricardo, why didn't you come home? Where are you? She settled, dejected, before the beehive fireplace where live coals took the chill off. How much longer could she hold out? The statements kept arriving. There was something called a mechanic's lien against the casa. There were properties that had been taken away by distant courts. Ricardo had owned this or that, sections of land, ranchos, mining claims, some houses. Now that wolf, Malachi Cromwell-Nast, among others, was attaching them. For what? She did not understand this country or its laws. Why was it necessary for Ricardo O'Rourke, a citizen of Mexico, to live here?

Someday soon, unless she found the gold mine, someone would throw her out of the casa. And then what would she be? How would she live? *Ah, Ricardo* . . . If only she could look into his eyes again, see Paradise again . . .

She had never gone prospecting, but this was not prospecting. She would look for a certain hoofprint in the dust, and then she would try to find others and see the direction they took, and then she would follow backward to the hole in the ground where the *viejos* dug out gold. She would look for this shiny rock, quartz, like the piece she held in her hand. What more was there to it?

She checked on the wounded mule one last time before going to bed, examining it by the light of her lamp. The mule whoofed and brayed softly and limped toward her, moving slowly but without much difficulty. She held the lamp over the injured flank; the blood had clotted along the six-inch ditch that creased its flesh.

"Paco, someday you will be fine. This thing I did to you, it was not on purpose. Please forgive me, Señor Paco."

The mule yawned.

She decided she would walk into the hills in the morning. She didn't need a prospector's kit or a mule, not if she stayed within a mile or two of Rio Blanco. If there had been a mine, the workers in Rio Blanco would have walked to it. So she would walk to wherever it might be. On foot, she could examine the prints of passing animals, study each once closely. Yes, there was something to be said for walking.

Before dawn, she made her toilet and dressed. The

air was cold, so she wrapped a shawl about her, and in a small kid-leather *bolsa* she placed Ricardo's revolver. That was all. She would be gone all day, but did not feel like eating. Maybe when she returned she would eat.

She hiked through the silent town at first light, heading eastward, the way the dying prospector had come. Tomorrow would be the man's funeral. She would attend; she feared no one else would, and she wanted someone on this earth to remember the man and bid him adios, and bless his soul. She would do that.

How strange Rio Blanco was this silent morning. Usually, smoke from breakfast fires filtered out of chimneys, old women in black rebozos might be seen on the streets, along with an occasional cart and saddle horse. But not this strange day, hours after word of a bonanza had exploded upon the town. The place was mostly deserted. Every hombre, including store clerks and hostlers and blacksmiths, had outfitted and vanished into the sinister gulches and ridges that hemmed the town. They were all gold-crazed, maddened by the sight of that ore. None had bothered to have it assayed; they saw gold in the quartz and raced into the hinterland. How many were gone? Three hundred? Maybe more.

She liked the velvety air, soft before the sun stirred it to life, fragrant with the sweetness of spring blooms, spiced with creosote bush, sweet with the hint of snow from the high country to the west, pungent with the eddying scent of water in the mountains. Now she saw two or three men loading their mules, and examined the animals sharply. They were not Ricardo's. She knew her husband's mules well, having groomed and fed and saddled them every day.

She wished she might wear *pantalones* so she might have freedom of movement, but she would not. She was a woman and a wife, and she would wear the proper things that were ordained from the beginning of creation for womanhood.

She did not attempt to look for the print of the strange hoof. Not yet. Not on this artery, where a thousand hooves had trampled every sign of the dying prospector's passage. But there would be a proper time when she was alone and off the path.

She spotted an escarpment ahead, a lofty overlook that would suit her purposes, and veered off the trail to reach it. She climbed a rough, rocky slope, wary of snakes, discharging debris that tumbled downward, violating the silence of the sweet dawn. She felt her heart hammer as she scaled a slope that she could barely manage, but when she topped out on the tawny caprock, she beheld the sun just bursting over the eastern ridges, some juniper, and a smooth flat area several yards square. It would do. She studied this aerie for snakes, found none, and settled on the smooth rock. All she had to do was be patient. The thief and her stolen mules would appear soon enough.

She smelled the creosote brush as the sun began to heat the slopes around her, and in the distance she could see the quiet buildings of Rio Blanco, all but abandoned in the gold rush. Then, even as she settled herself, she spotted someone coming, a man with three laden mules, his face obscured under a slouch hat. Ah, maybe the he-goat who stole her stock!

She stared intently, growing frustrated because she could not tell. Not even when the mules were immediately below her lookout could she say. But she doubted that these were Ricardo's because one was almost black. Only one of the three looked at all familiar, and she was simply too far away to say. This high lookout would not work.

Frustrated, she watched the prospector swing easily around a bend, and vanish. She faced a stark decision: Either she would have to sit at roadside and watch the traffic, or else abandon the project. It wasn't hard to decide: Her task was to find the mine, not find the thief. Eventually, she would spot her mules and deal with the thief, but just now she had a larger and more urgent purpose. Descending was harder than ascending, and more treacherous. But she balanced herself carefully, stepped from rock to rock, checked her skidding, and finally reached the dusty and manure-strewn path.

That's when she discovered another person on foot, without livestock, ambling her way. It was the last person she wished to see, one who evoked secret amusement, if not contempt, whenever she saw him. He wore plaid tan knickerbockers with high-top lace boots, a brown corduroy cutaway coat, and a blue silk bandanna about his bosom.

"Why, madam, I believe it's Mrs. O'Rourke," said Elwood LaGrange.

"Have we met?" she asked coldly.

He carefully removed his costly sombrero and smiled toothily. "Oh, we have now, whether or not we have before," he said. "But I won't tell a soul."

"Well, then, *buenos dias*," she said, and started by.

"I could not help but observe your descent," he said. "I am certainly curious about what took you up there."

"I was looking for someone to shoot dead," she said.

"Now that's the best idea I've heard all day," he replied. "May I walk with you?"

"You'll regret it."

"On the contrary, I imagine I'll fill a notebook or two."

She saw he was not going to be put off, so she pursed her lips and proceeded, unwilling to bestow so much as a smile upon the idiot.

Why was she not favored by God?

Chapter 6

Artie Quill would do. The fierce-eyed old scoundrel was just the right man for the task. He was cunning, smart, unscrupulous, and savage when cornered. But he gave all the appearance of bland good cheer and meekness.

Malachi Cromwell-Nast had a special task for the old sourdough, and now was slowly revealing the details. "You'll get two thirds, and I'll get one third," he said, watching Quill's bright cherry eyes light up.

At least for the moment, Nast thought. It wouldn't be hard to clean Quill out of his share. But one did have to hold out bait to catch the fish.

"Well, what's your secret?" asked Quill. "That mine's been hidden for a century."

Quill's nasal whine grated on Nast, who truly detested men who had no polish or cultivation, and detested uncivilized females even more.

"I have the mule. The one carrying that prospector, whoever he was. The mule has a unique rear hoofprint. Not only that, but the mule came from somewhere and might take you back to that somewhere, given a free rein."

"Hoofprint? Ah, a signature, a sign of passage!" Quill's berry-bright eyes lit with amusement. "I'm not sure I'm interested. There's hundreds of square miles, whole ranges, gulches, and ridges. Much of it is rock.

I'm not sure it's worth my time, especially for only two thirds. Now three quarters, that's a sporting chance."

Malachi Nast wrung his bony white hands. "You're the only prospector I'd trust," he said.

Quill smiled toothily. His snuff-stained teeth appalled the fastidious Nast.

"I guess I'd better find someone else," Nast said. "This is all probably a wild-goose chase. You're right. What's a hoofprint? It'll all be trampled over by the end of the day. So many rushing out there."

Quill was still listening, skepticism written all over his hairy face.

"Slim chance of finding anything," Nast said. "But I thought I'd make an offer. I'll grubstake you, as usual, and you get to take the mule."

"Is it yours?"

Nast nodded. "It is now."

"I thought so," Quill said, smiling. "Where is this mine? Nowhere. That gold quartz might have come off a ledge somewhere."

Nast shrugged. "Maybe."

"Where do you think it is?" Quill said.

"An easy walk from Rio Blanco."

Nast stared upward at the serrated walls of tan rock tumbling downward, thrown into disarray by gigantic forces aeons ago. Within a few yards of town was an utter wilderness filled with secret arroyos, twisting canyons, odd overhangs, strange little parks hidden behind clefts, steep inclines leading up to hidden alpine meadows. Up there was mystery and menace. That tumbled country had sucked men into it who were never seen again. That country contained lodes of iron that fouled magnetic compasses, poisonous springs that were surrounded by the bones of unwitting creatures, heat-blasted greasewood, remnants of mysterious ancient cultures.

Quill himself had explored much of it, escaping

only because of his obsession for blazing trails, checking landmarks, leaving signs pointing to exits. Nast knew that, knew that Quill was the man for the task.

"Three quarters," said Quill, licking his lips.

Nast sighed happily. The fish was hooked. "No, that's too much," he said. "I want more than a quarter for a grubstake. I'm giving you the keys to the kingdom."

Quill grunted. "A mule with an odd hind shoe. Good until the next shower."

"All right, you get three quarters," Nast said.

Quill's seamed face slowly relaxed, not into friendship but something darker, and veiled. He never said yes. He didn't need to.

Nast didn't shake hands. The prospector's paws were as horny as a toad's back.

"Go draw your kit at the hardware. Give this chit to Al Swensen."

"I want the mule too."

"If you succeed, yes. If not, you bring it back. I'll give it to another man to do what you failed to do."

Artie Quill licked his lips, which emerged from a sea of wiry facial foliage. He nodded.

"Be quick about it," Nast said. "Your slothful ways won't find the mine."

"Maybe we understand each other, maybe we don't," Quill said. "Where's the mule?"

Nast escorted the sourdough to a private animal yard, well hidden by adobe walls, and pointed.

Quill immediately haltered the mule and then studied the hind hoof and the print it left in the dry clay.

Then he dropped the hind leg and smiled. His lips, surrounded by gray bush, puckered into a winsome little smirk.

"I should demand ninety percent for my cut. This is worthless."

"You'll change your mind the first time you spot that print out there. But of course if you don't want to try . . ." Nast shrugged his shoulders, which bobbed upward within his spacious black suit, and then spread his hands in supplication.

Quill's cherry eyes lit up.

"Don't do anything I wouldn't do," Nast said.

Quill's smirk was satisfying.

The sourdough led the mule through the gate and into the alley, and Nast watched him go. If Quill hadn't been around, Nast might have gone out himself, unsuited as he was for prospecting. A mule that left a unique trail was worth the effort. From his window, which was cleaned daily and hadn't a mote of dust or a smear on it, Nast watched the gluttonous prospector head for Basil Baumgartner's hardware emporium, and within an hour Quill would be outfitted and out of town. Then all there was to do was wait.

The Lost Doubloon was the principal reason that Nast had made a headquarters of Rio Blanco instead of staying down in Silver City, where all the mining activity was. Now it looked like he had a good chance of locating the mine. The history was sketchy but enticing. Unlike all the others who were attracted to the story, he had done his homework in various places, including Mexico City, Durango, and Hermosillo.

The mine had yielded a fortune even before it vanished from known history. Its ore, milky quartz laced with native gold, had been easily reduced by milling, or breaking down the quartz, and then amalgamating the gold with quicksilver, which was then retorted off, leaving only the gold, and a lot of it. Nast had quietly surveyed Rio Blanco, and found the foundation of a great *arrastra*, a stone-built milling area where burros dragging a heavy stone around a circular path crushed the quartz. It had been a crude but effective way for the Mexicans to reduce the ore. They used a similar device to grind wheat or other grain, but none was grown here. He had quietly walked the byways of the sleeping hamlet until he found the milling work. It was in plain sight, though somewhat concealed by desert brush, for all the world to see, and yet only he, Malachi Nast, had found this positive evidence of the mine. But his attempts to trace pathways from the *arrastra* to the mine had met with failure.

So Nast had bided his time, finding other ways to get rich while he continued to hunt for the lost mine. Getting rich was easy. He found properties and claims that had been abandoned, or for which no annual assessment work had been done, such as those held by the O'Rourke widow. He'd snatched them from her, often without her knowing it. She wouldn't know what to do with them anyway. On some he had found small mineral deposits, and these could be exploited or sold to suckers. But his Moby Dick was still the Lost Doubloon. And now it looked like he might have it.

He rubbed his waxy hands, anxious about Quill, wondering whether Quill was the right man. But a survey of his options persuaded him that Quill was not only the right man, but the best man for what followed after discovery. Quill, for all his cunning and genius in the field, had a fatal flaw that made it easy to snatch away everything. Quill had located a dozen mines, a hundred ledges, and had a sense of gold or silver so keen he swore he could smell gold, smell other valuable minerals, and could find wealth with that long thick beak of his.

Artie Quill was something of a genius as a prospector, but a fool whenever he succeeded. For Artie Quill's recreation, whenever he laid claim to some bonanza, was opium. His first business was always to head for the nearest Chinaman, pay his way into a dark, suffocating den, purchase the little brown ball of the narcotic that could be settled into the bowl of a pipe, and remove himself to whatever paradise he wished to visit. Within days, or sometimes a few weeks,

Artie Quill would have lost his bonanza, sickened himself on the Chinaman's product, and found himself nauseous, broke, despondent, blank of mind, and dependent on shrewd observers of human nature, such as Malachi Nast, who by this means had collected thirty or forty good silver, gold, copper, and iron claims across the Southwest.

And now it would happen all over again if Nast's plans were to yield their expected fruit. He had, only a fortnight earlier, imported an opium den into Rio Blanco, and the Chinaman was already doing a good business among the drifters and prospectors floating through town. Nast owned seventy-five percent of the opium den, and was making some tidy income, though nowhere near what might be gotten from such an operation in a larger town. Still, it would serve its purpose and pay well if indeed Artie Quill once again triumphed over the lesser and dumber gold hunters and gave it all away.

Malachi Nast liked to cover all the bets.

Chapter 7

Elwood LaGrange was struck, at that moment, by one of those thunderbolts that only rarely befall any mortal. He saw before him a woman so sweet and dazzling of face and figure and carriage that he fell instantly in love. This Mexican woman had, in a glance, stirred every particle within him. He had seen her many times in Rio Blanco, but now everything was different.

There was more. In that same revelation he saw his whole worthless life for what it was, utter waste and futility. All this happened so fast, like a stroke of lightning frying his mind, that only in the following moments could he put anything into words, or express any of it as feeling.

But he knew, in the tick of a clock, that Guadalupe O'Rourke was the woman of the wildest and most yearning dreams that had ever pierced his calloused soul, and worse, he could never have her, never touch her, never win her, never even earn a smile or a kind thought from her lips, much less a kiss.

Still worse, he knew that his whole futile life had been a waste. He had done nothing of note, avoided striving, achieving, wrestling with great tasks. He knew he had always run away from the smallest difficulties, lied to the world about his vocation, which really was no vocation at all but simply the vapid amusement of a wastrel who clipped coupons from bonds for a living.

Still worse, he knew that so long as he was who he was, this incredible woman would never give him a second glance. He stared miserably at her, aware of the flood of loneliness he felt, a loneliness he had denied he ever felt, a loneliness he hated. He had no friends. Not one. He had no confidant with whom he could share his deepest feelings. He had no colleagues because he worked at no employment. He lacked even so much as drinking companions. He always sat alone in saloons or cantinas. He had shied away from even the humblest and simplest friendships, and hidden behind barriers of insult and superiority and scorn of everyone around him.

He had devoted his dull young life to doing as little as possible, and where had it taken him? Not to poverty, for he was comfortably fixed, but to loneliness and now self-pity. Even friendships require an effort. Courtship and love required even more giving of himself. He thought, chagrined, of all the hours and days and months he had squandered trying to be amused at the world, when he only was starved.

And there she was, walking away.

"Wait!" he cried.

She did, her eyes as cold as the Arctic.

"I . . ." He was speechless.

She turned to leave, but paused, seeing the desperation stamping his face.

"I was looking for someone to walk with," he said.

He watched that glacial gaze melt a little.

"I might be helpful to you. I could carry your bag."

She waited for more, a question in her eyes.

"You're looking for the mine," he said. "Everyone is. The whole town's looking for it."

"Then you know I wish to look for it alone."

"But I can help!"

"No, you can't help."

"We can look together. I can look out for rattlesnakes. I don't need money. I have an income. I
don't need a mine. I just . . ."

He could not for the life of him think of another
thing to say, and it was plain from the glacial stare that
he had not changed her mind.

"You can carry my *bolsa*," she said. "The revolver
is heavy."

He stared, not believing.

She smiled thinly. "If I find the mine and you are
lying to me about not wanting it and try to take it from
me . . . my husband will shoot you, if I don't first."

"I thought . . ."

"That I am a widow?" She shook her head.

All the passion and hope that had burst in him
slowly ebbed. She was married. Maybe O'Rourke was
abroad.

She started again, pausing now and then to study
the trail, as if she were looking for something lost in
the dust. She grew aware that he was watching, and
smiled curtly at him.

"You are looking for something?" he asked.

"The key," she said.

He resolved to look for a key. But there was only tan
clay and a thousand hoofprints, all indistinguishable.

"You have some idea where to look, madam?"

"No, and neither does anyone else."

She paused and pointed. Far up a yellow slope,
half a mile away, two prospectors were clambering
over talus.

"There must be hundreds looking," he said.

"*Sí*, and when word reaches Silver City, there'll be
five hundred more."

"What do you suppose the mine looks like?"

She shrugged, once again studying the earth as if it
might yield some secrets.

A faint trail, most likely worn by game, led to the left and climbed a rugged slope.

"I think maybe I will go up it," she said, turning off the main road.

Here the earth was undisturbed, with none of the marks of passage so plain on the main branch.

This trail rose swiftly, pierced between tumbled rock the size of houses, curled around projecting ledges. Within minutes they had entered a silent, private amphitheater rimmed by forbidding cliffs capped by rims.

He walked behind her, aware of how hard it was for her to negotiate the trail in her skirts. He watched her ahead of him, yearned for the impossible, cursed his own worthless life, and hated her absent husband.

Again she studied the ground, looking for what she called the key, but finding nothing but untrodden clay. They were scarcely a half hour from Rio Blanco by trail, but even closer as the crow flies. He thought the town might be just over that high ridge to the south. But in this maze, who could tell?

She paused and closed her eyes. "*Caramba!* We are close," she said.

But no mine, or tailings, or works, revealed itself to his eyes, and she wondered why she had said it, or felt it. For generations, people had hunted for that mine and had not found it or even found the road from the mine into the village. Every corner of this tumbled land had been poked and probed by shrewd men who could read signs of mineral in the rocks, who knew what colors to look for, what vegetation. But no one had ever found it, and sometimes Elwood imagined it was nothing but a myth.

"Why did you come with me?" she asked suddenly.

"I am lonely."

"Ah, lonely for a woman, I imagine." There was something amused in her face.

"You speak English," he said.

"Ricardo, my *esposo*, speaks both and required me to learn."

"And what brought him to Rio Blanco?"

He sensed reticence on her part. "Trading," she said at last, in a way that closed that topic.

They rounded a bend and plunged into a steep, shadowed canyon whose cliffs rose five hundred feet or more. It had been a waterway, with driftwood piled on ledges fifty feet above them. Now the trail rose steeply, winding them both as they struggled uphill. At every point where there was bare earth, she paused to study the ground, an obsession with something that puzzled him. Whatever she was looking for was not present.

"Why are you lonely?" she asked.

"Because . . . I never lacked for anything." He wondered if she could make sense of that. He wasn't sure he could, or that he could answer her.

The glacial cold had vanished from her eyes and had been replaced by curiosity. She was examining him now and then, as if tentatively accepting what she saw.

She stopped to catch her breath at a place where they could both sit on shelf-rock.

"What do you do?" she asked.

"That's the trouble," he replied.

"Why did you come here? To Rio Blanco?"

"For no reason. I just came, that's all."

She shook her head at that. "What do you want?" she asked.

He closed his eyes. He could not meet her gaze. He knew this day that a person who wanted nothing was not alive, just as he was not alive until an hour ago, when he discovered he wanted everything, especially this strange, secretive woman with the desperate look upon her face.

"I have walked enough. I am going back now," she said.

He stood. "I saw no signs of a mine, but I wouldn't know one if it stared at me from ten feet away."

She smiled at that, as if he had finally said something interesting to her.

Downslope, he talked a little, supposing he probably bored her. He talked about Dartmouth, about not trying, about not training for a vocation, about being given anything he asked for, clothing, travel, theater. It was just a matter of asking either parent, and he got what he wanted. Later, when he had cash in his pockets and was old enough, he experimented, drank too much, explored other vices, but no one cared, and he didn't care about himself, or the future, or what he might do with himself. The East had been a bore, so he came west, and the West had been a bore too, until this day, this walk with a married woman he could never have.

He spoke of some of this, censoring himself, and sometimes she turned to look at him solemnly.

"You are a person who needs to be brought to the table," she said.

It was an odd thing to say, but he agreed, without saying so.

They reached the road east of town, having exhausted themselves clambering through the silent wilderness.

She turned to him. "I will go back alone now," she said. "I wish not to be seen with anyone. Thank you for your company."

He nodded, handed her the fringed leather *bolsa,* and she strode purposefully toward Rio Blanco, a half mile distant, her lovely slim form growing smaller and smaller. He watched her go, the dead watching the living, and wondered whether for Elwood LaGrange there was a future.

Chapter 8

Guadalupe opened her door to Elias Bloom.

"You said you'd pay for the planting," Bloom said, twirling his gray felt hat in his hand.

"Did you have a burial?"

"No one knows him. So I put him under myself."

"I said I'd pay for a burial. A service."

"Now, wait a minute here," Bloom said. "I did it like you said."

"Headboard?"

"No name. So no headboard."

"You dug a hole and put him in. I won't pay until there's a headboard."

Bloom looked so angry she feared he would strike her, but then forced a smile to his sullen lips. "All right. I'll meet you there in an hour."

"What will the board say?"

"Pete Stark."

"No, it'll say, 'Unknown, Rest in Peace, Died, May 23, 1883.'" She thought on it. "And add this in small letters: 'He is missed.' That will comfort his spirit."

Bloom sniffed his superior sniff and retreated down the long hill. It was early evening, but the light lingered long that time of year. There would be light enough. She dug into her last reserve, hidden in a porcelain jar in the pantry, two ancient gold coins given to her by her father, as a sweet adios, at the time

Ricardo took her to the United States. They were doubloons. She felt one's weight and pocketed it, and wrapped a black lace rebozo over her shoulders.

A man deserved to be buried well even if he was a stranger and his name was unknown. Somewhere there would be relatives, maybe parents, maybe brothers and sisters. Maybe a wife or children. Someone loved this lone man, so she would take the sorrow upon herself.

She walked slowly down Casa Grande Street, hushed and deserted now because of the gold rush, past the western outskirts of Rio Blanco, through gentle hills, and then turned off upon a two-rut road that led to the cemetery. She found Bloom there, with a shovel, setting a black-lettered headboard into the yellow soil. To her surprise, Elwood LaGrange was there also, in a brown suit, his hair slicked.

"I saw him coming here, so I thought I'd pay my respects," LaGrange said.

Bloom straightened, done with his task. "Done. I want fifty dollars," he said.

She stared at the cabinetmaker and undertaker, saying nothing. He had daubed the headboard with black paint that was still wet, the words according to her wishes.

She waited for the man to lead a service or at least a prayer, but Bloom didn't. He simply stood, certain his own role was complete.

There was the fresh grave, mounded over with the yellow caliche of the district. Other graves, all Mexican, surrounded this place. None had stones. A few had black iron crosses. A few had withered flowers draped over them. It was a good place to rest forever, with layers of purple and tan ridges rising westward toward snowcapped mountains.

She turned to Elwood. "Would you give this man a prayer?"

LaGrange looked trapped. "Me?"

She nodded.

He saw there was no escape, walked to the head of the grave, and faced his two spectators. Plainly, it was a task he was not equipped to perform.

Then, as if something larger than himself took hold of his mind, he stared down at the dirt.

"Stranger," he began in a gentle voice. "We don't know who you are, so we have no name. But we know you lived a long life and had some luck. We know you'll be missed by someone; by us, for the loss of anyone diminishes us all. We know you found the mine and started the rush, but you didn't live to enjoy what you in your shrewdness and wisdom had uncovered.

"So . . . We're here to wish you bon voyage, to remember you, for we all want to be remembered. If you were lonely, consider us your friends. If you were desperate, consider us your harbor. If you were impoverished, consider us your riches. May God rest your soul and welcome you into his eternal Kingdom."

"Amen," she said.

She thought that was remarkably good. The strange man had an eloquence she never suspected, and maybe he never suspected either.

"All right," said Bloom. "I had to hire two diggers and make the box, and that's fifty."

She stared coolly at the man, whose instinct for commerce didn't allow even a decent interval between the burial and business.

"I have a doubloon," she said. "Here."

She dug into her *bolsa* and extracted the gold coin.

He fingered it, uncertain about its worth. "What's that?" he asked.

"It is a Spanish coin much in use in Mexico. It is worth eight *escudos* or sixteen pieces of eight."

"I don't know about this."

"It is worth more than all the gold in the ore this man brought from the mine." She couldn't resist the rest: "It is worth ten times the price of your soul."

He fingered the gold, smiled suddenly, jammed the felt hat onto his oily locks, and fled.

She turned to LaGrange. "Thank you," she said. "Every man, woman, and child deserves a good death and an adios. I would want such a thing, *si*?"

He nodded, his eyes on the hills. "There is no one who would say good-bye to me."

"Would you like to come with me tomorrow?" she asked. "Maybe we'll do better if we team up."

"I would do my best to help you," Elwood said.

"I know nothing about finding old mines. Maybe you do?" she asked.

"I wouldn't even know a streak of mineral in the rock," he said.

She smiled. "Then we will get lucky, *si*? I do have one small clue."

"What would that be?"

"If I see it, I will show it to you," she said, suddenly guarded.

"Maybe I know more than I think," he said. "I spend my evenings in the saloons where all the prospectors gather. I listen. I have never prospected but I know about color, and float, and what to keep an eye for."

"You will do that then, and keep us safe, and I will look for my own signs."

The crooked hoofprint.

She met him at the Cimarron Bank the next dawn; he was prompt. There was so much rough country to explore that she knew it could take years. But she knew a few other things too. The *viejos*, the old ones among the Mexicans of Rio Blanco, said the hole into Hell was close, not far, nodding sagely at this immutable wisdom. They didn't know how they knew it; only that it was so.

The hole that the Devil had used to escape Hell. That is what they called the Doubloon Mine.

LaGrange had outfitted himself in a way that only someone named Elwood could manage: He wore tan tweed knickers, long green, black, and red argyle stockings, black patent-leather walking shoes, a watch dangling from a gold fob, a pith helmet, tinted pince-nez, a canvas jacket bulging with pockets, and a boiled white cotton shirt pinned at the neck by a black bowtie. He also carried a knobby walking stick of polished blackthorn.

She thought she would enjoy hiking with such an apparition.

"I'll carry the picnic basket," he said, plucking the wicker from her hand.

The air that early was delicious, with freshets of cool eddying down from above, and the shadowed valley comfortable for hiking. Later, it would be fierce. She was sure her companion, this human armadillo, would scare off Gila monsters, and maybe even scorpions, as well as songbirds.

They followed the main trail eastward from Rio Blanco, passing the point where they turned off the day before, even as Elwood squinted knowingly at the jumble of rock, looking for telltale color; browns and reds indicating iron, or greens and blues suggesting copper salts. She, in turn, studied the ground, even though a thousand hooves had trod this trail since the prospector's mule had negotiated it.

Then, behind them and in a hurry, came a prospector riding a giant mule, and leading a smaller, scrawnier gray one. She turned. This one was a veteran sourdough, with a graying beard, a battered felt hat, ragged clothing, and an air of being comfortable in the wild.

She pulled to one side, and Elwood did too, and then she froze. The mule! It was the dead prospector's mule, the very one she had penned. The mule that Malachi Nast had commandeered, probably with fraudulent papers.

"Howdy," said the man, his gaze raking them both, focusing on Guadalupe's grace for a moment, and then startling at Elwood's outfit.

"A great day for javelina hunting," Elwood said.

The prospector guffawed, and dug his heels into his mule's flanks. The mule spurted forward, dragging the pack mule with it.

Guadalupe stopped, let the man and his beasts pass, her gaze boring into the man and his equipage, as if it were something to memorize. When at last the man rounded a bend and silence fell over them once again, she began hunting the earth for sign. It wasn't hard to find.

"Ah!" she cried. "See this!"

"See what?"

"This print!"

"What about it?"

"This is what I am looking for, this print!"

Elwood studied the print, seeing nothing, and finally smiled at her.

"I will tell you about all this, LaGrange," she said, resuming their forward travel. "Memorize this print right here, the odd one, heavy and wide on one side. Study it and know it and never forget it!"

Elwood LaGrange obediently bent on one knee and examined the print in the clay dust.

"Now, now I will tell you!" she said. "This might lead us to the mine."

Chapter 9

Artie Quill smiled as he passed the greaser widow and the fop. Word gets out of a gold strike, he thought, and everyone in a town, down to the saloon swampers, is out hunting for it, picnic baskets in hand.

There was plenty to amuse him this time, especially Malachi Cromwell-Nast, that tarantula who kept spinning his webs over western New Mexico Territory. Nast had spent years angling for gold and silver without ever outfitting himself and heading into the wilds to look for it. He'd never held a pick or a shovel in those waxy white hands. His principal business was euchring anyone who was sucker enough to do business with him.

This time, Nast was nuttier than ever, imagining that an odd telltale hoofprint might be found in hundreds of square miles of desert mountains, and that it might lead to the lost mine. That was the trouble with people who sat around in armchairs and supposed they had any idea of what the real world was like.

Coming across a hoofprint like that in a rocky wilderness like this was a one-in-a-million chance, and the worst possible way to hunt down the old Doubloon Mine. Did he think that such a print would weather more than a few days? Wind and sun and dust would obliterate it. Did he think there would even be hoofprints in country that was almost devoid of soil? Artie had never been in such barren and stony ground, where the lack of rainfall and snow had left the jumbled rocks largely unscathed, sharp-edged, and raw. The sun did more reduction than water in these parts.

Well, the hell with looking for the odd hoofprint. Forget the damned mule. When Nast told Artie that the mule was the big secret and the key to finding the mine, Artie had all but laughed in the man's face. Not that Artie wouldn't examine virgin ground if an odd hoofprint showed up, but he knew better than to waste time. There were, by now, a couple hundred mules, burros, and horses roaming over this arid wilderness, the property of their gold-crazed owners, leaving prints and dung in every arroyo.

Artie had a little secret of his own. He knew the snakebit prospector, whose name he would never reveal because that would give the game away. The dead man was Stud Malone, and Stud always swore there was a mountain of pure quartz gold over in the Mimbres Mountains and there were some old Spanish works there too. So Artie had kept his trap shut, and sure enough, no one else put a name to the dying man.

Plainly, Stud had found the old Doubloon over there, and that's where Artie was heading. Not to the Mimbres Mountains exactly, but to the arid canyons west of there, where Malone had poked around for years, cussing his luck. That was tough country, not much water, and a man could find himself three, four days from the nearest seep. It took a good outfit to survive, and now Artie had one, including Stud's own mule. It wasn't the mule's hoofprint but its homing instinct that might help.

The mule would tell him where water was, where Stud had camped, where there was something to chew on. All Artie had to do was keep a sharp eye on that mule and turn it loose whenever it showed signs of wanting to go somewhere. Artie understood mules. They were his pals. They listened to his windy comments and never argued with him. He knew Stud had hunted gold a hell of a lot farther away from Rio Blanco than Malachi Nast imagined, and that's where he was heading.

That too cheered Artie. If he found the Doubloon, he'd have it to himself. Nast wasn't going to get a dime's worth of ore from it. The Doubloon would stay hidden. Just getting there was so complex Artie wasn't sure he could manage it, at least not until he figured out the route, which would be a dogleg around more obstacles, mostly canyons, than he cared to think about.

Prospecting wasn't for anyone who liked company. Artie had a fine Sharps rifle slung from a sheath under his leg, a rifle he had occasionally used to scare off competition. Let some green prospector get shot at a few times, let a bullet clip rock inches away, and the smart fellow will decide gold's somewhere else. Artie smiled again. There were a few lone sourdoughs who came on anyway, after the warning shot, and were never heard from again.

All that burning day Artie Quill rode southeast, pausing only briefly in the mid-afternoon heat at a cliff side full of petroglyphs where he could duck the sun. Malone's mule bleated once, whickered, and tugged on his line, so Artie let him loose. The mule hightailed down a steep deer trail into an arroyo bottom and drank at a tiny seep that filled a hollow in the rock hardly a foot wide.

Well, well, well. This here mule of Stud's had seen the elephant.

Artie liked that. He watered his riding mule, and then dipped a tin cup into the water, pushed aside a carpet of whining bugs and some green scum, and tasted it. Not bad. An odd flavor. Enough slowly seeping down a granite face to save a life. He wondered if the seep was seasonal, whether it would dry out later in the summer, whether he could dig into the dirt below the spring and fill a cup of water. It was worth knowing. Artie believed in letting his livestock talk to him. Malone's mule had spoken. He also believed he was hot on Malone's trail, with the mule acting so familiar in this silent country. The hardpan was too rocky for hoofprints, but that didn't matter.

He saw no life; not even a vulture. The brassy blue of the sky was oppressive; he ached for a cloud, a thunderhead clinging to a distant peak, some cool forests to rest in, but here was none of that. Only yellow and tan and orange rock, an occasional greasewood or barrel cactus, a sandy watercourse showing the tiny imprints of small animals. And silence.

He didn't sweat. It was too dry. But the sun's glare was so hot he couldn't touch his saddle horn, or any of the iron buckles on his saddle, or the side of his tin canteen. He should have holed up, but he feared someone else among his fraternity of sourdoughs had figured it all out too and was ahead of him. So he pushed onward, not quite knowing where to start looking, but aware of the anonymous rock. When he saw black or red, green, blue, ochre, bright yellow, white, or any rock that shone or glittered, that's when he would stop and make a camp at the first good place, preferably well hidden, shaded, and watered.

Late in that furnace-hot afternoon, a rock slide tumbled downslope before him from somewhere near the ridge five hundred feet up. A shower of dun stone rattled and skidded and banged, disturbing the peace. Quill halted at once, and in one smooth sweep pulled his Sharps out of its sheath and aimed it up there. Something had done that, and he was ready to destroy it.

But he saw nothing. The stock of the Sharps burned in his hands, and the barrel would soon be too hot to touch. He squinted from sun-blasted eyes whose pupils had been bleached by years of abuse, and saw nothing. He jammed the Sharps back in its sheath, and pulled his canteen up. He sucked the hot water, sparing it for future use. He was seven or eight miles from that seep, the last water he had seen. He studied that cliff, now shadowed in the late sun, and waited a while, but he saw nothing more and proceeded gingerly forward, across the trajectory of the slide.

If some son of a bitch was up there, hunting him, then that son of a bitch would soon die.

He wondered sometimes what he would do if he found a real bonanza, not some ledge worth a few hundred dollars, but a big strike, one that poured coin into his purse. He had become so at home in the lonely wild that the thought of anything else, a great city for instance, seemed a novelty and left him uneasy. But he did have a little notion that he had been nurturing tenderly in his mind for a few years. He would like to own the biggest, best, must luxurious parlor house in San Francisco, with lush and exotic girls all under twenty-one and gathered from the four corners of the world; liveried staff, a fine selection of wines and liqueurs in the saloon part of it, a green baize poker table for those who might enjoy other entertainments, and a string ensemble playing chamber music. There, in a quiet and sensuous world, surrounded by his own bought beauties, he would enjoy the last hours on his clock.

Now that was something to dream about!

He came upon a steep, deep, and narrow canyon branching right, and took it, following a rocky waterway that plainly could rage twenty feet of water in a storm. He spotted driftwood high above him on the cliffs. This took him into a tiny hidden park, a grassy bowl of about two acres, surrounded by towering yellow cliffs. The sight startled him. He wasn't expecting the green. He hunted for the source of water that kept that grass verdant, and discovered a seep at the base of a cliff with a bit of water purling from a crack in the schist. There were no bones or any odor, and some bees hovered over the foliage. All signs that the water was good. He released Stud's mule, which trotted at once to the seep and lapped up water unhesitatingly. Stud's mule had been here before.

"Home sweet home, fellas," he said. But then he studied the rims, seeing nothing amiss. He realized, suddenly, that this was a safe, hidden haven. He did worry about storms high above, cloudbursts that would send water tumbling over a watercourse to one side. It was possible this little park would be swiftly submerged under just the right conditions. Uneasily, he studied the situation, and finally settled on a bench of flat rock to one side, five or six feet higher than the grass. Room enough for his camp and the animals if a deluge roared down on him.

He unsaddled the pack mule and let it water. The mules drank greedily, having been parched by the long day's ride in summer sun. Then he extracted a brush from his saddlebag and carefully groomed his animals, checked their hooves for stone bruises and lodged pebbles, and turned them loose. They would stay in the park and would not stray far from water. He watched them trot into the hock-high grass and begin to masticate it.

He was proud of his mules, treated them gently and with great respect. Unlike so many sourdoughs, he never abused them, never subjected them to thirst if he could help it. Nor did he overburden them. They were his traveling companions, partners in his enterprises, lifesavers, good listeners when he talked to them, and often they helped him locate water or grass.

He heard, in the distance, the faint rattle of falling rock, sprang for his Sharps once again, and waited warily, frozen in place, his sun-bleached eyes scanning the line, high above, where rock ended and bright blue sky began. But he saw nothing. Maybe the little slides were normal here in this eroded benchland west of the Mimbres Mountains.

Then again, maybe not.

Chapter 10

Sergei Gudonov swiftly loaded one of his stolen mules by candlelight, saddled the other, and then led both out of town, relying on his considerable knowledge of the stars to steer him. He didn't really need the second mule, but it might be handy. There was enough moonlight for him to make his way through a spooky desert dark, and by dawn he found himself two miles northeast of Rio Blanco, in an eroded escarpment he had meant to explore for months.

His plan was utterly simple. Let all those sourdoughs, with their advanced knowledge of minerals, hunt for the right-colored rocks. He had a better, more brilliant idea: He would hunt for ancient works, for signs of habitation. He would employ his vast understanding of archaeology, gotten from books and from Russian antiquarians, and that would lead him to the Doubloon Mine.

The Spanish hadn't mined in a vacuum. Every pound of ore brought to the surface required works. A windlass perhaps, ancient tailings, shoring, barracks, kitchen, stables, worn paths or roads. Works would tell the story; he would find the lost mine swiftly because he wasn't looking for gold; he was looking for evidence of mining.

The Spanish had little machinery and little iron, but they did have cheap labor, captive Indians who carried ore in woven reed baskets. He knew, if he looked, that he would find remnants of baskets, of kitchens, of human habitation, along with broken harness and tack, perhaps some mule shoes, and some timber works. He would also find graves. Spanish and Mexican mines routinely took lives, and the dead were tossed aside like used-up horses. There too would be remnants of Hispanic religion, the *santos,* the ornate iron crosses, perhaps mission bells long silenced and forlorn. The Church was woven through and through the lives of those people, and no such work as a mine would go unattended by all the insignia of faith and worship. A cross would be a clue.

As the earliest light began to shape the land around him, he tied the mules to an isolated oak and clambered up the rocky grade toward the ridge. He wished to greet the dawn, and to orient himself. The low sun would probe hillsides and canyons, its horizontal rays limning anything wrought by man, making his search easy. By the time he had clambered three or four hundred feet to the ridge, he was utterly winded, but the view caught his eye. Dawn is the quietest and sweetest moment. The sun, just breaking the rim of the east, shot its golden rays into the flanks of every canyon, the shadows throwing everything into relief, giving Sergei an extraordinary view. A great stillness embraced the land. The deep and mysterious silence of the wilds caught him.

From the ridge he could see tens of miles into a country so mysterious and jumbled that he could spend a life sorting it out. He stood, winded, in the wild, absorbing the awakening day. The sun caught and held the flanks of the unnamed mountains to the north, turning them pink and salmon in the hush. And then his eye caught something odd, something exciting. There, on that mountainside, brilliant in the new day's light, was a giant cross formed out of the mountains themselves, dark against the glowing light, a vertical canyon, perhaps with horizontal branches. He could not tell, but he knew at once that that sight, on such a morning as this, would have electrified a Spaniard.

Gudonov had no religion but science, and science he revered as reverently as any devout Christian approaching an altar. He had gotten his fill of religion in Russia; he knew it was nothing but mythology employed to prop up the regime and intimidate the poor and the oppressed. Once he had freed his mind of superstition, he had embraced that which is knowable and provable, and cast all the rest aside. But always with an understanding of the grip that superstition and priests had on the minds of simpler people. Now, standing there all alone in a lonesome land, he saw embedded in the distant mountain flanks an unmistakable symbol, and knew he would head for it, and knew that generations of Spanish and Mexicans had seen it and had been drawn there to that mountain range, five or six miles distant.

Excited, he took a compass bearing and then hastened down the rocky grade, recovered his mules, and started northwest, through a labyrinth that would have steered him astray but for the compass he used constantly in those cloistered arroyos and watersheds.

He saw not a soul, heard no other mortal, and sensed that the bulk of the prospectors had continued eastward, rather than turning north as he had. They were all too lazy or unimaginative to do anything other than follow the road, as if that dead prospector had taken a highway into Rio Blanco.

It was no easy task to reach that obscure mountain flank. Time and again he found himself in a box canyon, or in a twisting arroyo that took him anywhere but northwest. Stubbornly, he tugged his mules up precipitous ridges, trying to find shortcuts across drainages. His persistence paid off: At each ridgetop he marked his steady progress toward that obscure range of arid mountains.

By noon, he had worn himself down. In the next drainage he found some shade in an arroyo, and there he rested, letting the mules graze on some tender spring grass. He was committed; there was no way he could find his way back to Rio Blanco except by dead reckoning. That meant he must conserve water, look for springs and seeps, prepare for a foray that might last two or three days. He knew he was not far from town as the crow flies, but what might be three or four miles in a straight line would be ten miles of travel, up and down, round and about.

The midday heat had built, draining courage out of him. Suddenly, he was cautious. He hunted for shadow and found it; not that he was any cooler. The brazen sun had fired up the air in that arroyo until he could barely breathe. He allowed himself a good suck from the canteen and resolved to wait. Prudence demanded it. But his mind was on that black cross carved at dawn out of the mountain, and he knew he had already discovered the mine that would be at its foot.

He dawdled two hours. Then impatience overtook him and he plunged recklessly into the fierce afternoon heat, feeling giddy under the lash of the sun. He intended to climb across drainages once again, and worked his way upward over scorching rock, too hot to touch, until he reached a jumbled ridge. And there, not half a mile distant, was the obscure range, its foothills clawing toward him. He saw no sign of the shadowy cross that had bewitched him at dawn, nor did the gray rock give the slightest clue. But in the morrow he might see it again at dawn, and from the very foot of the obscure range.

He tugged his reluctant mules down a rocky grade, feeling the heat sap him cruelly, and knew he could just barely reach those foothills and then he would need to hole up if possible and wait for the murderous heat to abate.

And water . . . He was farther from town than he had intended to go without plenty of water.

He settled impatiently on sand in the shadow of a red cliff, in a silence so terrible he ached for any noise, even the slight whisper of a breeze. What had brought him to such a place as this? Overthrowing the Czars? Yes, exactly. And their cousins and every miserable parasitic nobleman in Mother Russia. And then he would usher in paradise. But even as he told himself that he would be midwife to paradise, his skeptical mind rebelled. He would cleanse Russia of its parasites, and then another generation would cleanse Russia of the next parasites . . . and the real reason he was a revolutionary was because he enjoyed the whole business.

He sat restlessly until the sun swung around, and suddenly he was no longer in shade but under the late afternoon sun. There was no escape. He collected his mules, which had drifted up the arroyo, snatching at rare bits of vegetation, and then he headed toward the silent mountains, now a purple wall before him, the sun arcing around behind them. In spite of the heat, he felt refreshed, and the mules did too. They followed along placidly as he worked up an arroyo toward the mountains. The worst of the heat had passed. By the time the sun was over the rear of the mountains, he had reached the lower slopes. There was no sign of the curious formation that had stamped a giant cross upon those slopes under the golden dawn light, and he could not say whether he had stuck the range somewhere nearby.

The solitude oppressed him. How much better it would be to sit at a table with friends and sip vodka and plan the revolution! He thought better of piercing into the mountains by following this arroyo, so he hiked once again to a ridge that clawed its way out of the highlands, and there, where his view suddenly widened to include hundreds of square miles, he studied the country. Again, the silence oppressed him. He felt, in that hush, that he was a hundred miles from any other mortal, though his rational mind told him some of the gold-crazed prospectors might be only a mile or two distant.

He pulled out his fine German field glass and began studying the foothills, not knowing what to look for or what an ancient Spanish mine head might look like. The light had grown soft and lavender, and the earth shimmered from the heat the sun-blasted rock was releasing as night swept near. Then he saw something. Not a mile distant, two drainages to the left, was a huddle of things that might be adobe buildings, maybe rock, definitely man-made, with rectangles and squares.

The mine, surely the mine! And he could make it before full dark. He glassed the silent, solemn structures one last time, burning them into his mind, as well as the immediate terrain, so he could orient himself even if dark befell him. There was an escarpment above he could home in on.

The Lost Doubloon? He sensed that it was. Hastily, with the waning light on his mind, he skidded down to his mules, dragged them up to the ridge, and then they plummeted downslope to the next arroyo, and then over the following ridge, his mind and body half-crazed. Nothing was harder than crossing stony drainages loaded with treacherous talus, and now he raced up the third drainage, a rocky defile that, he believed, would take him to the mine. To the gold. To revolution.

Just as full night settled over that silent land, he rounded a bend, found himself on level shelf-land, spotted the huddle of silent structures, most of them built from fieldstone with mud mortar. An ancient stone-walled well with a windlass stood below the structures. And beyond, a black rectangle stabbed into the cliffside, the whole tableau before him swathed in silence.

Chapter 11

Gudonov exulted. He penned the mules in a sun-bleached corral made of twisted mesquite limbs and set out to explore what he could in the failing light. By all appearances, this seemed to be an abandoned rancho, but he knew how cunning the Spaniards were at hiding their mines. The house was built of field-stone with mud mortar, and the rooms were entirely empty and oddly cold, as if it had been the Devil's habitation. Something skittered across the clay floor of the main room, and he resolved to be careful. An adobe barn was likewise totally devoid of anything. Not even a stick of wood. Several ruined adobe out-buildings yielded nothing else.

By then it was full dark. He located the well, which had a broken windlass without a rope, and peered into its gloom, discerning nothing. He headed for his pack and found a rope and tied his little cook pot to it, and lowered it slowly into the well. It hit something hard. He pulled it up. No water. He tried again, with the same result.

Maybe it had been a rancho after all, abandoned because of the lack of water. He would look further in the morning. So far, he had found nothing. Not even debris. Whoever once lived here had taken everything, and now the hulks were as cold and gloomy as death.

Meanwhile, he needed to care for the mules. He

surmised that he was less than a day's walk back to Rio Blanco; nothing to worry about. He had six quarts left, so he gave each mule one quart of water, using his cook pot. Not much, but enough.

He found no wood for a fire; the place was as naked of vegetation as the driest corner of the Sahara. He would sleep hungry, for want of anything to cook with. He debated where to bed, and finally selected the old corral itself, guessing that the mules might discourage rattlers. No manure lay in the corrals; sun and wind and rain had long since sluiced away every sign of animals and left only hard clean clay.

He didn't like this place, this evidence of a failed dream, and slept only fitfully, awakened frequently by strange noises, or by nothing at all. He didn't believe in ghosts, and laughed at spectres, and couldn't understand his malaise. He took comfort in the stars, familiar constellations, and in the certitude that he would soon find the Lost Doubloon and he could turn it into a revolution. The Smith and Wesson Russian would have a special destiny, the handgun that extinguished a Romanov emperor, but for now it would be handy to keep wild animals at bay. He set it beside his sleeping bag.

At first light, he rose with a start, and then quieted his heart when he realized he was utterly alone. No one was staring at him from mournful eyes. It must have been a small animal, maybe a coyote. He drank a little from his canteen, and soon was ready for the day. He hoped the brightening light in the east would soon reveal the giant blue-shadowed cross on the slope above, but his angle was wrong, and as the sun climbed he saw nothing but the anonymous flank of arid mountains. He patrolled the outlying areas of the ranch and found a burial plot, seven graves in all. One headboard lying on the clay was all that remained, but its legend had weathered away, and he could say only that something once had been painted on it. A few flecks of black clung to the silvered gray wood. A family of peons had lived and died here.

He ached for a meal, hot tea, and finally tried wrestling the mesquite from the corral, but the pieces had been cunningly interwoven, and did not yield.

This was no mine. There was not even disturbed earth in the anonymous hillside that might suggest something buried. No ruts left by ore wagons or carts. No tailings. No fuel for a revolution here. He had decisions to make. On examining the terrain, he concluded he was still east of the somber dark cross he had seen, and even though it would take him farther from Rio Blanco, it would be worth crossing one or two more drainages until he reached the mysterious place at the foot of the cross. He could always make it back to Rio Blanco by evening.

So he haltered the mules, threw a saddle blanket over the pack mule, cinched the packsaddle over it, collected the lead lines, and set out on a course that would take him farther from Rio Blanco. If he found a timbered gulch, he would stop for breakfast. He had a fine habit of sipping China tea each morning, a habit that brightened his mind and spirit as he prepared for the day. Now he yearned for tea and a samovar to heat it.

He took one last look at this desolate place and pitied the erstwhile owners. Some Spanish don had taken up all the good level land and had forced these poor peons to subsist in arid mountain desert country that couldn't support them.

Ah! He would someday take revolution to every country! He would change the world! He would free peons and serfs and slaves and the poor from the iron grasp of greedy plutocrats, landlords, and nobles, who lived at ease and enjoyed privilege at the expense of the desperate masses. It was a good dream, a fire that flickered steadily in his commodious mind, and he was not too modest to believe he might set the whole world afire with justice. If he had been the president of this republic, he would have forbidden these poor, ignorant peons from taking up a rancho on such hopeless ground. He would have reserved all such land for the state, just to keep the ignorant out of it.

Poor miserable creatures, men and women with rough hands!

He pulled out his pocket watch. He would work along the base of the mountain range for exactly one half hour, and then, no matter what, if he found nothing, he would retreat to Rio Blanco and water. He had not been a Cossack for nothing and would not endanger himself. Risk, always, any time, any place. The world didn't belong to the timid, who eked out their miserable lives in fear; but foolishness in the desert? Never.

So he tugged his hungry mules and they followed reluctantly, abandoning the old rancho and working once again across giant drainages, steep inclines followed by treacherous plunges into arroyos that made him feel like a dwarf. And always, as the sun rose, he kept an eye on the golden mountain ridges, looking for that mysterious blue cross, that sign that would have fired the imagination of any Spaniard or Mexican. But he saw nothing familiar, not even a vulture riding the thermals, even as the heat of the day began to build. That eerie silence once again oppressed him.

At exactly nine-thirty, he stopped. His half hour had expired, and now he had to work steadily toward Rio Blanco—and water. He had an iron discipline, wrought by intelligence. He took one last reluctant look, spotted an odd disruption of nature halfway up the tumbled slope, realized it was a massive, mineralized ledge, a red streak that began abruptly and stopped abruptly in the midst of featureless dun-colored rock.

He debated.

Red could mean many things. Iron oxides, which

were often associated with gold. Cinnabar, a mercury ore. It could mean nothing.

He withdrew his fine German spyglass and studied the formation, fascinated by its abrupt endings that must have been the result of faults. Below it, several house-sized tan objects stood, too distant to make out. Buildings? Huge boulders that had tumbled from above? He slowly glassed the country below, looking for faint two-rut trails, and saw none. The Lost Doubloon had disappeared over a century earlier, but the ruts of the *carettas* carrying away its ore would surely remain.

His gaze returned to those giant dun lumps below the outcrop, and he sensed they were man-made, orderly in form. He glanced at his timepiece, and at the sun, which was blazing down now, scorching through his white cotton shirt, building up midmorning heat. By afternoon, the whole area would be a furnace.

He weighed the prospects. So far, over half a night and a day, he had followed a dogleg, first northeast out of Rio Blanco, then northwest toward these obscure mountains. He had traveled only ten or eleven miles in all, but the trip back to Rio Blanco, due south, would be much shorter, encompassing the third leg of the triangle. He was no more than six or seven miles from Rio Blanco, a matter of a few hours even in this almost impenetrable terrain.

He studied the country leading up to that outcrop, and saw it was rough and steep, but still negotiable in two or three hours. Add an hour to be conservative. He could be there at two in the afternoon, no later. Look over the buildings and outcrop in a half hour. There would be a trail leading away, toward town. One that no doubt had been worn by thousands of pack mules bearing gold ore. Be off by two-thirty, in Rio Blanco before nightfall.

Water was the risk. But if he gave his mules each a quart at the probable mine site, drank a little himself, and saved back a quart for his return, he would be fine. What's more, when it got too hot, he would find a shady nook and hole up until it cooled. His mind was a match for any desert.

His mind made up, he began the climb at once, probing up on a roundabout path through treacherous talus-laden slopes even as the heat thundered on his flesh, sucking away moisture. He was shockingly thirsty, but refrained from touching his hot sheet-metal canteen. There would be time enough for a drink once he got there, and likely a well or a spring near the buildings.

Thus he toiled, resting frequently, letting the mules, whose tongues hung out dry, pick the pace. It was not two when he finally reached that outcrop, clambering wearily over a last cruel ledge that scraped his hand, but after three, and the heat was roaring in his ears, hammering his temples, and stupefying the mules.

There was nothing there. What he had thought were buildings were nothing more than huge slabs of rock that had tumbled from above. There was no sign that any mortal had ever been there. The red of the rock was more a morning trick of light than a reality. The rock was more brown than red, and stratified, which meant it probably had been laid down in an ancient sea. He thought it might be iron-stained limestone. He pocketed a piece of the stone, and would test it later.

From this lofty aerie he could see vast distances, but this day white haze obscured the terrain, so he felt cloistered and isolated. He led his mules to a shadowed place, and let the steady breeze cool him. They were all desperate for a drink, and he knew neither he nor the mules could go much further without water. So he got his cook pot and canteen, and carefully gave each animal a quart, holding the pot tightly to avoid disasters. Then he drank most of a quart himself. He shook the canteen. There was perhaps a quart left.

The mule carrying the packsaddle brayed piteously. A quart hardly wet its throat.

He waited a while, giving the animals and himself a rest, and then led them due south, on a compass bearing that would bring them by evening to Rio Blanco. But it was not possible in that terrain to hold to a compass bearing, and he found himself detouring giant claws of land, or circling upslope to avoid precipitous gulches.

Resting carefully, conserving strength, he made his way one mile, then another, without seeing much change in the land, or any sign that he was approaching the broad valley where the town nestled. He topped another ridge that formed the roots of the mountains, continued along a high plateau, enjoying the level land, and then came to a dead halt.

Before him, stretching as far as he could see right and left, lay a yellow canyon half a mile wide and fifteen hundred or two thousand feet deep, with precipitous walls that afforded no passage down, or up. The bottom did contain a little green vegetation, saltbush mostly, tucked into the shadiest corners, but no water. Nothing but a sandy waste down there, and the sun a murderous force that would permit him no mistakes.

He was blocked. And if he didn't find a way out, or water, blocked and dead.

Chapter 12

At last! Malachi Cromwell-Nast held in his hand a thick manilla packet from the City of Mexico that had wended its way north for months, it seemed, and finally arrived in Rio Blanco. It was from a certain attorney at law down there, Miguel Otero, with whom Nast had been in contact for a year and a half.

He swiftly broke the red wax seal, opened the envelope, and extracted a letter and some documents. He turned first to the letter, written in elegant Spanish, and learned that Ricardo O'Rourke, citizen of Mexico, had been executed by firing squad over a year before for treasonable conduct against the government of Porfirio Diaz. The specific charge had been supplying five hundred Sharps and Winchester carbines to insurgent and rebel guerrilla groups in the State of Sonora. The *rurales* had caught him delivering the rifles, manacled him, and shipped him south to Mexico City in an oxcart under heavy guard. The president had imposed a 100,000-peso fine upon O'Rourke, who was sick and emaciated after the long, brutal trip.

It was a ransom. Pay or die. The gunrunner O'Rourke had failed to come up with the cash and had met his fate one dawn, according to information Otero acquired by bribing military officials. O'Rourke had been blindfolded, tied to a post before the famous pockmarked wall of doom on the northern outskirts of the city, shot in the heart by a squad of ten blue-clad soldiers, and swiftly buried in a pauper's grave. The case had never been made public.

Nast grunted. O'Rourke's true occupation, gunrunner and munitions supplier to anti-Diaz guerrillas swarming over Sonora, was known to his widow, but few others knew it or even suspected it. O'Rourke had let the world know he was a land and mining speculator. She didn't know she was a widow, and Nast wasn't going to tell her. Not yet. She knew only that her Ricardo had set out on a "business trip" two years earlier and never returned.

The other document was a fair copy of President Diaz's death sentence for O'Rourke, and the fine that was to be paid to the Republic of Mexico in 180 days if the criminal was to escape death. It was undated. That was an old Mexican money-raising tradition. A life for a hundred thousand pesos. Nast studied it, absorbing its details. That document would be most useful. If the Widow O'Rourke was sitting on a pile of cash she didn't know about, Nast was going to encourage her find it and pay the ransom.

He tucked the Diaz proclamation into the breast pocket of his black broadcloth suit and braved the sullen heat of early evening, making his spidery way up the gravelly grade to the hilltop mansion that overlooked Rio Blanco. The lady probably would be home, wearied from her wanderings. She and that Eastern fop had wandered out upon the wilds, bearing a wicker picnic basket. It amused him. They were looking for the lost gold mine.

The manse had fallen into disrepair ever since she had discharged her servants for the want of funds to pay them. That was fine; he would soon be fixing it up, whitewashing its exterior, putting alabaster statuary on the grounds. He favored Grecian women in diaphanous flowing robes, with Cupids on either side of the Doric pillars at the portico.

It was seven, an appropriate evening hour to do business. He knocked and waited.

But the door opened at once, and he beheld that striking young woman in the doorway, dressed in dark gray silk, which accentuated the gold of her flesh. She eyed him coolly. There was no friendship between them.

"Señora, I have most important news of your husband," he said.

"Ricardo?" Her face lost its color.

"Yes, good news."

She nodded him in, her face a mask, her carriage proud. He headed for the familiar parlor, streaked with the last of the sun falling across the blue and gold brussels carpet.

"Ricardo is in Mexico City, a prisoner of the Diaz government," he said. "He needs money."

"Ricardo! Alive! Oh, Madre de Dios!"

She slumped into a settee and buried her face in her hands, unable to stop the flow of tears.

"Ricardo, mi Ricardo," she cried.

Nast waited quietly until at last she was able to resume their discussion. She controlled her feelings less well than most women, but he would be patient. Soon, she gazed up at him with those lavender eyes, and smiled.

"He is alive," she whispered.

"It's a terrible place, this dungeon, and he needs cash," Nast said. "See? This came from a barrister, Señor Otero, down there who keeps an eye on business matters of mine in Mexico. It is the sentence, drafted by Diaz himself. There is the matter of a large fine, upon receipt of which your husband might be freed if it is the will of the president. One can not quite be sure," he added cautiously. "Diaz has a will of his own."

He handed her the proclamation, uncertain

whether she could read, but indeed she could, though only a few well-bred Mexican women could manage it. She scanned the document.

"Guns! This is how he is charged? Guns! He is a businessman," she said warily. "Import and export."

She knew better, but Nast did not press the point. Obviously, Ricardo O'Rourke had urged her to use discretion at all times. "Diaz wants a hundred thousand pesos. That's twelve and a half thousand American dollars."

She stared at him. "I have nothing."

"Richard O'Rourke invested heavily. Surely you have access to his funds, his property."

"No, I have nothing. *Nada*. I need help raising such a sum," she said. "But I will raise it. I will get this *dinero* somehow, some way, and take it myself to Porfirio Diaz and give it to him and then take Ricardo away from there. This I will do. Maybe I will just go and petition the president. Surely he will hear me."

"Ah, no, Señora, he might count you as guilty as your husband. No, you will want to negotiate from here, send the funds by courier, and wait until your husband is safe."

"How do I know this? Why haven't I heard this before? Why does all this come from you?"

"Señora, a while ago I quietly took a hand in the matter, seeing you alone and in need, and made inquiries. Everything in the City of Mexico is secret, and so was this document, and it took great effort and a few gold pieces placed in the right hands to acquire this information."

"But how do I know this is so?"

He plunged his hand into his pocket and withdrew a small silver Maltese cross that was suspended by a delicate chain necklace. He dropped it into her hand. She studied it, turned it over, and sighed, fresh tears welling in those lovely eyes.

"It is truly word from him. I will send him word also," she said. She rose, vanished, returned, and dropped a small silver image of the Virgin of Guadalupe in his hand. "Send this to him. He will know everything."

"I will do that, Señora. It will take two months or so for the mail to reach the City of Mexico."

"I do not have the money," she said. "It will take time. Tell this Otero that."

"You might have some of it. You might gather what you have and offer it to President Diaz. Maybe he will accept and free Richard."

"These properties he has, they are in Ricardo's name. I cannot raise any money."

"Well, let me see about that. There's power of attorney, you know. You might sell this house too. Or mortgage it."

"It is not mine; it is Ricardo's."

"Ah, but things can be arranged. Leave it to me. We'll find a way to bring your husband out of his captivity. All it requires is money."

"Money!" Her face crumpled upon that news.

"I will find out what is deeded to Richard O'Rourke and see what can be done," he said. "Meanwhile, remember him in your prayers, and remember me as well, for I will need divine strength."

She nodded, and rose. Plainly she wished to be alone.

"Give me a few days," he said. "Meanwhile, gather such funds as you can."

She accompanied him to the door, and as he left she shot him a look so penetrating and desperate, from those wounded eyes, that the moment lingered with him long after he hiked through the gloaming to his shadowed parlor.

Everything had gone just as planned.

Nast had, in fact, accumulated over two or three years a list of all of O'Rourke's ranching and mining properties in New Mexico, and knew their approximate worth. O'Rourke had speculated in mining claims and timber and water rights, mostly as a cover for his true occupation, running guns and desperados. But to Nash's astonishment, these properties had all been sold before his last journey, as if O'Rourke feared something or needed a lot of money. Various trips to the clerk and recorder at Silver City had confirmed O'Rourke's sales. The man could have made a living developing these holdings. One silver claim alone showed great promise. But O'Rourke was plainly a man with a passion, and that passion was to free Mexico of Diaz, and he wanted all that he owned converted to cash, probably hidden where no one could get at it. That money had to be somewhere. Probably in the mansion, whether Guadalupe knew of it or not.

Nast supposed the mansion and its outbuilding and grounds were worth a couple of thousand. She didn't have the faintest idea what she was worth or what she owned. That was plain from the months of virtual starvation she had endured, waiting for Ricardo to return.

There she was, desperate for money. She needed a hundred thousand pesos to free Ricardo before he was shot. That was the dilemma Nast laid before her. It would be interesting to see how she came up with it. He was sure the money was lying around, even if Ricardo had not told her where it was. And if she found it, he would soon pocket it.

It was all paying off, his years of effort. He had grubstaked scores of prospectors and profited from their wayward ways. Not one bonanza found by those sourdoughs he had financed had remained in their hands. He was now worth, on paper at least, a hundred thousand dollars, but that was only a beginning. With a little luck he could pocket the ransom and commandeer the Lost Doubloon, and reach his goal: He intended to become a millionaire.

Chapter 13

Guadalupe sat numbly, staring out the window at the quickening light of a new day. Somehow she had known. Every time he took one of his trips, she lived in dread until he returned. Maybe it was those green cat's eyes, or that lithe, feral walk, or the small secret habits of his. Maybe it was simply because he had said so little about his purposes, made those swift trips, never voiced an opinion in public about politics or the dictator-president Diaz. At parties, *bailes*, fiestas, he was the soul of discretion.

He was a dangerous man, *sí*! A very dangerous man, a leopard, a panther, a jaguar, slick and feline, pouncing and killing his prey. That was what had stirred her soul and her loins, this danger in Ricardo.

A man who ran rifles! A man who took Henrys and Spencers and Sharps rifles and ammunition to the hot-eyed rebels in the mountains, the angry ones who wished to unseat Porfirio Diaz. The president of Mexico had created great prosperity—but only for the rich, and the poor were worse off than ever. And Diaz had dealt harshly with all opposition, making himself all but a dictator for as long as he wished to govern.

Something about her husband set her heart on fire. He was taking steel to the enemies of Diaz! He was risking his life because he had a tiger's heart and a soul that flooded with passion. Such a man, such a man! Never had she been so impassioned, so enthralled by any human being. And he was hers, all hers.

Ah, Ricardo! Now he was rotting in some dungeon in the City of Mexico, waiting for her to rescue him, alive only because Diaz had perceived he had money, and money was useful to men such as the president. Ah, Ricardo, you and your *fusils,* caught by *rurales* and hauled in irons for hundreds of miles to the capital of the republic, if Mexico could be called a republic under Diaz. God forbid you should become a martyr.

A hundred thousand pesos, a fortune beyond imagining. She would raise it somehow. She would buy Ricardo's liberty and safety. Someday, she would take her lover in her arms and hold him, and feed him well and make him strong, and delight him as she had before, in all the ways she knew.

What to do? Jesús, José, Maria, what to do? She had nothing. She thought narrowly of Nast and didn't trust him. Why had the news of Ricardo's imprisonment come through Nast? Why? Was he an agent of the government, of Diaz himself? Were it not for Ricardo's silver Maltese cross, the very emblem she had given him and that he wore always, she would not have believed a word Nast said.

But that cross, that familiar fat little cross, so unlike any other, now lay in her palm, a message from her husband and lover. She had to believe Nast, at least a little. It made her dizzy to think of what she must do; garner a hundred thousand pesos and then exchange them for Ricardo's liberty, and all without allowing deception or treachery, for such a swine as Diaz would stop at nothing and might take the money and not release Ricardo.

This great house, those bits of land, what were they worth? She knew she couldn't get two thousand dollars for the whole lot, even if she had title to them, which she did not. Ricardo had always shielded her from his business affairs, and now she knew why. If he had any other assets, accounts in banks, gold, anything, she didn't know of it. She had to free him. She had to find a way.

The Lost Doubloon Mine. Somewhere nearby was a fabled fortune. The Hispanic people of this town had told her a few things that the Anglos didn't know. They said the mine was just a brief walk from Rio Blanco; that the miners walked to their homes each evening, a short distance down the slopes and into the town. The lost mine was here, not some great distance away. But whenever Guadalupe asked where, where, where, they turned secretive, shrugged, and said they had no idea. It was an evil place, the Devil's hole, and they did not wish to discuss it. That was the story handed down from the ancestors, and it was worth only a shrug.

She knew their minds! She knew that these, her compatriots, now citizens of the United States, secretly believed the mine was the jaws of evil, that he who entered through its portals brought only death upon himself and his world. That was the fiery lesson, and it lingered long after everyone had forgotten where the mine might be.

Somewhere, not far away, was the answer to her prayers.

She wandered aimlessly through the silent, empty casa, pausing at last at a niche in the wall where the image of Mexico's patroness, the Virgin of Guadalupe, rested in her halo of gold leaf.

"Oh, most blessed Mother, Ricardo needs me. Have mercy on me out of your infinite kindness, and help me," she begged. "Intercede for us. Poor Ricardo. He suffers so, and all because of that swine Diaz, who burdens the poor and favors the rich and haughty. Take pity on us."

But she was not comforted.

It would be just another bright spring day.

It was one thing to dream of Ricardo, another to devise means to help him. Poor man, lying wasted and pale in some pestilent hole in the City of Mexico, choking on the foul air. Helping him would not be easy. But what good did it do to remind herself of that? She would take each hour as it came.

She wrapped a thin white rebozo over her and plunged into the early morning, walked down the grade to town, and then through the almost-deserted city, where everyone had suddenly turned into a gold-seeker.

It never occurred to her to ask herself why she was looking for Elwood LaGrange, the least likely man in Rio Blanco to uncover a lost mine. But that's where she was headed. One thing about him: He was well fixed and probably wouldn't steal it from her, though one could never know what gold did to people. Another thing: He had an earnest desire to be helpful. She knew she had a certain effect on him, something she could read in his face, and she intended to exploit it. He would be a handy puppy. Another thing: He was not dangerous, and he was probably intelligent. Another thing: He was a gentleman who would protect her. Another thing: She had utterly no feeling for him, felt no attraction to him. He stirred nothing within her.

She found the overdressed Yank in the restaurant, sipping coffee and grimacing, wiping his puffy lips with a soiled napkin.

He spotted her and rose abruptly.

"Ah! It's you! I was just thinking of our admirable little jaunt yesterday, Mrs. O'Rourke. May I interest you in joining me for a morning repast?"

She surveyed him as he stood there in his brown tweeds and canvas puttees and shiny shoes and boiled white shirt and pince-nez, and wondered what madness had gripped her.

"Come to my house, Señor, when you are done. I have business to attend."

"As you wish, Mrs. O'Rourke. I'll be there directly. Is it a new word for my collection?"

She permitted herself a smile.

By the time he arrived a half hour later, she had changed into her oldest and least valuable dress, one with a generous scoop of neckline that bared her smooth caramel neck and a little of her chest. She would use what she had shamelessly, if that was what it took to attract Elwood LaGrange, who would be her factotum and helper.

"I am going to search for the lost mine, and I want you to be with me," she said.

"The lost mine? Why, Mrs. O'Rourke, it's a myth."

"I am going to find it. Will you come with me?"

"Madam, I would be honored."

"Good. Then you can carry the lunch basket and the canteen."

The puppy picked up both items and they headed out the door. This time, she steered him away from the town below, and toward a canyon that opened behind her house. It occurred to her that maybe this old mansion had been erected at the very throat of the gulch that took miners to and from the mine.

"I've never been this direction," he said.

"Then you'll see the land with a fresh eye. We must find the mine."

"You make it sound urgent."

"More so than I can tell you. I need that mine, and right now too. And if we find it, I plan to keep it all."

Elwood laughed gently, the amusement of a skeptic. She didn't mind. Out of sheer politeness he would surrender the mine to her, even if he discovered it. He had no *cojones,* and his silky smooth hands had never held a hammer or a pick. She knew the sort.

Anything for a lady, even carrying baskets and tools and canteens, like the meanest burro.

"You don't object?" she asked.

"To your keeping the mine? Well, you'll have to promise me a big nugget as a souvenir."

"Maybe I won't," she said. She knew his type. The more she abused him, the more he would yearn for her. This Yankee burro was quite the opposite of Ricardo, who knew how to make a woman float in the air.

The manse below them stood, actually, on a bench overlooking Rio Blanco, but now they reached the end of the bench and plunged into a narrow yellow canyon, bone-dry and hot even though most of it lay in shadow, even in midday. She discovered not the slightest sign of human passage in the stony ground. No trail, no scarred land, no ruts, no middens or rock or markers. The canyon rose steeply and led deep into a gash in the mountains. None of the rock, which was a dun sandstone, seemed mineralized. She had hiked here from time to time, until one day a puma leapt across her path and raced up a slope. She had never entered this place after that, even though it opened on her own casa.

"Mrs. O'Rourke, I don't know much, but I know that this sort of sandstone, laid down in a sea bottom long ago, is not a likely place for gold. We need to find igneous or metamorphic rock," he said.

"Whatever that is."

He smiled. "We don't know much, do we? I'll try to learn. Then I can help more."

She nodded, secretly disheartened.

A silence enveloped them, so total that not even the whisper of a spring zephyr caught her ear. The canyon deepened until they were perhaps five hundred feet below the rims above. And nowhere did she see anything that looked like a mine.

The rock slide shocked her. High above, yellow dust

and a rumble caught her eye, a rattle and then a thunder of rock avalanching downward. Elwood grabbed her and pulled her back, his reaction even faster than hers, his body shielding her, and together they watched a mound of disintegrated stone pile up on the trail and billow dust and debris, enveloping them in a cloud of grit.

He held her quietly, somehow much calmer than she.

"It makes a man wonder," he said.

Chapter 14

The thought struck Sergei Gudonov that he might die here, scarcely half a day's walk to Rio Blanco. And if he died, so would the yearning of millions of serfs. They might not know it, but he was their salvation, the one with the vision and courage to lift them from misery and chains.

For a moment a vast pity swept him, not just for himself but for the world, which would lie unredeemed by revolution if he perished. But that passed. Not for nothing had he been a Cossack. He stared into that awesome abyss, knowing that somehow he had to reach its floor. There would be no water up here; there might be some down there.

He felt the thump of his heart pushing thickened blood through his protesting body. Ah, for a drink! He still had that last sip or two, but he must save it until his own death loomed. Only then would he taste the nectar. His mules stood, heads down, plainly near their limit.

Downslope then, alongside that abyss, until he could find a trail. Wearily, he shuffled through the furnace heat of afternoon, working his way along the lip of that canyon, trying to conserve energy. Oh, for cool, cool water.

He did not know how far he and the listless mules had thus traveled when he discovered the faint sign of a game trail descending from the lip of the canyon. Tiny hoofprints dotted it, perhaps those of desert mule deer. One look at it made him dizzy. If he took it, he would descend along a steep and frightful trace, sometimes only inches wide, with a sheer precipice along one side and cliff along the other. He could not see where it went or what obstacles it encountered. He knew once he started down, there would be no turning back, no way to turn the mules around. The canyon floor lay perhaps a thousand feet below and showed no sign of moisture. And yet a game trail always existed for a reason. It was the way to somewhere game needed to go.

He stepped gingerly onto the incline, which at that point was soft dirt sloping at a terrifying angle. The mules didn't want to follow. He yanked savagely at the line, and with a piteous bray the pack mule stepped forward, skidded twenty feet, and scrambled to a halt at the edge of the abyss. The other mule, unburdened, found the passage easier.

The first hundred yards posed no great difficulty other than the sheer terror of falling off the trail and tumbling, bouncing, careening to his death. The mules twitched and stepped gingerly, small mincing steps that bespoke their own terror. Then the trail, still descending at what seemed like a forty-five-degree angle, suddenly narrowed to a foot of width, the precipice on one side, the cliff on the other, and no way to turn around. The narrow passage ran perhaps thirty feet.

Parched he was, but now suddenly he felt a sweat rise to his flesh. But he was a military man. He inched along the passage, leaning into the cliff, one foot at a time, careful, so careful, where he placed each boot. He tried not to look off to his left, where there was only a void and the hazy far wall of the canyon half a mile across. He feared a snake or any surprise. He paused, his heart hammering, and reached for his canteen, but it was strung on the packsaddle. The mule had refused to budge.

Angrily, he tugged the line, almost toppling himself, but still the mule would not move. In a rage, Gudonov yelled, yanked savagely, and the mule followed two steps and stopped, its packsaddle pressing against the cliff.

"You will come!" he yelled, fury boiling through him. This mule he would shoot with his Smith and Wesson Russian revolver. He would not tolerate disobedience of any sort in any animal.

He yanked savagely, dragging the mule toward him. The mule, surprised, plunged forward, the packsaddle striking the cliff, and then the mule's front hoofs stepped into space. The mule screeched piteously and toppled over the edge. One last terrified bray caught Gudonov's ears as the mule somersaulted down, struck rock, careened out into space, and tumbled to its doom, somewhere below, far out of sight.

Gudonov stared, sickened, desperate. His own rage had doomed the mule, and he knew it. Doomed himself. He had always had an uncontrollable temper, and now it had destroyed him. Death now. The pack and the canteen went with the mule. His heart hammered. A sickly silence engulfed him. Behind him, the remaining mule stood easily, unburdened. Gudonov did not try to drag it behind him, and simply started downslope again. The mule trotted easily along the narrows, surefooted so long as no pack was forcing it off the thinnest of trails.

Then the mule was safe, standing behind him. He would let the mule pick its own way down. On leaden legs he walked and skidded and tripped downward, rounding bends, once dodging a snake that blocked the trail. He passed brushy areas, creosote brush, acrid in the sun, rabbit brush, prickly pear cactus. The remaining mule nipped at fodder now and then, but made its way down the terrifying slope. At one point, there was no alternative but to skid down an incline Sergei guessed was sixty degrees, but he managed it, and so did the mule, which braked itself with its forefeet as it skidded.

There was not any relief, no easy moments, no easy passage, until suddenly he found himself in deep shade, the far rim of the canyon at last shielding him from the cruel sun. Ten minutes later, he guessed, he reached the rocky and sandy floor. He set out at once to find his dead mule and pack, but could see nothing, and finally concluded that the mule had landed somewhere partly up the cliff. He sank to the ground, an oddly cool spot, trembling. He might be only four or five miles from Rio Blanco, but it might as well be a hundred.

Water. His tongue felt glued to his mouth. He found a pebble and stuffed it into his mouth, trying to generate some saliva, but it didn't help. He spit it out. He hunted for a stick; something to dig with if he found damp sand. But nothing was in sight. He staggered down the canyon, clinging to shade, letting the mule look to itself, and by this means managed another half mile. At one point he found a low area rimmed with brush, and tried to kick away sand, but he found no dampness, and could not find a stick worthy of the name to dig with.

He rested again, trying to quiet his tripping heart, which had speeded itself the thirstier he got. He forced himself to his feet. It was cooler now, the cliffs casting blue shadow across the whole canyon. But he was too desperate to notice. He managed another two hundred yards, and tumbled to the gravel, where he lay with the mule above him.

Mule's blood. He would cut the mule open and

drink red blood. But he had no knife. His pack had vanished. He knew now that Sergei Gudonov had come to the end of his mortal life, a victim of his own impatience and haste and anger. He had violated every principle of surviving in the desert. He had rationalized his every move farther from water. He had, in a rage, sent the pack mule to its doom, and with it his last quart of water. He had only himself to blame.

No! It wasn't he who was to blame. It was the rich and powerful, who had driven him to hunt for gold to overthrow them. If the world's arrogant swine, the Romanovs and their kind, had been civilized rather than barbaric, he wouldn't be here trying to find the means to throw them out.

Thus satisfied as to who took his life, for he was already thinking of himself as a dead man, a victim of the Czars, he staggered down the giant canyon, the mule wandering behind him. He began hallucinating. Ahead was an oasis, a spring, a river. Ahead was a fountain of cold water, glimmering in the sun.

Ahead was a man.

No, a chimera.

Yes, a man.

A man leading a burro laden with driftwood collected from this canyon, the debris of a thousand floods.

"Señor?"

"Water."

"*Agua?*"

"Damn your hide, water!"

Gudonov spotted the small soldered tin canteen suspended by a cord from the man's neck, snatched it, uncorked it, and poured paradise down his parched throat, not pausing until he had emptied it.

And then he fell to the clay.

"Señor . . . "

The man struggled with English, but with much

pointing he made himself clear. Something called Miragro Wells lay a short distance away. The Mexican man would take Gudonov there, water the mule, refill his own canteen. Gudonov sat stupidly, feeling the water work in him, feeling his pulse slow and blood begin to move in his parched body.

The man was a woodcutter, the sort who gathered firewood for the stoves in town and sold it for a pittance, the sort of peon Gudonov intended to liberate with the revolution. Here was one of the oppressed, one of the world's poorest of poor, sent by Fate to rescue the revolution.

After a while, Gudonov stood shakily. The sun was fading away and night loomed. The little man smiled and led Gudonov along the cooling canyon. It seemed a long walk, longer than he had understood, but before full dark, they rounded a bend and he beheld a small verdant flat, crowded with cottonwoods and lesser trees, and there was a pool at the foot of the cliff, where a spring purled water.

The desperate mule raced ahead, ripping the lead rope from Gudonov's fingers, and when Gudonov arrived, he found the mule sucking and slurping water. Unseen creatures fled into the dusk. This pool sustained life for miles around.

The woodcutter watched approvingly, and then filled his pillaged canteen.

"Where is Rio Blanco?" Gudonov asked.

"Rio Blanco?" The man understood that much anyway. He beckoned Gudonov to a patch of wet sand, and drew a map. Another hour's walk down this arroyo. Then a right turn into a giant side canyon that would take him to a ridge and down a well-marked trail. After that, four hours of walking to Rio Blanco.

"I will repay you. I will set you free. I will overthrow the swine who have made you a poor woodcutter in sandals and white *pantalones*," he said. "I will give you freedom!"

The woodcutter pointed at himself. "José Maria Aguirre," he said.

"You will no longer be a woodcutter. Soon you will be your own master. I will give you a new world."

The woodcutter stared, smiled without comprehending, and left Gudonov there at the spring, alive to witness another day.

Chapter 15

Artie Quill met the hushed dawn happily. On this day he would find the Lost Doubloon Mine. This stretch of dry foothills was where Stud Malone had hunted that mine for years, and now Artie was hot on the trail.

He stretched, appreciating the hazy light. He hated nights. In the quarter of a century he had been a lone-wolf prospector, he had never gotten used to sleeping on the hard ground. His body rebelled. Worse, he had always been obsessed with the belief that someday something would murder him in his sleep, so he often sat awake through the night, his back pressed into a rock wall, his rifle in hand, his senses raw and ready. That nocturnal death was something foreseen, mystical, and dreaded, and the longer he lived, the more it governed his nights, so he hated to go to sleep and be vulnerable, no matter how exhausted he might be.

But last night he had dozed at least. And here he was, alive and well with the sky brightening. Whatever lurked in his future that would strike him dead as he slept had held off yet another day.

He built a tiny fire using sticks from the brush abounding along a damp drainage, and made some coffee in a speckled blue pot blackened by smoke. Coffee was all he would need until evening. He rarely ate more than one meal a day; it saved him endless time and energy out in the wilds. The mules grazed peacefully as he sipped and watched the shadows shorten as the sun climbed.

He would leave his own mule here and take Malone's, hoping to read a few clues from its behavior. He relished what was to come. He alone had recognized the dying Malone in Rio Blanco, and he alone knew where Malone had spent a decade hunting gold. This day he would work north along these foothills, probing each arroyo, and tomorrow, if he found nothing, he would work south. But he was a man brimming with instinct, raw feeling that overwhelmed him, and he simply knew that this would be a bonanza day.

He led Malone's mule out of the hidden park. His own mule wanted to follow, and Quill finally let it, rather than picketing it in the park. In the cool of the morning he led them north, poking into one gulch and then another, making it thorough. He pushed clear to the head of each gulch, in one case a box canyon, looking for old Spanish works. A mine usually left telltale signs: tailings, ruts, a hole in the ground, decaying sheds or buildings, human debris.

But all he found this soft hot morning was silence and desolation. Most of this rock was not even igneous, but sedimentary, not a likely area for minerals to collect, unless he stumbled on the dark carbonates of silver that were deposited in limestone areas. He was faintly annoyed, but he had spent years as a prospector being annoyed, knowing how cunningly the earth hid its treasures and how often the sort of rock he was looking for outcropped from anonymous sandstone that overlaid the bonanza belts.

He retreated down a long arroyo feeling out of sorts, and when he was able, headed for the next one, the fourth canyon of the morning. He paused a half mile north at a minor depression, not a true arroyo but a watercourse even so, that obviously didn't drain much of the mountains above. He would have passed it by as an obviously futile side trip, but Malone's mule didn't want to pass it by. His big mule ears rotated upward, and he started that direction, so Quill let him. Artie Quill knew enough to let a veteran mule show him a thing or two about country the mule knew well.

"All right then, damn you," he said affectionately, for Artie Quill was a man with a vast respect for mules and an intuitive understanding of them. Malone's mule clambered confidently up an unlikely shallow watercourse hemmed by two anonymous claws of the foothills, and then topped a shoulder that revealed a breathtaking arroyo quite invisible from below. Now the arroyo plunged into a steep-walled canyon and the rock turned into a striated pink and brown. Quill marveled. From the foot of the range, looking straight up that minor valley, all this was invisible. His heart lifted. Far above, a raven circled, a rare sign of life in these arid wastes.

This was a relatively dry canyon, without driftwood tumbled down from the mountains above, or signs of flooding. It curved slightly north, or left, and Quill eagerly clambered up it, his heart pounding from the exertion. He looked back and discovered he had climbed six or seven hundred feet from the tableland below, and the canyon would take him still higher, and fast.

He spotted the brown spoor of another mule or horse, and the sight angered him. Someone had been here not long ago. This spoor was not desiccated; not yet. Was it the spoor of Malone's own mule? Maybe, but it didn't seem right. Quill extracted his Sharps from its saddle sheath. Some rat might be up there ahead of him, and that just might be fatal for the rat.

He paused to catch his breath, feeling giddy. He was now in a cramped canyon with towering walls that offered no way up them. Brush clung to the walls here and there, along with an occasional piñon pine and live oak that had found water in the cracks of the rock. Giant slabs of rock had tumbled into this canyon, forcing Quill to dodge around them. He liked the look of the rock up here, sensing he was drawing ever closer to something beyond his wildest imagination.

A few minutes later, he was not disappointed. Around a bend he discovered the mouth of a mine probing into a seam of glistening reddish brown rock that looked like it might have iron oxide in it. A dark hole gaped in the wall of stone that vaulted upward, a hole without shoring of any sort. Nearby, on a sloping bench too small to contain much, were the fieldstone ruins of a storage shed and a pen for animals. Pressed against the cliff were the roofless remains of a bunkhouse, now a heap of crumbling fieldstone, most of it no doubt tailings from the mine, roofed with earth and a few logs from the timber high above.

Malone's mule whickered cheerfully, as if this had been a pleasant home for him. Quill shoved him and the other mule into the gateless pen. They wouldn't drift, not unless they got thirsty. The Lost Doubloon for certain! No wonder no one could find it. From below, on the flats west of these mountains, it was invisible, and not even the lower drainage offered a clue to the vaulting canyon above.

Quill plucked his Sharps from its sheath, and did what he always did. He squinted toward every ridgeline, every outcrop, every possible hiding place where some son of a bitch might lurk. Once in a while he had spotted Indians, sometimes Hispanics, and sometimes another prospector. He had tangled with more than one, and still had his hide intact, which said something for his caution.

Satisfied, he headed for the gloomy hole carved into the cliff, aware that Malone had died from a rattlesnake bite to his leg. That was not going to happen to Artie Quill, that was for sure. He peered around in there, seeing nothing, but that didn't mean a thing. He thought he'd find some wood and build a hot little fire inside that hole and see what slithered out. He was in no hurry. He had found the gold, and all he had to do was smoke out a few snakes.

There wasn't much wood around. These cliffs were naked rock. But for aeons water had brought wood down from above, and Artie knew he'd find some with a little patience. An hour later, he had his blaze going about ten feet inside the bore, and then he backed away and waited. He saw no snakes, but most of the smoke was simply pouring out the front, and it might not drive away the serpents.

What happened next startled Artie Quill.

A man and a mule bolted out of that hole, coughing and gasping. The mule shuddered, sucked air, brayed piteously. The man wore the worn clothing of a prospector, and carried a pick hammer, which he dropped on the ground while he sucked fresh air into his lungs.

When the man finally recovered enough to examine Artie, he flew into a rage.

"What the hell are you doing, building a fire in my mine?" the white-bearded old geezer yelled.

"Chasing snakes."

"There ain't any snakes in there. Now get out of here!"

"I'm staying."

"This ain't your mine. This is my property."

Artie Quill smiled.

"You heard me," the man yelled, which only triggered another violent coughing fit, which sent him to his hands and knees.

The mule recovered faster. It was saddled with a pack frame and some ancient panniers, half filled with rock. It wheezed, and then stood immobile, blinking at the bright light of day.

The miner stood, his fit having died down, and approached Quill.

"I don't know who you be, but let me tell you something. You don't go building fires in mine heads. You could've killed me and Rosie here."

"This is the Doubloon, right?"

"What's that?"

"An old mine."

"This is my mine."

Artie lifted his Sharps to the man's breast and shot him. The miner looked shocked as recognition filled his face, and then he slowly slid to the ground and oblivion. Artie watched him spasm for a moment and then sag into quietude. He lay in a small patch of sunlight; everything else was shaded by the cliffs.

No man was going to take the Doubloon from Artie Quill.

Artie headed for the wary mule loaded with ore, and pulled out a piece of it, and then another, and another, and another. It wasn't like any ore he knew, maybe a little red or orange. Funny color. Not copper, not lead, not silver. Or maybe it was. Damned if he could tell without a field test or two. He hiked over to his mules in the corral, dug through his gear, and pulled out a small wooden box with stoppered vials of chemicals carefully packed within. He took out his blowpipe, a spirit lamp, a platinum forceps, and a small mortar and pestle. He ground the ore into smaller bits, lit the spirit lamp, plucked up a piece of ore with the forceps, placed it in the flame, and blew gently, with uncertain results. Then he placed some of the powdered ore in an iron spoon, added some carbonate of soda, and heated it over his lamp, holding a gold half-eagle coin just above with his forceps. The gold was swiftly coated a silvery white.

It wasn't a gold mine at all. The ore was cinnabar, and that white sheen on the gold coin was quicksilver.

Chapter 16

Guadalupe O'Rourke mystified Elwood LaGrange. By turns she was fierce and sad, and sometimes her composure seemed to disintegrate. Some terrible thing was tormenting her, but what it might be he hadn't the faintest idea. He knew only that she was hunting for the mine with a frenzy that seemed forbidding. And sometimes she stared at Elwood as if he were a worm.

Slowly, carefully, they worked up the steep canyon until they topped out on a vast plateau high above Rio Blanco. They had seen nothing that might suggest a mine. Not that either of them knew much about that. But still, there ought to be some clues such as heaped rock, a brush-concealed entrance, the scrape of iron wheels over a rocky trail, anything unnatural or out of place. But the stone walls of the canyon were just as nature had carved them, and in that entire four-mile hike to the plateau, they never saw so much as a *maybe*.

"We will lunch now," she said after they had gazed over the huge, glowing prospect, with vistas running fifty miles in most directions, all of it shimmering in the midday sun.

Her meal was as simple as it was elegant. She unstoppered some hearty Madeira and poured it, and then passed him some white cheese and a chunk of crusty bread that tasted somehow sweet to the palate. A soft summery breeze toyed with her jet hair, and under that benign sun her warm flesh glowed with such a splendor that Elwood dissolved within himself. This distant, glorious woman so entranced him that he could only sit there and wish he were someone else, someone who might win a smile and a touch and a glow in her eyes.

"I am not much of a man to find a lost mine," he said. "I would have walked right past it."

"We will find it because we must."

"Because you need it we'll find it?"

"Yes! That is how life is. I must find it, so I will."

For a moment he thought she might tell him what was driving this fierce need, but she didn't. Her face softened.

"You are good company, and now that we have looked in this place, we will try another and another . . . and another."

The cheese, which he suspected was Mexican goat cheese, tasted soft and pungent, and went well with the crisp bread that he suddenly was enjoying, as if her presence had made it the most luxuriant and delicate cheese in all the universe.

"What next?" he asked.

That resolve that he marveled at filled her face. She stared at distant horizons lost in haze fifty miles away, her secrets as obscured as the distant terrain. "We will walk until we find the next canyon going down toward Rio Blanco," she said.

It seemed intelligent to him.

He was filled with a strange ardor, and as he ate he fantasized: Walking down the next canyon he would see something, something out of ordinary, something exciting. He would point. They would scramble up a rocky slope to a brushy place, and peer into a black hole braced with mining timbers.

She would smile, sigh, draw him into her arms, and kiss him, and he would for that moment be in paradise itself.

"What are you thinking?" she asked.

"Of finding the mine. I want to. There is something so urgent about this that I dream of it."

She eyed him somberly. "I need the money. I need to help someone."

The look in her crumbling face was so terrible that he ached to hold her, comfort her, but he could not do such a thing.

That feeling returned to him, the one he had experienced when he first encountered her, when she accepted help from him. He had seen his whole worthless life pass before him, his dabbling and fiddling and wasting of time. Now, once again, he wanted to make himself worthy of her caring, even if all it would ever win for him was a smile, a moment of gratitude.

"I will find the mine for you. Maybe I can help in other ways. You'll need to claim it, stake it out, either sell it or arrange to mine it. I don't know much, but I'll find out."

The gratitude with which she patted his hand and smiled at him transported him into realms where he had never been in his short dull life.

"Tonight I'll talk to miners and maybe talk to one of the lawyers, and tomorrow I'll tell what I found out."

"Elwood, you are kind," she said.

He sighed. It wasn't the sort of thing a woman would say to someone she loved. But of course she didn't love him. Why should she? And yet that knowledge didn't keep him from yearning for her.

She packed up the remains of the picnic and he took the wicker basket. They started along the naked plateau, more or less paralleling Rio Blanco, invisible far below. He enjoyed striding beside her, feeling her purposeful gaze, which raked every rock, every cliff, every crease in the land. After fifteen or twenty minutes on the windswept plateau, they struck a great dip, and off to the right the land clearly dropped into a chasm leading off the plateau in the direction of Rio Blanco.

She turned unhesitatingly.

"We could be trapped," he said. "We might arrive at a cliff or a drop we can't climb down."

"We will find the mine," she replied, and raced down off the plateau until they were swiftly engulfed in yellow rock looming upward to either side of them. Then she slowed.

"We will look hard," she said.

At first, there was nothing to see but anonymous sandstone. But then the canyon became more interesting. On one side was a gray fine-grained rock Elwood thought might be gneiss, and on the other was the sandstone, heaved up at a steep angle. But he marveled at how little he knew of geology. It had been one of those things that had slid past him when he was younger, something not worth knowing. Now, suddenly, everything was worth knowing, and he peered sharply about with an innocent's eyes, discovering marvels at every hand. Brush and driftwood caught hundreds of feet above him on a cliff; pine trees growing from fissures in the rock; an eagle's aerie near the west rim.

"What is this gray rock?" she asked.

"I don't know. Maybe gneiss."

"Does it have gold in it?"

"I don't know."

Desperately, he wanted to know.

"Why is this gray rock on one side and sandstone on the other?"

He had ideas, but dared not plunge into upheavals and watercourses that over aeons had sluiced out a fault in the earth.

"Guadalupe, when we return I intend to find out many things. I'll try to help you."

He felt sheepish, confessing to his vast ignorance, but she didn't see that at all.

She smiled at him. "I believe you would," she said, and he felt comforted by that strange, assessing gaze.

He wondered where in Rio Blanco he could find a geology text, or at least someone well enough versed in the mysteries of the land to teach him some rudiments of the earth sciences. He doubted he would find much, but Silver City would be a good place to search.

They stopped here and there to study likely places in this canyon, including one where a heap of driftwood had piled up into an impenetrable thicket that hid a recessed rock wall under an overhang. But behind the mountain of debris was blank gray rock, without even a crack in it. In aeons past, this canyon had carried a lot of water that had swept boulders and trees and gravel before it. But they found no sign of a mine, no sign of works or habitation. The canyon leveled out, and late that day they walked along a broadening gulch that debouched east of Rio Blanco a mile or so. The entire trip had yielded them nothing except the knowledge that no mine existed where they had walked—as far as two rank innocents could tell.

Dusk caught them as they approached Rio Blanco. They hiked through a deserted and dark town, and by the time he had escorted her to the gloomy mansion, it was full dark. He could barely see her beside him. Her house seemed solemn this evening.

"It has been a long day," she said, twisting away in a manner that would not even let him take her hand or say good-bye. But then she thought better of it and turned.

"You have been most kind. I would not have done this alone."

"I think you would have, Mrs. O'Rourke."

"*Sí,*" she said tautly, "it is so," and he wondered anew what desperation was compelling this feckless hunt for a mine that probably was only a myth.

"*Mañana?*" he said.

"Would you be willing to meet me at dawn at the bank, Mr. LaGrange?"

"You are very serious about this."

He did not see her tears, but did see her softly wipe her eyes in the darkness. "It is my only hope," she said.

He left her with that mystery spinning webs in his mind. This, her only hope? What terrible thing was she facing, and why did she need a gold mine?

It had been a very long hike, perhaps ten miles and much of it up and down. He would soon be in his bed and sleeping soundly. He was ready for it: a bite to eat at a saloon and then he would collapse.

But no, he would not do that. Before he met Guadalupe, he would have done that. But now he had a task before him, and for the first time in his life he would set to work when he didn't much feel like it.

He tried the Bella Donna Saloon first, and asked the barkeep where he could find a prospector's handbook or a geology book.

"Sorry, Elwood," the keep said.

He tried the Casa Grande House next, and got only a shrug from two patrons and the barman. After that, he tried the Bixby House and the Mint Hotel's bar, and no one could help him.

But then he ran into the attorney, Horace Crown, having a late supper in the Mint's restaurant.

"I'm looking for a geology text, Horace."

"Ha! Think you'll find the lost mine, eh?"

"It crossed my mind."

Crown chuckled. "I'll meet you in my office in ten minutes. I have a prospector's handbook that'll turn you into a sourdough in a flash."

And that was how Elwood LaGrange spent an entire night getting himself educated by candlelight, so that he might be of some use to the woman he adored but could never have.

Chapter 17

For some reason, Elwood was not happy with his mustache. It had always been his pride and joy, a bristly honey-brown color with lush tips he carefully waxed so that it hung to either side of his mouth like little scimitars.

Now he stood before the oval mirror of the marble-topped vanity, dissatisfied with the way he looked. The little scimitars looked silly. He wondered why he had ever worn them. He thought maybe Guadalupe didn't like them. She had never complimented him on his grooming or attire, even when he wore his best plaid knickers, his purple bowtie, lace-up boots, green cut-away coat, boiled white shirt, and creamy beaver caballero hat.

He frowned, peered this way and that at his soft young face, and sighed. He laid out his toiletries, poured hot water from a pitcher into the vitreous china basin, and began massaging yellow soap into his mustache until he knew the hair had softened. Then, carefully, he scraped a corner of the mustache off, and then more, and then the scimitar on either side, and finally that thick portion under his nostrils. He stared. The naked flesh was whiter than the rest of his face, making him look like a tenderfoot. It would take a few days to tan the color of the rest. He thought wildly of buying a theatrical mustache and pasting it on with spirit gum, and then thought better of it.

He did not make a handsome sight. Most of the night he had studied the prospector's handbook, burning four candles in the process, and didn't set the book aside until the wee hours. He had slept only briefly, but at least he knew something about looking for minerals.

He had agreed to meet Guadalupe at the break of dawn and continue their exploration. This day they would head west, along a well-traveled road that eventually curved south and followed a tortuous route to Silver City. Few prospectors bothered to hunt in that terrain. The rock didn't appear to be mineralized. There was daily traffic on that well-traveled route, and no doubt the arroyos had been pawed over many times. But Mrs. O'Rourke wanted to explore it, and was even adamant about it. The canyons west of town were an easy walk to Rio Blanco, and that fit with what she knew: The ancient miners had walked from the mine to the town.

She was waiting, once again with her wicker basket, a white shawl covering her neck.

"You look different . . . ah, it is the mustache," she said.

"What do you think?"

She smiled, reached out, and touched his face with a gentle hand, drawing a finger over the newly shorn area.

He felt weak at the knees.

They hiked through a great hush, but not at a leisurely pace. The determined woman was going to find that mine, and that meant scouting many square miles of the country around Rio Blanco. He was amazed at her ferocity. It was as if a life depended on finding the bonanza.

She turned at the first northerly gulch, and they walked through a broad valley that rose swiftly toward the foothills. But this area was covered with soil, not rock, and dotted with gambel oak. The sun burst suddenly over the rim of the world to the east, and the long light lit the narrowing canyon ahead, painting it rosy and then salmon on one side, while plunging the other into lavender gloom. He thought he had never seen the world so sweet and gracious.

He was in an ebullient mood, all because of a moment that had hardly lasted five seconds. Her fingers softly touching the place where the mustache had been evoked something in him so joyous that he could find no word for it. He, a would-be lexicographer, was stumped for a word that might define the tiny tendrils of tenderness that bloomed and ached through him.

Far ahead, the tips of blue snowcapped mountains caught the golden light, serrating the purple heavens with gold teeth. Was this paradise? Not a breeze stirred the air, and the country lay peacefully in the cradle of the newborn day.

The soil overburden ended abruptly with a ledge of tan rock, and they pierced into a stony gray canyon with a dry watercourse down the center of it, flanked by juniper and cactus.

"Today we will find the Doubloon," she said with such certitude that Elwood was startled. "Maybe here. I have a feeling about it."

"Do you always get feelings?"

She eyed him gravely. "I was given the gift of visions, the inner eye. It is a special gift given by God to a few of my people. I see things that are not clear to others. I am not quite seeing the mine, but it is hovering behind a veil, so close now I sense it. When the moment comes, I will see it, and maybe I will be transported to the very place." She eyed him. "But that is not anything you would know about."

He understood nothing of that. Occult knowledge fascinated him, but he was also a skeptic. How could she know anything beyond what her senses revealed to her? If she really did know such things, or felt occasional revelations, then she was given gifts unlike any he had seen in New York and the East. He could name a few professors who would have been envious.

"I spent the night learning minerals," he said. "See? I brought the handbook."

"Minerals? What good is that?"

"They are signposts leading us to the mine, Mrs. O'Rourke."

She smiled. "Then you have secret knowledge."

"We should look for float. Those are bits and pieces of ore that have broken loose from the mother lode and have been washed and driven downslope, far from the ore."

"Ah, then we shall look. I am still looking for those unique hoofprints too."

"Good. Most gold ore is quartz, which is shiny and crystalline. It can be many colors, from transparent, like glass, to gray to brown, depending on the impurities in it. If we find pieces of quartz that are rounded and weathered, that means the float is very old and has been smoothed by nature; recent pieces have sharp edges, and if we find those, we know we're close to the source."

She smiled. "You have been studying, Mr. La-Grange."

"It's book learning, not field experience, but maybe it'll help."

"I am already looking at the ground."

They hiked more slowly now as they penetrated the gray-walled canyon. Now and then, they plucked up something from the canyon floor and studied it uncertainly. But nothing looked like quartz.

"I think it's easier to find a mine," she said. "I could pick up a thousand stones and see nothing."

"A good prospector can see things we can't," he

said. "Like pyrites. Gold is often found in sulphurets and other minerals. There are all sorts of tests, but we haven't the tools and chemicals to perform them. But we can look for float anyway."

"What does a sulphuret look like?" she asked.

Elwood shook his head. "All I know is that a sulphuret is a metallic pyrite, iron, copper tin, other metals. These ores deteriorate in the sunlight and air, and the gold leaves them and is washed into creeks."

She smiled wryly at him and shook her head.

"I learned less than I thought," he confessed, feeling blue. He had thought he might conquer geology if he tried hard enough.

"You have already helped," she said.

She bent over and picked up a dark stone, but it was only a fine-grained rock he thought was schist. He wouldn't bet on it. Not after one candlelit seance with a prospecting manual.

"We should look for the mine head," he said, tacitly acknowledging their innocence of anything that might help them field-test rocks.

They poked and probed their way up the gray arroyo, finding little to excite their interest, though there did seem to be some evidence of industry there in the shape of heaps of rock. But the piles were not associated with any digging or hole in the cliff, and Elwood thought they might simply be the remains of an old quarry. He wondered whether he had seen such stone in the buildings of Rio Blanco, and remembered that the bank had been erected of a similar gray stone, probably a granite.

"I think we won't find the mine anywhere near here," he said.

"We will look."

It was the way she said it that gave pause. She had been filled with boundless energy this trip, marching determinedly toward anything that might be a mine head, any cliff that showed promise of a vein of quartz, like a dog running ten miles for every mile its master walked.

But the day yielded nothing. By late afternoon, they had emerged from the gray canyon and started for Rio Blanco, both silently mulling their chances.

"I will go out tomorrow. But I won't ask you to join me," she said. "You have done enough."

"But I enjoy the hunt."

"No, you've done enough. I am feeling, well, in-debted to you, and have no way of returning your kindness . . . and interest."

"I don't ask anything of you."

She eyed him. "Why don't you?"

"I am pleased to be in your company. I've made a friend."

She hesitated, finding meaning in what he said. "There is nothing, nothing in it for you, Señor La-Grange. Nothing."

Had she sensed his true feelings? Of course she had, and she was shooing him away.

"You need someone with you, Señora."

She didn't reply, but the hauteur in her eyes told him he should not have said it.

He desperately wanted to continue with her even if the passion blooming in him was doomed. He knew it was doomed from the start anyway. She was the first woman who had ever accepted his friendship, the first woman ever to take an interest in him.

Maybe he could try a different approach. "I will help you for a part of the mine if we find it," he ventured.

She pondered that a while. "I like that better," she said. "I will pay you a thousand dollars if we find the mine and it can still produce."

He nodded. Now it was a business arrangement. She had shifted it away from dangerous ground.

Chapter 18

Sergei Gudonov watched enviously as the woodcutter wandered away through twilight, perfectly at home day or night in a wild and terrible land. Why was it that he, Gudonov, one of the most intelligent mortals on earth, could not deal with this forbidding land while a simple and stupid peon could?

He thought maybe only a person of low and cunning intelligence could live in the wild; great intelligence like his should be employed in cities. He would settle at the Miragro Wells this night and hope to survive the ordeal. If this was the only water for miles around, then all manner of fearsome beasts would come here and drink, and among them might be catamounts and wolves. This desert spawned mountain lions six feet long, lithe and terrible creatures that could kill a man with fang and claw. He knew also that this desert harbored herds of vicious peccaries called javelinas that could surround prey, including men, and butcher them for dinner.

He eyed the spring uneasily. It purled from a granitic wall into a small pond that was rimmed by vegetation, except where animal trails reached the water. The pond drained into a small swamp and there the water vanished, but below were a few stately cottonwoods and a great deal of brush.

He drank again in the deep quiet, cupping his

hands and lifting sweet water to his cracked lips, his body not yet recovered from the parching it took earlier that day. His surviving mule cropped grass a little ways off; it would not stray from feed and water, so he saw no point in tying it.

He decided to spend the night well away from the water, perhaps in the cottonwood grove nearby. Or maybe he could walk up the canyon a little and press his back against the vertical cliff. That seemed better. He would sit all night against that wall, well away from the spring. He would find a stick and some stones to beat off predators. Everything had been lost when his pack mule plunged off the trail, including his Smith and Wesson Russian, and now he was defenseless apart from such weapons as he could devise.

By deep dusk he had a long stick in hand, and had collected a pile of stones he could throw. He did not like the thought of spending a whole night in this forbidding place. Uneasily, he sat on the hard and cruel ground, propped himself against the cliff, and watched the stars materialize out of the deep of the night. In the swamp, bullfrogs began their rhythmic croaking, lulling him into a moment of peace. But not for long. He heard a strange screeching, the bray of his mule, the tumble and thud of animals moving, and he sat rigid, his staff in hand, ready to defend himself.

Then, nothing. After a while, the bullfrogs started their music. He sat rigidly, fearful of the rattler he could see in his mind's eye, slithering slowing along the base of the cliff, looking for dinner at the spring and finding a warm human being in his way.

All that terrible night, strange sounds violated the peace, and terrible shapes and shadows crossed his vision. A spare moon crusted the land with white, making the spring the haunt of ghosts and spirits and hobgoblins. He knew what was needed to abolish evil spirits and wild animals, but he had always laughed at exorcism. There was neither god nor demon, nothing to exorcise. What he ought to do was compose a lyrical poem, using the tongue of Mother Russia, and thus vanquish the horrors of this alien wilderness. But not even his enormous brain would permit him to make a poem this evil night.

At one point, after more fluttering and a scream, he arose, his long club in hand, and roared, striding around through the pale and white wasteland roaring imprecations, swinging his club at phantoms, cursing the thousand evils lurking there with watchful eyes. Ghosts! He saw a hundred ghosts, crowding to the lip of water for a drink, transparent and white in the moonlight. He knew who they were, the ghosts of the world's oppressed, the little people he would set free with the gold he would find.

Then, suddenly, he was weary, and settled into his rocky chair, his back against stone, fighting off sleep, determined not to let any animal, known or unknown, creep murderously upon him. He was born to transform the world, and no animal of this vicious wild would stay him.

And so the night dragged by until an early light cracked open the darkness. He was exhausted. He drank again, washed his face in the cool water, rose to look for his mule, and girded himself for a walk of six or seven hours without a canteen or a map, other than one drawn in the sand, and no certainty that the miserable peasant knew what he was talking about.

He studied the small patch of grass for the mule, and didn't find it. But maybe it was sleeping. He spotted an iron-gray mound that looked like a sleeping mule off to once side, and approached it. It was indeed his mule, stretched out on the grass.

"Up," he roared, and booted the buttocks of the mule.

It didn't move.

He kicked again, and his foot struck dead flesh. Chilled, he circled around to the other side, where he could see the mule's head better, and there discovered the mule's throat had been slit, neatly, with a sharp instrument, one ear to the other, and the gray hair below the incision was soaked with blood.

A paralyzing chill hit him, and momentarily drained his strength. He looked fearfully around. If that peon had done this, he would thrash that woodcutter half to death. Wildly, he studied the benign cottonwoods, silent and somber in the dawn, their leaves and limbs still black in the dusky dark. He waved his big stick menacingly.

"I will kill you," he yelled, but no one answered.

There was no one present at Miragro Wells. No one except ghosts.

He drank again, drank until he could hold no more water, because what he drank would have to last him clear to Rio Blanco, and then started down the broad valley, hastening to escape that place of the dead and the damned.

He worried his way through a silent dawn with no breeze, no bird, no living thing, not even a lizard, to suggest he lived in a world full of life. Fear drove him, fear not only of that spring, but that he would miss the turnoff described by the woodcutter.

But when he came upon it he recognized it at once, a steep canyon at the right, with a clear trail in its bottom, and he turned. From now on he needed only to follow the trail, and he would end up in Rio Blanco by noon. With the rising sun, his hardy spirits returned, and he put the haunted night behind him. He knew what had killed that mule. There were hundreds of prospectors hunting that mine, swarming over this huge wilderness, and one of them had found the mule and killed it, thus disabling a rival. Sergei grunted. If he ever found out who the culprit was, he would slit a throat himself. On this disastrous trip he had lost two mules and his entire pack, while finding no sign of a mine.

The trail took him up a narrow canyon whose walls cramped his spirits, and then over a ridge, just as the woodcutter said, and finally down a long slope, with vast views cropping up here and there, distant mountains hazy in a blinding white world. He studied the cliffs as he hiked, looking for telltale signs of human activity, but nature here was silent and anonymous, juniper and cactus crowding the trail, naked rock and patches of piñon pine high above.

He would regroup, get a new mule and gear, and head out once again. Nothing would keep him from that mine, and the gold that would underwrite the transformation of the whole world.

By noon, on a particularly sizzling day, he dragged into Rio Blanco, desperate once again for water. He paused first at one of the shallow wells that watered the town, and drank from a dipper, and then headed for Casa Grande Street, intending to re-outfit at once. When he swung around a blind corner and found himself on the main thoroughfare, the sight astounded him. A mob of prospectors hurried in and out of the few stores in Casa Blanca, while mules, burros, horses, buggies, wagons, and one stagecoach jammed the city.

He stopped, startled, and realized that word of the dying prospector's gold ore had reached Silver City, fifty miles south, and now the rush was on. Cursing, he pushed through the throngs and into the hardware emporium, suspecting the worst. He was not wrong. Everything remotely useful for camping out and prospecting had been stripped from its shelves, and men were cussing the store clerks for not having an infinite supply of picks and axes and shovels and hammers and tenting and cook pots and knives.

"But sir, how can I find a mine without so much as a Dutch oven?" one bald gent was saying.

Sergei knew he'd find the same story in every shop in town. The livery would not have a single four-footed animal. The grocer would not have beans or coffee or side-pork. The dry-goods man would not have boots or jackets or blankets. Sergei watched all these fools clamoring and whining and complaining, and headed abruptly for his small adobe house. He knew what he had to do, and once he was rested and deep darkness cloaked him, he would do it. Before dawn, he would be out of town once again, with some-one's outfit in tow.

But first there was the propaganda. Weary as he was, he set aside his bodily needs and headed for the saloons and any knot of gold-crazed fools he could find.

"I will tell you," he said over a lager, "zis prospector, I saw him as he lay dying. That snakebite was not new. Many hours it took for that leg to swell up, for that venom to kill that man. He had traveled far, I tell you. I knew zis. Who else was a medical corpsman for the Cossacks and knows such things, eh?"

They understood. These mobs, which Gudonov es-timated as between three and four hundred feverish gold-seekers, would wander far from Rio Blanco, far, far beyond the areas where the lost mine might lurk. For the sake of the revolution, he must steer them down a fool's trail.

Chapter 19

Fortunes could be made without even leaving the office. Malachi Cromwell-Nast understood what drove men, and simply put that knowledge to use.

No one thought of him as a rich man. He took care to keep his office furnishings modest and practical. He took space on the second floor of the Cimmaron Bank, and made sure that his desk was battered and his swivel chair squeaked, and the lithographs on his walls were cheap. It was useful to appear hard-pressed and to conceal his mounting fortune from prying eyes.

The lithographs indeed featured images of Uncle Sam, or Motherhood—a winsome grouping of sturdy boys and girls gathered about a loving and heroic woman, or the American Eagle. All these helped create the impression he sought to give others, including the brute occupying one of his squeaking chairs.

The gent's name was Arnold Schwartz and he was eager for employment. He had a low brow, a sign of low intelligence, but had massive shoulders and arms, plainly the result of hard work. The man had spent much of his life in a Pittsburgh foundry until he was fired. Nast knew why Schwartz had been fired. He had been a labor agitator. He came from a coal-mining family, which was good.

"You'll do," Nast said. "You're going to be my eyes and ears for now. Later, I may have special tasks for you.

You'll visit any camp you find, talk with any prospector you come across. If any has ore, you'll snatch a piece of it one way or another, and then remember which ore goes with which prospector. Is that clear?"

"How'm I gonna cart all that around?"

"I got a burro for you. There's not a mule or horse to be had, but a burro I can get in Mextown. You'll carry your gear on it. You'll carry a pick and shovel and look like a miner even if you've never dug for gold in your life. Is that clear?"

"What's it worth?"

"It's worth a dollar a day, plus two dollars for every tip that's worth my consideration."

"What do ya mean by that?"

"It means I'll be the judge of whether to pay you. You will be my spy. I want news. I want tips. I want samples. If anyone finds that mine, I want to know about it. If anyone's got mineral, I want a piece of that mineral. I won't buy worthless or old news. I want new news and news worth two dollars. And I don't want you out there more than three days at a time. You come back every three days. I may have other tasks for you."

"Such as?"

"Such as what you do so well. Agitate. You have big fists. That's why you're here, as far from Pennsylvania as you could get."

Schwartz grinned. That was good.

"You are dumb as a stump about this desert. Learn how to survive. For your sake, not mine. If you kill yourself, you'll save me a wage. That's exactly what you mean to me. An expense. Give me a reason to think more of you, and you'll have your reward, and a lot more than two dollars."

Schwartz smiled.

"Look for Artie Quill. Gray beard, shifty eyes, crooked smile, heavily armed. He has a foul breath. All you have to do is talk with him for three minutes and if you can't stand the air, that's Artie. I've shown you his tintype. I want to know everything that Quill is doing. Spy on him. But watch out. He shoots strangers. Quill and I have a grubstake arrangement and I want to make sure he's keeping his end of it."

"He don't look so tough."

"He's a lot tougher than any foundryman ever thought of being."

Schwartz snorted, disbelieving.

"All right, your gear and your burro are at Beaumont's Livery Barn. Tell Augie Beaumont I sent you."

The brute lumbered out, shaking the floor with each heavy step.

Nast watched from his window as Schwartz headed down Casa Grande Street.

Maybe, maybe not. The brute would have to prove himself.

Nast knew he would have to hire several more snitches to keep an eye on things. A gold rush required intelligence. There were miners swarming over hundreds of square miles, and Nast needed to know what was happening out there. Snitches were worth the money.

He returned to the task that had absorbed him for days, finding the source of Ricardo O'Rourke's fortune—and what had happened to all that wealth.

The Mexican gunrunner didn't own a thing in Mexico, and for obvious reasons: Anything O'Rourke possessed down there was likely to be confiscated by the Diaz regime. That left the gunrunner and revolutionary the option of buying property north of the border. But he was a Mexican citizen and couldn't homestead land here, so whatever he bought had to be patented land or a mining claim. With all his loot from running guns, he had plenty of cash, but Nast had been unable to find a single property still owned by O'Rourke. He had examined the tax rolls and the recorded deeds of every county in New Mexico, and there were none. That was a great mystery. The man was rumored to own ranches and mining claims, water rights and orchards.

Still, when O'Rourke was in town, he always had cash; often gold he exchanged for greenbacks at the bank. If his fortune was not in real property, land and buildings and mines, then it must be in something else. And Nast ached to know what it was. It was plain that Guadalupe didn't know of it. If such wealth actually existed, she would swiftly have come up with the funds to ransom her husband. But she was as much in the dark as Nast.

And that was why, this hot day, he decided to pay a social call on Mrs. O'Rourke to offer his specialized services to the woman. If there was an O'Rourke fortune to be found, Nast would find it. He found no one at home midday, and tried again late in the day. This time she opened the door.

"Señora, I wonder if you might have a moment. I thought to see how you are progressing, and offer my assistance."

"Thank you," she said. "I am doing well."

She didn't invite him in. She looked weary and was dressed in that picnic attire she wore these days. She seemed reluctant to talk.

"I was wondering how you are coming with your efforts to put the ransom together."

She shook her head.

"Perhaps, Señora, I can help. One thing I know how to do is look through papers. Perhaps I could look through your husband's papers and find ways you might take advantage of his wealth."

She shook her head again.

"Ah, are you saying no? Really, I can find properties, determine their value, show you how you might market them."

"Mr. Nast, my husband has no papers. There is not a paper in this house."

"Ah, no papers? No business documents? No . . . will?"

"Nada."

"But surely . . ."

"Thank you for your interest; now I must prepare a little supper, frijoles perhaps."

"But Mrs. O'Rourke . . . ," he said, reaching for something, anything. "Time is running out. Who knows how long President Diaz will have patience? Your husband's in more and more danger with each passing day. We must find a way to collect the ransom and get it to Mexico City."

She stared at Nast, her eyes smoldering in the twilight. At least she was listening.

"Perhaps he has a safe, a strongbox. I'll help you look. If we find some papers, perhaps we can raise the money."

"Nada." Something in her changed. "You think I am hiding something. Or telling you untrue things. Good night, Mr. Nast."

She swung the heavy door closed. It snapped shut. He heard the bolt fall and knew she had locked her home to him. He stood there in the dark, on that veranda, slightly irritated. He prided himself on his ability never to succumb to emotion, so he swiftly retreated to that cool hardness where his mind worked best.

She was lying. There would be private papers. One way or another, he would find out what Ricardo O'Rourke owned. A gunrunner wasn't going to leave documents around, but that didn't mean he didn't possess them; didn't mean he had no property.

Slowly, Nast retreated from that dark and stormy porch and walked down to Rio Blanco, his mind actively engaged in resolving the issue. There were papers in that house.

Then he knew what he would do. Utterly simple. He would see for himself. She had taken to hiking with that fool LaGrange, and while they wandered the hills looking for the Lost Doubloon, he would pay a visit. He would take a little gift with him, of course, a subterfuge, an excuse if he were caught. But he wouldn't get caught. That great quiet adobe building slept silently through the middle of each day, its owner gone.

Oh, he would search. He would study each wall, remove each painting hanging there, lift up each rug, check any desk for secret compartments and spring-loaded doors. He would study the back of closets, the upper reaches of any pantry, the recesses of any cold cellar. And when he was done, she would have no secrets from him, and he would surely know what Ricardo O'Rourke had done with all his wealth.

Heartened by that little plan, he hastened back to his office, which was really his home because he often slept on a bunk there, and resolved to pounce the next time the lady wandered out of town with that idiot from the East. He had rooms, but preferred to live in his office. Like most men who had given their souls over to business, his office was more home than his rooms, and his office had become his mistress and family and church.

No papers! The little tamale could lie persuasively, her face filled with hurt innocence. But he would have the last laugh.

Chapter 20

Artie Quill probed the cinnabar mine, found that the shaft rose steadily through dark metamorphic rock for fifty feet until it hit a crosscut that stretched in either direction along a thick seam of cinnabar. The miner had been off to the left, and had been driven out by Artie's fire that was intended to drive away any snakes.

It wasn't the Doubloon, and that irked him. But it might be worth something if he could latch onto it and keep it hidden a while, especially from Malachi Cromwell-Nast. He retreated to daylight, contemplated the dead miner, whose blood had soaked into the ground, and decided to conceal the evidence. He dragged the miner deep into the mine and left the body there. He lifted the heavy packsaddle from the small mule, and dragged it into the mine and left it beside the dead miner. Back in daylight he scouted for some brush to hide the mine entrance, found very little in that stony canyon, and finally gave up trying to hide the mine head.

He eyed the mule tenderly. Mules were friends of all prospectors, lifesavers, beasts of burden, loyal comrades in the wilds. This one was small, gray, nondescript, and shied away from being handled.

"Whoa, there, gal," Artie said. "I'm taking you with me. You're heading for grass and water, You and me, we're old friends. I'd never hurt no jenny mule."

Artie rubbed her ears and scratched her jaw. He had a way with mules. "I'll call you Rosie, sweetheart. You're just the prettiest little thing ever stood on four legs."

It was love at first sight. The mule calmed under Artie's tender ministrations, and soon trotted along behind as they worked down the canyon to the base of the foothills.

Artie fumed. He had been so sure he had found the lost mine that it hadn't even occurred to him that it might be something entirely different. Stud Malone, who had scouted all this country over and over, never told him that cinnabar might be found in these foothills. Malone talked gold, and once in a while silver, but the man's heart was set on gold. There were prospectors like that: A man wanted silver or turquoise or platinum or gold and nothing else would do. He might find a mountain of copper or tin, but that wouldn't do.

But Artie wasn't like that. Loot was loot.

There was nothing to do but hike to the next arroyo and try once again for the Doubloon. It looked to him like there might be fifty or sixty canyons cut out of the flank of this range, and he would have to probe every one of them. Somewhere around here, Malone had found the Doubloon and had gotten some ore out of it before a rattler nailed him. And by God, Artie was going to find it, and then he and Rosie could retire.

The foothills abruptly changed as he worked north, from gray rock to red and brown, and he sensed a giant fault had cleaved the land into totally different belts. The red rock was harder, less eroded, higher and newer. He preferred the redder rock; it looked to be granite, and that might harbor quartz, and quartz. . . . His mind raced. He wondered why he had wasted time in that grim gray area. Now he was homing in, and soon Stud Malone's secret would pop out.

He turned into a broad canyon with vertical red walls a half mile apart, and swiftly discovered he was not alone. Here, in the silty sand, were hoofprints by the hundred. A fear and rage cut through him, and he paused to try to count the numbers of mules that had left their prints in the dust and clay. But they were beyond counting. He reminded himself that he was in the midst of a gold rush, and that these mountains and valleys were crawling with sourdoughs, and that one or another of them might get lucky.

Artie felt rage build up in him. That mine was his. He alone knew the dead man, Malone, and knew the man's little habits and the area he poked through. Artie grimly set out to find the interlopers and chase them off if he could. He had his ways, and they were effective.

He veered at once toward the south wall, the shadowed wall, where his movements would not be noticed. The moment he left the worn trail up the center of that giant gulch, the travel was rougher, but he didn't mind. He pursued a tortured route around slide-rock, tumbled granite boulders, talus, and steep little hollows. He was looking for a game trail that would take him to the ridge above, where he could work toward the mountains and keep a sharp eye on anything below.

The thought of a bunch of rivals poking through this likely canyon irritated him, and he decided sharp, decisive action was needed. This canyon, above all the others, was the likeliest spot for a mine. His gaze raked the walls and hollows as he walked, his sight begging to find the telltale tailings or squared shadow that might mean a timbered mine shaft. But he found only piñon pine and juniper in thick carpets, and sometimes had to wrestle his way through the juniper, which lashed and scratched him.

His mules followed dutifully. Rosie was a gem, never complaining or balking. He paused for breath, and drew his rough hand over her head, waggling her long and delicate ears. He and Miss Rosie were going to get along just fine.

Then, at last, he found what he was looking for, a game trail barely six inches wide, with tiny hoofprints on it, desert mule deer, and fresh too. A well-used trail from the canyon floor to the rim. He took it, and found himself climbing in dizzy steps, until his lungs howled and heart banged relentlessly. But he was gaining the ridge a couple of hundred feet above, and there he would have a view, the sort of view he needed to plan some further action.

He faced a terrible barrier at the last, a four-foot red ledge he had to climb over and somehow bring his mules over after him. He could see no way. The ledge was easy enough for a deer, but no mule could manage it, especially one with a packsaddle.

Was it all for nothing? He turned carefully, not wishing to lose his balance and fall into that heap of rock below. That's when he spotted some mining activity across the chasm, several men, tiny dots, industriously doing something. He eased around Rosie until he reached his pack mule and dug into the panniers for his brass spyglass. He found it easily and telescoped it to its maximum, and then hunted for the miners in the tiny circle of magnified terrain visible to him. He had trouble finding them, and made one annoying sweep after another without pinpointing them, but just before he exploded into wild rage he caught a glimpse, and a moment later had them in his sight.

Some prospectors were running tests on some ore. Five bearded men, breaking down what might have been quartz. One was running some amalgamation operation, where crushed quartz ore was mixed with mercury, which amalgamated with the freed particles of gold and later could be separated with a simple distillation process. So they'd found gold. So they were using quicksilver. Artie's mind raced to the cinnabar mine he had so recently claimed.

Was this the Doubloon Mine? Artie agonized over that as he glassed the wall of rock on the far side of the canyon. He saw nothing resembling a mine, but that didn't mean much. The old mine might have been nothing but an open ledge. Or maybe these gents had carted the ore down from someplace high up. He raged at the very thought that they had gotten to the mine before he did.

He knew there would be a rush; probably a thousand greedy men were scouring a few hundred square miles, and they ranged from store clerks to old sourdoughs like himself, with a few accountants and doctors and whiskey drummers thrown in.

He didn't even know how the hell he'd get off this deer trail, much less deal with it.

"Hey, Rosie, we're going to turn around," he said. Rosie yawned, revealing a long pink tongue and brown-stained choppers. He eased around Rosie to the pack mule. He had to turn that one around first, and he knew what that entailed. Ever so carefully he lifted off the panniers and set them on the trail. Then he loosened the cinches of the packsaddle and slowly, carefully lifted it off the mule, which arched its back. Its shoulder muscles shivered. Artie watched where he was stepping. One false step into thin air and he would scream his way through three or four hundred feet of air, and then bounce like a rag doll off ledges and boulders.

So far, so good.

Now to back the mule ten feet or so to a wider spot, maybe eighteen inches across. He crowded the mule back until it took a mincing step, and then another and another, and then it began backing too swiftly and Artie stopped it with a yank. But eventually they made the tiny widening, if it could be called that.

"All right, swing it," he said.

Artie's mule understood, and began mincing around, its ears flattened back, one hoof lowering onto thin air until he found purchase, and then, suddenly, the mule was turned. Artie went to get Rosie, and to his astonishment Rosie had already reversed herself and faced downslope.

"Rosie, you are a wonder mule, the sweetest longears ever to gaze upon the likes of Artie Quill."

Getting that packsaddle back on would be a hell of a task because the trail wasn't wide enough. He thought he just might reconnoiter before getting into all of that, so he left the mules where they stood, and worked down that slope for twenty yards. There was a side trail, one he had missed because it was little used, sloping upward toward the ridge. He hiked it, finding the grade simple and easy, and clambered out on top, on a high and handsome escarpment where a man could stand in the wind and own the world.

It took but a little while to bring his mules up, and to drag his packs and saddle to the top and saddle his critter. He found shelter in a cup of rock, and brought the mules there.

Then he unsheathed his fine Sharps buffalo rifle, and a box of brass shells, and hunted for the right forted-up overlook, with a good exit if he needed one. He soon found just the spot, and began glassing the miners down below. It would be an easy shot.

Chapter 21

Elwood LaGrange met Guadalupe at dawn the next day, but this time he was dressed differently. His plaid knickers weren't the thing to wear in a desert wild, where everything had needles and stickers. Today he wore some blue-jean cloth dungarees with copper rivets reinforcing the seams. They had been made by a San Francisco company with long experience supplying clothing to miners.

The pungence of the stiff fabric had delighted him as he pulled the dungarees on. To this he added a new chambray ready-made shirt, pale blue, that would breathe air through it during the heat of the day, and about his neck was a green gingham bandanna. A flat-crowned straw Panama completed his costume, and made him feel better-equipped to wrestle with tough slopes and a blazing sun.

He must had startled her, because she stared hard at him before she nodded, her gaze pausing at each new item. He could tell in a glance that she was out of sorts. A melancholia clung to her this day, far more than the previous days, though he had noticed a certain sadness clinging to her for all the time they had explored together. He wished he could help her, or heal her, or at least offer her a little comfort. But whatever her burden, she kept it locked within, her grief hidden behind those proud lips and eyes.

This day she wore the same battered gray skirts and a fresh white *blusa,* scooped at the neck and puffed at the shoulders. A soft white rebozo completed her costume, and now she wore it as a head scarf that disciplined her glossy jet hair.

"That is good," she said, her gesture embracing his new clothing.

"I think it will be better after these have been laundered. This jean cloth is going to scrape the skin off me."

"That hard fabric will last a long time," she said.

"Where to this day?"

"West again. The next canyon out of town."

He was agreeable to that. She knew the country far better than he, so she would choose the locale of each day's march.

He plucked her wicker picnic basket from her golden arm and they headed west along the rutted road, in the sweet silence of the dawning day.

No one was on the road, so they hiked peaceably away from Rio Blanco, keeping their thoughts to themselves. He sometimes wondered if he would ever have a real conversation with her, the kind of conversation that true friends enjoy. He decided she would never open herself to him, and whatever secrets she bore would always be hers alone. But he was content just to be walking beside this lissome woman whose mysterious troubles had lit fires in him.

They hiked a half hour in companionable silence until the first rays of a newborn sun shot light upon the noble range of mountains northwest, gilding their flanks with gold.

"This is a good place to live," he said, surprising himself because it had never occurred to him to stay.

"Why do you say so, Mr. LaGrange?"

"Because each day is painted in different colors."

"Is that enough?"

"I grew up in the East where there is green forest and meadow and plenty of rain. But forest conceals. It is only in these austere lands that one faces one's own self. I think I like the desert because it makes one honest."

She weighed that. "I have never heard of such a thing," she said. "But I have heard the desert is where one comes closest to God, and that is why the Hebrew prophets retreated to the desert to hear the voice of the Divine."

They passed the giant watershed they had examined the previous day, and a half hour later reached a new drainage, a golden arroyo, brightened by a low sun that wrought pinks and lavenders and purples in every shadow. He thought he had never seen such a palette of warm color in nature, and imagined he was walking into a magical place where any artist would become famous without half-trying.

He had no idea whether such a rainbow land would hide minerals. He was content this morning to hike up a sandy gulch between golden arms of rock, with every shadow painted sea green or tawny peach or chocolate brown or azure. A little gambel oak thrived in the few places that caught rain, and in some areas, patches of cactus in spring bloom shot bold yellows onto the amazing canvas.

He knew, suddenly, that for the rest of his life he would remember this magical place, where God had applied a mad, delicate, and bold paintbrush to everything in sight. He studied this purple and gold panorama, looking for telltale signs of mining, but saw nothing. Neither did he expect to find a mine in sandstone country, but one never knew. Nature was a bag of tricks.

She seemed this day to retreat deep inside herself, and whatever was passing through her mind occupied her far more than the terrain. It was as if the mine she sought so badly might be found in the landscape of her heart rather than this real world on this bright spring day. By noon, they had traipsed deep into this rainbow canyon without seeing the slightest evidence of habitation. The heat built, as it always did this time of year. This was also a drier area than the others, and they found no sign of a seep, and very little sign of wildlife.

They came to a point where the canyon narrowed, and then they walked between two smooth red walls of rock and into a hidden park beyond, with coarse grasses dotting a small plain of perhaps ten or twelve acres. He pointed to a copse of scrub oak and brush in the shadow of a cliff.

"Lunch?" he asked.

She seemed to emerge from some distant place, and nodded. He was ready to sit. The unwashed jean cloth had chafed some places on his thighs, and he wondered how he would endure the long walk back to Rio Blanco.

She had filled the picnic basket once again with goat cheese, plus a bottle of Madeira, two brown pears, and a long hard loaf of black bread. And this time, she had included an old table linen for a ground cover.

She set out the meal silently, as if she wanted to live this day apart from him. He drank from the tepid water in his canteen, and handed it to her, but she shook her head.

She watched him eat, but didn't touch the food she had placed on the cloth before herself. She sat wearily, her long gray skirts tucked around her thighs, her rebozo loose over her bosom gauzing her warm flesh, her thoughts some millennia away.

"I learned a few days ago that Ricardo is alive," she said. "Maybe alive. I was given a small token that he always wore around his neck. It was brought from the

City of Mexico, where he is a prisoner of the president, Diaz."

"Your husband?"

"*Sí*, Ricardo. For two years I waited and he did not come home. I thought he was dead. I knew what he does. He supplies arms to guerrillas in Sonora who want to overthrow Diaz, a dictator even if he calls himself El Presidente. He does nothing for the poor and humble and desperate except grind them down under his heel. Diaz was once a poor man himself, but he betrays his people. Ricardo, he wished to help fight this man. That is in him, helping, and running guns. Soon after he married me, we came here, safe from Diaz, and his *rurales,* the provincial police who torment those they can abuse.

"Here he could buy arms, good rifles and ammunition and other things needed for the revolution, and then ship them by the light of the moon to those who were waiting. He is like that, a great green-eyed cat who can run with the moon."

Elwood sat quietly, awaiting whatever would come, not wanting to know how much she loved her Ricardo, but knowing she would talk of it anyway. At last she was talking, sharing her secrets, all the barriers that lay between them shattered now.

"He was a man, oh, what a man," she said, "my Ricardo. Afraid of nothing. Full of humor, like his Irish people, and full of songs. He could sit down and make a ballad and sing it. He would sit beside me and sing songs to me, and these came flowing out of his mind."

She sipped some of the Madeira now, memories dancing across her face.

"A few days ago, when Nast dropped Ricardo's little Maltese cross into my hand, he brought some news. Ricardo was being held for ransom. The *rurales* had caught him and put him in irons and carried him in a cart clear to the City of Mexico, where he was condemned to die as a traitor. But then Diaz said that Ricardo might live if much money were paid for his release. A hundred thousand pesos." She stared at him. "Eight pesos to a dollar. Twelve and a half thousand dollars. I do not have it. I have nothing."

"That's why we're looking so hard for the Lost Doubloon."

"Yes. Every hour of every day, his life is in greater peril. Someday, if no money comes, they will take him to the wall."

"To the wall?"

"The place, an adobe wall, with a post before it where they tie the prisoner and then . . . shoot him as the snare drums roll."

"Good God."

"This tarantula, Mr. Nast, I don't know how he found out about this or got Ricardo's cross. He says he wants to help me, but I don't trust him a bit. He wants to take from the widow."

"Widow?"

Her eyes filled. "Ricardo. I think he might be dead. I think this ransom is a story of Mr. Nast. But I don't know. How can I know?"

Tears slid down her cheeks.

He reached across and held her hand.

"Then believe he lives," he said.

"I have the vision that shows me what is true. So far, I know nothing, no vision comes, but I have a bad feeling."

"And if we do find the mine?"

She seemed to come out of the world she was inhabiting within, and she gazed sadly at him. "I will go to the City of Mexico and find Ricardo and bring him home, whether beside me or in a coffin I don't know."

Chapter 22

Guadalupe thought that this rainbow-colored canyon was affecting her mood. Her marriage had been a rainbow, all the brightest colors of life. Ricardo was a rainbow, the miracle of sun pouring through the rain. Now, as she lunched with this Anglo man, she thought of rainbows, and purple storm clouds, and yellow sunlight.

"Mrs. O'Rourke, I have a competence, not a large one, that reaches me each month. It would be enough to take you to Mexico City, and for me to go along as your protector," LaGrange was saying.

She stared. He was offering her a great gift.

"Oh, *gracias*, but I cannot . . ."

"We would find out about your husband."

She smiled bitterly. "Not unless we have money. It would take much money to find out about my husband. The regime keeps its secrets. Everything is for sale, including information."

"I might see about borrowing the twelve thousand you need. We need to do something, and hunting for a lost mine seems the least likely to get us anywhere."

"You? Borrow?"

"I can't get into the trust fund, but perhaps I could borrow the money and pay it back. I am living on three thousand a year."

"But Elwood . . . !"

She was touched. This man she knew so little about was offering to go deep into debt for her; much too deep.

She reached over the picnic basket and touched his hand. "I cannot let you do that."

"I've never wanted more to do something. This is the first time in my entire life I've felt I simply have to do something."

"I won't accept, but you are most kind. Never have I met such a man who is so kind."

He gazed gently at her. "It's because of you. I want you to have your life back." He paused. "To pay the ransom and bring him back to you. To your kiss."

The way he said it, she suddenly knew he loved her, loved her so much that he would sacrifice himself to bring her husband home to her.

"Elwood," she said. "Please . . ."

"I will tell you a strange thing, about gentleman C's. Have you ever heard of that?"

She shook her head.

"In our universities, students receive letter grades, with A the highest, and C means an average grade, neither very bad nor very good. Well, in some schools, including the place where I studied, called Dartmouth, there are all sorts of young men from families with a lot of money, and I was one of them.

"Those young men, including myself, thought it was terribly uncouth to strive for high grades. That was a sign of new wealth, of bounders who had just arrived at affluence. We laughed at the young men who worked hard, got A's, and sought good positions after they graduated. We didn't need good positions. We were the sons of old and wealthy families. So we did just enough work in college to earn ourselves a C, while we devoted ourselves to more important things, such as sculling, drinking, flirting. . . ."

She stared at him doubtfully, not really grasping much of it.

"The point is, all my life I've never really tried. Never believed in anything very much. Never committed myself to anything. Until now."

Something in this stirred and disturbed her. "You should not try for my sake. I am not . . . please understand."

She knew from someplace deep in her heart that he loved her, and that she had stirred something in him, and for the first time he was truly striving toward a goal. A goal she could never give to him.

"Señor LaGrange, you are very kind, and you have been valuable for me. I would hesitate to look for the Lost Doubloon alone, but with you at my side I have no fears. We have covered much ground. I wish to give you a thousand thanks, *mil gracias*, but you must understand. . . ."

He nodded. She thought he did understand. And she did care about him.

She liked him better in this plain clothing. At last he had abandoned those gaudy plaid knickers and all the rest of it, in favor of miners' jeans and a plain shirt, as if he had joined the rest of the world, and was no longer a man apart.

"We will find the mine and free your husband," he said. "And I will not rest until we find it. I am going to do everything in my power to restore you to the life you once had."

He would do everything in his power. She marveled at it, coming from a man who, until a few days earlier, she'd regarded as the most hapless fool in Rio Blanco.

He began to pick up the debris and fill the wicker basket.

"Let's find that mine," he said.

That afternoon, she continued to marvel at the change in Elwood LaGrange. He walked resolutely up the canyon for another three miles until it pinched out in a box, and all the while he plunged from one side to the other for a close look at anything out of the ordinary. But this rainbow canyon was mostly sandstone, and not a likely place for a mine, and by mid-afternoon they both knew that no gold mine would be discovered this day.

And yet she had discovered something: an Elwood LaGrange who was emerging from a cocoon like a chrysalis. She found herself glancing at him furtively, aware of a lithe if unworked body, a handsome lean figure, an upright posture, and an ease that can only come to someone who had all the assurance of his social caste.

The trip down the canyon went faster because they weren't scouring every bush and rock.

"I've been studying," he said. "Silver is sometimes found in argentite, which looks tarnished, but when you cut it open it is bright. But Stromeyerine is lead-gray. Pyrargrite's a ruby silver color, and horn silver looks like wax, and when you cut it, it will tarnish to a gray-violet. Stephanite's brittle. And Iodargyrite's a yellow earth . . . silver is malleable, and that's one of the best ways to tell whether you found some."

She was laughing in spite of herself. "Pretty soon you will be the best geologist in Rio Blanco."

"I intend to be," he said.

The way he said it would have once surprised her, but not now.

"Can you identify any of those ores?" she asked.

"Not a one, but I will. Before the next few weeks pass, I will be able to identify most ores. There's a place in Silver City I can go and learn. They have shelf after shelf of samples."

"Why? What's in it for you, LaGrange?"

"A ransom," he said.

Something tugged at her heart when he said it.

They reached Rio Blanco at dusk, exhausted from an unusually long trek.

"Tomorrow, we try another, eh?" she said.

"I'll be here."

She watched him slip through the dark. Rio Blanco remained strangely empty, with so many tromping the distant ridges looking for a mine that may have never existed.

She trudged up the slope to the great casa, and found herself troubled. Something didn't seem right. Her powerful intuitions were setting off alarms in her mind. She paused before the great door on the veranda, feeling the wrongness, yet unable to tell what was disturbing her. She peered into the windows of the darkened house and saw nothing.

Finally, she opened the door, half-expecting something evil, but the place was silent. Still, she knew someone had been there. It didn't smell right.

She walked boldly from room to room, finding nothing amiss. She lit a coal-oil lamp and searched, but everything was in its place. She paused at the cherrywood desk, sensing that the prowler—she was sure there had been a prowler—spent time there, poking and probing. The prowler had found nothing because nothing was there.

She raged at Malachi Cromwell-Nast, who had spent an hour or two this day trying to dig up Ricardo O'Rourke's secrets. She knew it. She didn't know how she knew it. Nast would be disappointed. He could not understand a man like her husband, a man who lived as daringly as any mortal could live. He had bet on the revolution and once he had made that bet, Ricardo spent everything he possessed to further the cause. There was no hidden wealth, apart from a few minor things. She thought he had a few lots somewhere, or maybe a little gold in a bank, mostly for emergencies. Gunrunners sometimes needed some traveling money fast.

There was nothing in the waxed cherrywood desk, and now there were the smudges of hands that had probed and tapped and pushed every corner of it and had found nothing. She found a rag and wiped the wood angrily until it shone again.

Why had he done it?

Furiously, she wrapped a black rebozo about her and plunged into the night, so charged with energy that the day's long trek had no effect on her weary body. She swept down the long road, plunged into Rio Blanco, stormed to the upstairs offices of Malachi Cromwell-Nast, and pounded on the door.

He opened, a lamp in hand.

"Why Mrs. O'Rourke. Do come in."

"Why did you do it?"

"Do what?"

"Why did you ransack my house?"

"I don't have the faintest idea what you're talking about."

"There was nothing in the desk, was there? Nothing at all because Ricardo had nothing there. You don't understand. I told you and you didn't listen. You didn't believe me. He has no property." She paused for breath. The oleaginous financier gaped, at a loss for words this time.

"Don't you ever enter my house again, do you hear? Never! Next time I will shoot."

He shook his head, and then gave up talking.

She whirled away, and she heard the door click softly behind her. She didn't know his scheme, but soon enough she would find out.

Chapter 23

Artie Quill slowly glassed the handful of miners in the valley far below, studying what they were up to. Long experience with prospecting told him this was no lost mine, but a ledge of some sort they had discovered and were now evaluating. He spotted some burros grazing nearby, some picks and shovels scattered below the seam, and some field-test equipment they were using. Probably they had found gold; they appeared to be amalgamating some samples.

He compressed his telescope and eyed the prospectors through the sights of his Sharps rifle, drawing a bead on this one and that, and then thought better of it. If they had found the Doubloon, they would now be dead. The Doubloon was his and no one else would ever extract a dime's worth of gold from it. But this was just a five-hundred-dollar quartz outcrop. He studied the ridge behind him, noted a clear getaway path over the top and into the next canyon, and decided that would do.

He returned to his redoubt, amused at what would come. When the sights of his Sharps were squarely on the amalgamation pan, he fired. The pan bucked, scattering contents. Men paused, tiny figures peering this way and that, unsure of where the shot had come from or what to do about it. Quill jacked out the shell and loaded another, this time picking what appeared to be a box of DuPont giant powder about fifty yards from the ledge. Oh, ho!

He squeezed and hit the wooden box, which blew a giant fireball of white lightning that flattened all the prospectors down there. A big thump boomed back at Artie, along with a shock wave that slapped air against him. Some of those closer to the blast were rolling around on the soil; others held their heads. The noise must have deafened them. Artie laughed.

"Well, Rosie, look at that," he said to his new lady friend.

Some of the miners were up now, applying bandages to those who had been hit by debris. He imagined that outfit would be boiling out of there with its tail between its legs, and one or two would be newly deaf.

Serves 'em right.

He watched a while more, while the uninjured plastered the wounds of the injured, and then backed away, careful not to skyline himself. That was a good morning's work. He yawned and slid the Sharps back into its saddle sheath. He stole one last glance at that outfit, figuring they'd all hightail it back to Rio Blanco and never be seen in these parts again, which suited Artie Quill just fine. Someday he'd take a look at that ledge, but not just now. He had a fabulous old mine to find.

He plucked up the lead lines and led his mules down the far side of the ridge, and then walked parallel to the ridge, studying the new terrain far below. He spotted no one. This land was so huge that it could absorb a thousand gold-crazed prospectors hunting for the mine, and they would scarcely see one another.

The only question was, where did Stud Malone find that mine? For once, Artie began to doubt that it was anywhere near here even though this was Malone's favorite stamping ground. Malone's mule was offering no clue at all, docilely moving along with all the passivity of a well-trained beast of burden. That mule obviously knew this country, but little good that did.

Quill glassed the new valley carefully, finding no other sign of mineralization or mining or habitation. He was getting tired of this game. It probably would be better to hunt for other prospectors and see what they came up with and then take it away from them. If he continued this slow study of every canyon along these mountains, he might miss out. Someone would find the Doubloon and Artie would be a month late finding it out. Besides, he was too far from Rio Blanco. The Doubloon was associated with the town, and he was twenty miles from there as the crow flies, and forty miles by the time he figured all the twists and ups and downs.

He had a little one-man cinnabar mine all to himself; he'd gotten that much out of this trip. But he could not claim it or go near there for several years.

It was time to collect the mule he'd left in the hidden park and head into town for a spell. Time for some booze and some gossip and a dark-haired dolly or two. He surveyed the high country, discovered a long ridge that would take him where he wanted to go, and then began the trek back to the park. He was a loner, and liked loner country most of the time, but once in a while Artie Quill needed some liquid refreshment and some company.

He spent the rest of the next day extracting himself from the foothills, and didn't see a soul the whole time until he came across a lone man tugging a laden burro along. One glance told Quill this one was no veteran of the canyons, but the greenest dude in the West, in stiff new clothes and squeaky boots that no doubt were torturing him. What interested Quill the most was that this gent had no pick or shovel or even a prospector's hammer.

"Well, what's the word?" the man said when they met on the trail. "You find any gold?"

"Mister, you must be new here. If I found gold, I sure wouldn't be telling people about it. I'd get it claimed and registered with the land office first."

"I'm new all right," the fellow said. "I don't know a thing about it, but maybe I'll find the lost gold mine. You got any clues?"

Quill laughed. "Why would I share them if I did? Friend, you'd better just skedaddle back to town and forget it."

"I'm Arnold Schwartz," the man said. "And you?"

Quill just laughed.

"You have any idea where to look?" Schwartz asked.

"What are you looking for?"

"The lost mine, and any other gold strike around here."

That struck Artie Quill as mighty strange. "Schwartz, if I knew that, I wouldn't tell you."

"I pay for information."

"You pay? Pay?"

"You tell me where there's a strike, and I'll give you a half eagle."

"A strike, eh. All right, I'll take a half eagle. I know where there's a little one. You head out this road. . . ."

He ended up drawing a map that would take this pilgrim to the canyon where he had scared off a few prospectors.

"There's a ledge there. Some exposed quartz with gold in it. The crowd operating it will probably shoot you on sight. All right, how about that eagle?"

Schwartz dug into his britches and extracted a five-dollar gold piece and handed it to Quill, but with a strange intentness that chilled Quill. The gold piece was almost buried in Schwartz's massive and scarred hands. Those were hands that had seen a rough trade. Quill eyed those enormous shoulders and beefy arms and piano-leg legs, and suddenly knew Schwartz could squash him with one blow.

"I never forget a face," Schwartz said, and dropped the gold into Quill's hand.

"Neither do I," Quill retorted.

The lumbering greenhorn trailing a little burro started east again, and Quill watched him narrowly. Something didn't add up. That galoot was not looking for mineral, but something else. Uneasily, Quill watched until the man rounded a bend and vanished, and even then Quill watched his back. He eyed his shiny gold piece, wondering why the man was laying out that sort of money to be guided toward a strike, even a minor one. The man was buying information. The man was someone's bird dog. That was an interesting thought.

The half eagle would buy him a fine old time.

In Rio Blanco, Quill first took his mules to the livery barn, bought them a two-bit bait of oats, then treated himself to a one-dollar room at Jessie Goodrich's boardinghouse, and saved the rest for a beef dinner, a few good drinks, and a whore. Somewhere along the way, he would have to talk with Nast and tell him that the Lost Doubloon was not exactly making itself known, and he needed more grubstake money. Nast would whine and fork over.

He washed up, trimmed his beard, applied witch hazel and talcum, being a delicate sort who was offended by body odor when in towns, and headed for the Tia Juana Café, the traditional abode of prospectors. It was actually an eatery and saloon, so he could have his steak and some whiskey too, but what he starved for the most was news. If someone had found the lost mine, he wanted to know about it.

This night the place was jammed. There were plenty of prospectors sitting around, and Quill knew in a glance that they were not outbound, but returning men who had scoured the hills and come back in for outfitting and refreshments. He knew a few, but there were plenty of strangers too, mostly pale clerks with putty-soft fingers and city fools in wire-rimmed spectacles who thought they could latch onto a fortune without knowing a thing about mining.

He headed straight for Wilbur Meridian, a murderous old coot who was probably a robber but masqueraded as a prospector.

"Anyone find that lost mine?" Artie asked without preamble.

"Quill, if they did, they ain't telling us about it."

"That's all I wanted to know. Anyone make a strike?"

"I ain't heard of none but a few three-hundred-dollar ledges here and there, copper and lead mostly."

"That's enough to buy beans," Quill said. "How many are out there?"

"Some say a thousand, but that's horsepucky. The living and the dead don't amount to four hundred."

"Dead?"

Meridian smiled, revealing a gap-toothed gum.

"You know of anyone buying up ledges?" Quill asked.

"Haven't heard of it."

"I ran into a greenhorn paying money for information."

Meridian hee-hawed.

"This gent was big enough to flatten a man with one swing of his fist."

"A bullet is the great equalizer," Meridian said.

They thought alike. The man was like a brother.

When it came to information, the evening was a bust. Quill learned nothing. The Doubloon remained lost. Prospectors roamed every cranny of the country, but nothing of consequence had been found, or at least no one was talking about it.

Quill shrugged. He expected as much. He ordered a T-bone, downed some Old Crow, and headed for Minnie's Parlor House and a two-dollar tickle.

Chapter 24

Sergei Gudonov found little comfort in his barren room. He opened a tin of beans and ate it cold, loathing this American product. He was faced with a dilemma: how to advance the revolution now that his entire prospecting outfit had been destroyed and could not be replaced. Even if he had money, which he didn't, there was not a shop in Rio Blanco or Silver City that could outfit him, and not a burro to be found that would carry his gear.

He knew he would have to put his enormous intelligence to work and outwit these fools that were roaming every gulch for fifty miles around. He sat quietly on the stuffed cotton mattress of his black iron bedstead pondering his dilemma. The revolution cried for gold, and he intended to provide it, but how?

He calculated the odds: There were now perhaps five hundred men poking and probing the countryside hunting down the lost mine. Some of them were gifted prospectors, but most of them were fools and knaves. If the mine actually existed, the chances that one of them would find it before he did were very strong. He was but one and they were many. Maybe the best thing would be to put them all to work for him, at work for the revolution, though they would not know it.

He liked that idea. He could go back out into the

field himself by various means. He could steal an outfit in the dead of night and take off. He could rob the
Cimarron Bank, but that was a foolish notion. His ac-
cent would betray him. He could kill the owner of an
outfit and seize it. He would be glad to do this if the
owner was a rich man, but he would be reluctant to
kill a poor man, which would violate his revolutionary
principles.

He did not like his choices. If he stole an outfit, there
would be a good chance he would be found out and
maybe put to death. He was aware of the sort of vigi-
lante justice meted out to horse thieves and others of
that ilk in this raw frontier land. No, there must be a
better way, and that way would be to harness all these
industrious prospectors to the service of the revolution.

Ah, there was something. Let them thirst in the hot
sun, starve, toil, fend off vipers, test rocks for minerals,
feed their mules and burros, and parch themselves
from a lack of water. All but one or two would return
vanquished, broken, their funds gone, their dreams
shattered, wondering why they weren't lucky while
someone else indeed was lucky.

But there would be someone, or some small group,
that would find that mine. He could either take it
away from them by force or by persuasion, and turn it
to the service of the revolution.

But these Yanks had no thought of revolutions,
and not even the most eloquent arguments would
persuade them to turn over their wealth for a noble
and magnificent cause, larger and finer than mere
affluence. What pigs they were, seeking their own
happiness, oblivious to the suffering of the masses.
He despised Americans, so busy pursuing their own
lives. Yes, this was all leading in a single direction,
so obvious that it didn't even take his magnificent
intelligence to draw the right conclusions.

He would need to kill the discoverers of the Lost

Doubloon Mine, and do it in such a way that he would acquire the mine himself. The end justified the means. The gold would free millions; what if one or two people died for such a splendid result? Yes, a killing of those who found the mine would be entirely justified.

And he need not even leave town or hunt any further. Instead, he would prepare for the time when he would be required to act. He would need a perfect plan, one beyond suspicion, and then he would wait like a black widow spider for the moment to sting his prey. Having reasoned his way to that, he sat back on his bed, vastly satisfied with his plan. Of course it was only a rough outline. He must prepare, exquisitely and with all the intelligence of his enormous brain, to do the job sublimely, and to gather the mine into his own hands in a stroke of fate so perfect that no one would know what transpired. He would work out the details, and consider all the contingencies, over the next several days. Meanwhile, he would study the prospectors as they returned, as well as those departing for the wastelands, and make his plans.

The scheme did not fill him with joy. Murder would be a grim and tragic business. He was familiar with all of that; a soldier attached to the Cossacks is not innocent about life's hard realities. He believed in nothing supernatural; it was not God he worried about. It was his own tenderness that might afflict him and drive him to drink. He had killed in war, but this was not quite war.

He was out of money, and hated the thought of having to labor for a wage. A man of his intelligence ought not to spend a minute, an hour, at the service of some employer. He would be wasting his valuable mind and body clerking for some fool of a shopkeeper. No, there must be a better way. Whatever it was, he would need to find it fast or starve.

Then it came to him: He would form an alliance

with the town's richest man, the oppressor of hundreds, the bloodsucker who soaked up rents and fees from the humble and miserable, a man who stole bread off tables. And in time, Sergei Gudonov would show this bloodsucker what it means to be a revolutionary. Gudonov was a little vague about how some alliance might be arranged, but it didn't matter.

He freshened himself and hiked up Casa Grande Street to the upstairs chambers of Malachi Cromwell-Nast, and entered the austere and slightly shabby office. The hour was late, but Nast was at his desk, sans his cutaway coat, a black sleeve garter reining in his shirt, a lamp shedding buttery light over ledgers.

"Yes?" said Nast. "Oh, it's you, Gudonov. How's your revolution progressing?"

The greeting startled Sergei. Was there nothing this spider didn't know about every stranger in Rio Blanco?

"Not well. I need to arrange a living." He could not bring himself to say he wanted a job.

"And what is it you do?"

"I am a problem solver. Give me a problem and I will apply my abilities to it."

"What sort of problem?"

"I never turn down a task."

"And what do you want for this service?"

"As much as I can get."

Nast frowned. "We are fencing. What do you want from me, aside from my money? And how do you propose to be of value to me?"

"I am a man filled with ideals. I want to free the oppressed serfs in my native land. I want gold to do it. I will find the means."

Nast smiled, processing all that. "You favor all revolutions? Would you favor overthrowing Diaz in Mexico?"

"He is a pig, grinding the poor under his boot."

"Then you can help me," Nast said. "Sit down, Gudonov, and we'll talk. That chair squeaks, I want a new one, but who can get anything delivered to this place? In Rio Blanco is a certain widow . . . ah, wife, of a revolutionary now being held for ransom by President Porfirio Diaz. He wants a large sum, a hundred thousand pesos, and the wife lacks the money, and each hour, the husband moves closer to death by firing squad. She doesn't know where and what her husband's assets are, and she's frantic. And foolish. She thinks she can find the lost mine, get some gold, and rescue him. I try to help. I thought he had mining property, but I can find no record of it. That means he probably keeps his funds in silver or gold or jewels or currency, hidden somewhere, probably somewhere in or around the mansion. If we're to help the lady, we must find this man's treasure. She resists my efforts to help."

"So that's the story of Mrs. O'Rourke," Gudonov said.

"I see you keep yourself apprised of events here."

"And you want me to find out where O'Rourke hides his assets. How do you know there are any?"

"The house! The servants—of course she dismissed them now. The style. The carriage and teams."

"What are you proposing? Exactly?"

"Why, to rescue O'Rourke, of course."

"And what's in it for me?"

"Maybe nothing," Nast said, but it was a question. "Why should there be anything in it for you? You're a revolutionary, aren't you?"

"What's in it for you?" Sergei asked.

"Charity," said Nast. "Now, if you'll excuse me, I'm due at the home of Mrs. Cushman for our weekly Bible study group."

"Your what?"

"Mr. Gudonov, I don't know much about Russian religion, but here we study the Word carefully, imbibing its knowledge and fashioning our lives to the wisdom we discover in it. This week we are examining First Corinthians, a book I strongly recommend to you. It teaches the value of love."

Nast rose, his spidery frame casting thin shadows upon the walls. It was a dismissal.

"One last question, Mr. Nast. Why do you believe O'Rourke has a fortune concealed here?"

"Where else, Gudonov?"

"Why do you think he has a concealed fortune at all? Most revolutionaries don't. They spend everything! Go into debt because they believe in a cause."

"Why don't you ask Mrs. O'Rourke?"

Nast slid by Gudonov, lowered the wick on the coal-oil lamp, and gestured his visitor toward the door.

Gudonov tripped down the dark stairwell and into the night, marveling at the contradictions and paradoxes that made up the heart and soul of Malachi Cromwell-Nast.

It had been an amazing interview.

Gudonov snorted. As a person of superior intelligence, he had spotted Nast's game at once, when Nast accidentally gave it away, calling Guadalupe O'Rourke a widow and then correcting himself.

Nast simply wanted any wealth around that mansion, and had a fine little scheme for getting to it, if it could be found. Ransom indeed.

Chapter 25

Guadalupe was about to prepare for bed, but she sensed something wrong. As if someone were lurking out in the dark around her house. Sometimes she had these visions. Ricardo had given her a five-shot revolver and told her to use it if she must. She would be on her own when he was away on dangerous business.

She pulled the revolver from a drawer, checked the loads by the light of the sole lamp, and then slipped through the darkened house. Downstairs, in the moonlit parlor, she peered out the window and saw a figure standing in moonlight not far away. She knew the man.

She slipped to the kitchen and retreated into the dark yard, circling around in a way that kept her mostly out of sight. Her heart was hammering. But she was not one to cower under her bedclothes and await the worst. She had fire inside, and maybe that is why she and Ricardo lit bonfires of love together. She watched the man, who was standing very still, surveying the establishment.

Then he turned.

"Put up your hands," she snapped.

The man was startled and started to retreat.

She squeezed, sending a shot searing past his ear. It shattered the silence.

He stopped and turned slowly.

"So, it is you," she said. "There are no more mules to steal."

"I don't know what you're talking about."

"You stole the mules. You are the Russian."

"You don't even know who I am."

"I have inner vision. I know things my senses don't know. You are Gudonov and you stole my mules and maybe I will kill you. Why are you here?"

He began sliding his hands toward something at his waist.

"Hands up. I don't miss."

He stopped whatever he was doing. "Actually, I came to help you."

That was a novelty she hardly expected. "Help yourself, you mean."

He relaxed slightly. "I am going to lower my hands. I will not talk with my hands in the air."

"Then you will not talk at all because a bullet will enter your mouth."

He kept his hands up. He was a strange figure, with a huge mushroom-shaped head and coarse features.

"You have a fortune hidden here, and you are in great need," he said. "I thought I would help you find it."

She laughed. "Nast sent you. He thinks that too. He ransacked my house when I was gone yesterday, and found nothing. Now tell me, what did he say to you?"

"That your husband is a prisoner of Porfirio Diaz and being held for ransom and if the ransom isn't paid soon, he faces execution. That your husband hid wealth, currency, gold, silver, who knows? And you think there is none. He wishes to help you find it."

She laughed. "So he can have some or all of it. I don't know his scheme. Maybe Diaz wants fifty thousand pesos ransom and this man Nast tells me it's a hundred thousand so he can keep half. Who knows?

But Nast never did anything for anyone else in his life. That much I know."

"Your husband is a gunrunner."

She didn't respond.

"A revolutionary, overthrowing an oppressor, yes?"

She refused to answer.

"I am also a revolutionary."

"That doesn't exempt you from a bullet. Now leave or you will be shot. Maybe in the back. And if you ever return, I will not wait for your calling card, *si*?"

She waved the revolver, and he flinched.

"Señora, you probably have a fortune in your house. I am expert at detecting such things. I was born with certain gifts of intelligence. I have the biggest brain known to science."

"That doesn't mean there is any sense in your big brain. Ricardo keeps nothing. He lives to overthrow evil. When I needed money he handed it to me from his pocket."

"Nonetheless, Señora, you really don't know whether he has a secret stash."

"You are wasting my time."

"Señora, I am doing this for your sake. I mean, looking for your husband's fortune. We must save him."

She laughed.

"I will make you a proposition. Let me search. Right now. If I find your husband's fortune, you will give me some part of it. Some significant part. I leave the amount to you. And then you will have the rest to free him."

She thought about it. "*Sí*. I am tired of prowlers in my house. I will hold the lamp in one hand and the revolver in the other, and if you make one false move it will be your last. You will find nothing."

He lowered his hands, and she watched intently,

ready for anything. He walked to the mansion, and she followed.

"Enter there, and light the lamp," she said, waving him into the kitchen. "Then back away."

He did exactly as told.

She lifted the lamp and motioned him toward the parlor. "Start here," she said.

He proved to be an expert, lifting rugs, looking behind paintings, studying the backs of closets. He spent time with the cherrywood desk, his familiar hands looking for a compartment to spring. Then, startlingly, one did spring. He stood back, smugly. She peered inside the tiny compartment and found it empty.

"*Nada!* So I have told you!"

He nodded. Her revolver never wavered, and sometimes he glanced at that black bore pointing his way.

Room by room, he searched, and she secretly marveled that eyes and hands so skilled, and a brain so large, could find places to look in floors, walls, ceilings, furniture, lamps, art, cabinets, and even the flour bin. But an hour later, with the oil in the lamp almost gone, the house had been examined in ways she'd never imagined, and there was nothing to be found.

"I told you this is so," she said.

"I will look outside tomorrow, with your permission."

"No, I do not give it. There is but an empty pen where you took my mule. Some sheds. We will look now, and when you find nothing you will leave and never return."

He nodded. Now, with a fresh lamp, she steered him toward the outbuildings, and once again his gifted hands hunted for hidden troves. And all the while her shining little revolver never wavered. He scraped manure away from the ground, pushed and poked adobe, ran fingers over poles and beams, probed deep into the tack room and the feed bins, scaring off rats that slipped away in a flash. Then he was done.

"Nothing. *Nada*. Are you satisfied I tell the truth?" she asked.

He didn't reply directly. "I have done you a favor," he said. "Now you know what you did not know for sure."

She agreed, but wouldn't admit it to him. "Go, and do not come back unless you want a bullet for a welcome."

He smiled, his face pleasant in the soft light. "Nast was wrong. I will tell him."

"He won't believe it. He does not understand Ricardo. What makes a man like my husband live and breathe? I know. You know. But Nast cannot think of life as anything more than getting possessions."

"What makes anyone who desires to make the world a better place live and breathe?" Sergei said.

She almost liked him. But he had stolen and prowled and would do so again, even if for a cause.

"Go."

He turned, and vanished in the dark. She swiftly extinguished her lantern, not wishing to be a target. Then she ghosted back to the veranda, and waited there for a while. But he did not return. The revolver felt heavy in her hand, and she shuddered. She would have used it if she must.

What a strange eve it had been, escorting a robber through her home so he could see for himself that she had nothing to rob. She wished Gudonov had found something, some way to pay off Diaz and rescue Ricardo. How desperate she was, Ricardo in mortal peril, her own beloved facing the wall, the crack of ten rifles. If only the Russian had found something. She would have taken the hundred thousand pesos and given the rest to the man. All she wanted was the ransom, the gold that bought life.

This Russian would not be back . . . unless he'd

found something he hadn't revealed to her, something he would sneak back and steal. But she could not let her mind dwell on things like that.

The Russian was right. He had done her a favor. Now, the only thing standing between Ricardo's execution and his life was the lost mine. She must find that mine, and fast. She must find it and claim it and defend it before a thousand skilled prospectors found it. She must have it, without it she would be helpless. . . . The thought of Ricardo lying in some dungeon in the City of Mexico brought her to tears. What was he thinking? Was he trying to reach her? Why had no letter come? Was he all alone, without help? Did no one care? Was he ill? Did they feed him? Had they tortured him? Who caught him and how? Who took him away from Sonora? If she did find the mine, and sold it, could she get money to Diaz fast enough? What was the schedule of his doom? By what slow progression did the sands in his hourglass run out? When would that swine Diaz tire of toying with his prisoner, and nod to the executioners?

Ah, Dios, time had stopped.

Tomorrow, she must find the mine! There was no more time left!

Chapter 26

Artie Quill didn't feel happy. The fact was, no one had found the Lost Doubloon. No one knew where Stud Malone's rich ore had come from. He had prowled Malone's favorite haunts and come up with a ledge being gouged out by some tenderfeet, a little cinnabar mine, and a lot of nothing. He sighed. His grubstake was about used up. He would have to brace the old tarantula, Cromwell-Nast, for some more provisions, and suffer through more of the spider's insults and lectures.

But in fact he was flat, having squandered his last boodle in the arms of Short Polly, a midget over in the parlor house. This hungover morning he would deal with Nast, or maybe rob him. It didn't matter which. He dressed slowly so as not to offend his head, which was already swollen with a migraine that pulsed with every twitch of his eyes. Some Java might help. Gingerly, he drew up his britches and then pulled a canvas shirt over his grimy union suit, and headed into a blinding spring day. His eyes sprung a leak, he blinked, and pulled his slouch hat lower to shade himself from the searing sun.

He lacked cash for coffee or for breakfast, so extracting some from Malachi Cromwell-Nash became his first order of business, headache or not. He ascended those creaky wooden stairs slowly, hanging onto the stair rail, and eventually found himself before the pebbled glass door of Nast's lair. He entered, finding Nast hunched over his desk studying correspondence.

Nast looked up. "I've been expecting you. How was Short Polly?"

Quill tried hard not to be startled. Nash always knew everything.

"I have a headache," he said.

"After all that Old Orchard, I would think so."

Nast set down the letter that had absorbed him and peered at Quill. "You've come to report and beg for more money."

"Something like that. But I made some progress. I know where the Lost Doubloon isn't. It isn't where Stud Malone—he's the one found the mine—usually operates."

"The Mimbres foothills."

"How do you know that?"

Nast smiled. "Tell me what you found. Do I own half of anything?"

Artie Quill sighed, ran a horny hand through his shaggy hair, and shook his head. "No, 'fraid not this time. There was a ledge being worked by some greenhorns."

"And you scattered them like quail."

It was no good being startled by Nast. "That's not far from the truth of it, Malachi."

"Just for fun."

"They sure skeedaddled."

"And you have nothing else to report to me?"

"No, that was it for the whole trip. I came back in to town to resupply. I thought we could work us a little deal, same as before, you get half of anything I find."

"Like the cinnabar mine?"

"What, what?"

"The cinnabar mine. You shot the owner, dragged him into it, stole his mule, hid the saddlebags of ore, and got out of there."

Artie digested that slowly, gradually putting pieces together. Someone had been ghosting along behind him, someone who reported to Nast. The someone who had caused some rock to skid down a cliff once or twice, which had troubled Quill.

"Don't know what you're talking about," he said.

"I not only own half the mine, I own half the mule. Her name is Rosie, is it not? I will enjoy owning the rear end of Rosie."

"You got me baffled," said Quill.

"I have a cyclops eye, Quill. I have mysterious ways of knowing all things. I suppose you want more money from me."

Quill was about to shake his head, but Nast lifted a spidery hand. "You can have what you need. You're the best prospector around, but that's not why I'm provisioning you. The reason is, Quill, that you know exactly what to do in the wilds. You knew exactly what the choices were at the cinnabar mine, and you made the choice. So I will provision you once again. All you have to realize is that nothing escapes me."

Quill felt like killing him, but smiled instead. "I need a hundred."

"Twenty. That will feed you and the nag for a couple of weeks."

"I need more than that. My clothes are wore out. My boots have holes. My packsaddle's falling apart. I need some new gear."

"Then we'll all celebrate when you find the lost mine."

Nast wheeled in his swivel chair, spun the dial of an oversized enameled safe decorated with fat cupids in bold tints, along with the Holy Grail, and swung the black door open. From within, he plucked up two ten-dollar greenbacks and handed them to Quill.

"There now. I get half of whatever you find," he said.

Quill choked back a retort, uncocked his fist, which

he was about to use on the back of Nast's head when he saw enough cash in that black box to finance a year's trip to Argentina, and smiled. But Nast was already noting the transaction in a ledger, and then handed the ledger to Quill.

"Sign there," he said. "So I have an acknowledgment of the grubstake."

Quill had done all this several times before, and dutifully scratched his name with a nib pen.

"Now go forth and multiply our wealth," Nast said. "That's a minor revision of a Biblical verse."

Quill didn't care where it came from; he stomped out, headed for the Rio Blanco Mercantile, and loaded up on laxatives. The one thing that plagued him out in the wild was getting plugged up, and the one thing that helped him was a good dose of salts or herbs. This time, he bought a two large tins of *cascara sagrada*, a packet of senna, and a bottle of castor oil. The *cascara* in particular was a dandy, and reamed a man out proper. By Gawd, a little *cascara* made a new man. There were times out in the wild when he would have traded a gold mine for some *cascara*.

After that, he turned to less important things, such as buckwheat flour, a pint of Old Orchard for snakebite, some side-pork, saleratus, sourdough starter, some beans, a tin cook pot to replace one that had burned out, salt, a box of lucifers, a yellow-back novel that would serve more than one purpose, such as wiping his butt or starting a fire, fifty-two-caliber rifle cartridges, and a sack of oats for his critters. There would be enough left to redeem Rosie and the pack mule from the livery stable.

That done, he collected his animals and loaded up. But the truth of it was that he didn't have the faintest idea where to go. The mob had all headed north into foothill country and mountain ranges, where the earth had been upended. Or east or west into other ranges. The only place no one went was south, where an erosion-carved hinterland stretched anonymously for a hundred miles, broken by a few buttes and humps, and not much else. Water was scarcer there than anywhere in the whole area, likely to be so alkaline as to not be potable.

He ought to head north, if only to keep track of what all those greenhorns were finding or not finding. That was the mineralized area, with some proven strikes. He had covered much of the eastern reaches, without luck. West? A temptation. Pretty sandstone, some of it upended into scenic buttes and ridges. Not prime territory to unearth a gold mine. Water there, here and there, if one knew how to look for it, often a foot or so under the surface and revealed by the plants in the area.

He scowled. The blinding June sun was pounding at his eyes and inflaming his headache. Casa Grande Street was all but deserted; no one but mad dogs prowled in the noonday sun. But then Artie Quill saw something that interested him. Sitting on a bench under one of the galleries that shaded the boardwalk sat an Indian, immobile, staring at nothing, his hair in braids, his face the color of rust. Apache, Navajo, Pima, who the hell knows? The black flat-crowned hat suggested Navajo, but this was well south and west of their haunts.

Quill had a quick and intuitive mind, and concluded that the Indian on the bench staring at nothing was no accident, and might even be the very ghost who had slipped along behind him the last time out. The cyclops eye of Malachi Nast.

Quill laughed. He'd just see.

He headed the most unlikely direction, south, into the parched hinterland, just to see what sort of shadows were tailing along behind him. On this side of town there were a few jacales belonging to the Mexi-

cans, pens fenced with mesquite, adobe houses with
ocotillo ramadas and bright chilis hanging from the
walls, a snoozing dog or two, and a scattering of runty
chickens. No one was about. It was siesta time. He led
his weary mules through the quarter and into oblivi-
ion. That was the best description he could think of;
empty hills, mostly naked, hollows with dried grass in
their bottoms, occasional outcrops.

He continued some while in this direction, intending to circle north after a mile or so, but first he would
lay a trap. And that required the right terrain. He
plodded onward through a grim silence. Not even
birds floated the sky during the noon of a New Mexico day. The sunlight was so bright it leached the blue
out of the heavens, until all he could see was the
whiteness of this lonely land.

Then he spotted what he was looking for, a sharp
turn in the gulch he was following, and an outcrop
where he could conceal himself and his mules. He
headed that way, found a perfect observation point
above the surrounding country, hobbled his mules
in a hollow, and waited. There was not a lick of
shade. Just yellow rock too hot to touch. The sun
boiled water out of him. His tongue turned dry.

But the waiting was worthwhile. Almost like a ghost,
the Indian slipped along, somehow hard to see, as if
by some magic he could meld into the land. But there
he was. Following Quill. Nast's cyclops eye.

Artie was amused. He slipped over to his packsaddle, withdrew his Sharps, checked the load, and
returned to his hilltop redoubt. The shot would
be almost a thousand yards, but Artie didn't doubt
he could do it, and with one bullet.

Chapter 27

Elwood took one look at Guadalupe the next dawn and knew there was trouble afoot. She greeted him sternly from a face that radiated pain and fortitude. She handed him her wicker basket, and he slung his canteen over his shoulder and took the basket.

"Where to?" he asked.

She shrugged.

He didn't like that shrug. Maybe after they had walked a little, she would talk. Just now, she was so forbidding that he didn't venture a word.

Dawns were new to him. All his life he had kept late hours, arising no earlier than ten, as people of his social caste often did, and retiring around midnight. He had never experienced dawns. But now, in these wanderings with Guadalupe, he had discovered that dawns were the sweetest moments of all, hushed and peaceful and ripe with promise. He could watch the gray light brighten into color until the world was tinted. But most of all, he loved hiking beside the woman he loved, a love that bloomed each hour even though he could never have her. It was paradise just to be with her, to snatch a few hours of companionship with this great-hearted woman in such need.

"We've never gone south," he said.

He expected her to reply that no gold would ever be found in rolling arid hills covered with silty yellow soil, where hardly an outcrop of rock could be found. But she simply nodded, surrendering the choice to him.

Rio Blanco lay hushed and empty. No smoke from breakfast fires rose in the still air. Not a soul trod the clay street. Not a horse or mule or burro was to be seen. He led her past a silent smithy, past a harness maker's shop, past a wagon yard, and past some adobe homes with squash gardens beside them. A cur lifted its head, stared, and settled into its slumber again. A purple glow caught the town, and then lavender, and then oddly, gold and yellow, and by the time they were out of town, the sky had blued and the empty hills had settled into tans and ochres.

"Bad night?" he asked.

She nodded.

They walked another half a mile before he ventured to try again. "Word about your husband?"

"No."

He led them up an unused gulch, over a hilltop, and down again. Rio Blanco vanished, and they were now in a lonely sea. No land seemed more empty. The light itself became painful, and Elwood wished he had something more than a large-brimmed hat to protect his eyes. He peered about fearfully, afraid that he would lose his bearings and be unable to find town again. A distant peak, due north, would orient him.

He felt her presence beside him. She was suffering, and when she suffered, so did he.

"Guadalupe, perhaps we are not doing the right thing, wandering around looking for a lost mine."

She didn't reply.

"Maybe you should go to Mexico City and find your husband and arrange an interview with the dictator."

He sensed she was listening, even if she wasn't inclined to talk.

"A woman's pleas often win over a man's will," he said.

She wrapped her white rebozo over her to ward off the glaring sun.

"I think you should go," he went on. "I know you lack the means, but I will provide them. I can do that much. I will go with you, be your protector. I wish I could pay the ransom, but I have only a modest fixed income. I think it's the thing to do. Let's abandon this . . . this absurd search for a mine we wouldn't know if it was before our eyes."

She was listening. Something softened in her. She glanced his way, seeking something inside of him.

"Have you any contacts there?" he asked. "How do you know where to bring the ransom?"

"I have the name of a lawyer, a certain Señor Otero, given me by Malachi Nast."

"And that's all? Who is he and how does he fit in?"

"I don't know. I am to get the ransom to him. Then Ricardo will be freed. That is all I know."

"And what proof of this have you?"

"Ricardo's Maltese cross. The very one I gave him."

"No message from him?"

"The cross was enough."

"Was there a date given? A time you must be there with the money for Diaz?"

"*Nada,*" she said.

"There must be a date. This doesn't sound right to me."

She didn't respond. They hiked through rising heat now; the country rose and fell, never flat, never precipitous. He thought of a lonely sea.

"Señora, what happened last night?"

"They come looking for Ricardo's gold!"

"Who?"

"Nast, and now the Russian."

"Why?"

Scorn laced her reply. "They want it. They tell me they will help me, that Ricardo has gold in the house, or maybe dollars, and they'll help me, so we can ransom him. But Nast wants it for himself, and the Russian wants it for his revolution. Some revolution! Steal from the poor to overthrow the rich."

"They broke in?"

"Nast did, while I was gone. The Russian would have, but I caught him."

"What happened?"

"I made him look for it."

She told him that Gudonov found himself tearing her house and outbuildings apart under gunpoint, while she held a lamp.

She laughed bitterly. "Now he believes me."

"And now you wonder. Where is Ricardo? Is he safe? How do you reach him? You are dealing with a greedy old man who sees a way to fatten his purse."

She nodded, and then smiled gently at him.

"Thank you for offering," she said. "This trip to the City of Mexico, I will think about it. It is a long way, many weeks, and very hard, and there are many *bandidos.*"

"I would do anything for you."

"Why?"

"I cannot honorably say," he said.

She reached across to him and held his hand, and he felt her strong fingers grasp his. He felt in her grip a great tenderness; not love, for she could not give it, but something almost the same as love. In that moment, as in his other epiphanies when he was with her, he felt himself lifted and transformed.

"I will take you," he said. "We will go and save him."

They topped another low ridge and peered down upon a broad valley, almost lost in heat haze. He wondered where they would lunch, for this was not the sort of terrain that offered shade, and shade was what they would desperately need by noontime.

Still, in the bottom of the shallow valley was a line of gray vegetation, probably saltbush, a desert shrub that could grow to great heights and flourished in saline flats. Maybe they could find some shade there, a mile or so distant.

This great valley meandered out of the mountains in the west, and probably ran water from those mountains in wet seasons. It seemed the loneliest place Elwood had ever been. They descended a shallow grade, and headed toward a band of white, a river of sand that lay flat in the valley. The sand was bordered by towering brush, mostly saltbush, and back from the arroyo, mesquite and ironwood, but there were other shrubs too that Elwood wasn't sure he knew. Perhaps water lay not far below the surface, feeding this luxuriant growth.

They followed an animal trail through the dense brush, which seemed almost a forest after hiking over the naked land, and found themselves out upon that pancake-flat white sand, the dry watercourse that wound from the mountains.

He had never seen such brilliantly white sand. This sand was whiter than anything he had seen in nature. It glared up at him, drawing tears to his eyes. It lay packed and flat, save for the prints of animals, mule deer, perhaps javelinas, and creatures he could not identify.

"I will go blind here. It's too white!" she said.

"I'll look for some shade. This brush is ten or fifteen feet high. We'll find a bower."

He headed across, toward the far bank, where the gray-green brush towered.

"Aiee, this is a white river," she said.

"*Rio Blanco.*"

They stared at each other. They were standing in a

river of bright white sand, a river a hundred yards wide, with regular banks of dense shrubbery. All that was lacking was water, and judging from the brush, it was not far down.

"Madre de Dios," she whispered. "Elwood, do you know the history?"

"A little."

"Rio Blanco was the town where the gold mine was, but it was struck by the Black Plague, and most of its people died. Do you suppose . . . that the ones who didn't die left Rio Blanco and made a new town nearby, away from the plague?"

"And the old Rio Blanco is around here somewhere?" he asked.

"And the mine is somewhere near here also?"

They hiked along the white river, not knowing which direction to travel, more and more aware that the name Rio Blanco was apt, in fact perfect.

"Which way?" she asked.

"Up, upstream," he said.

"Why?"

"I don't know."

They walked up the white river, the caked sand hard underfoot, studying the thick brush along the banks that hid whatever lay beneath it. And for a mile, they never spoke a word.

Chapter 28

The glare off the white sand was so brutal that Guadalupe could barely see, and her eyes hurt from squinting. A glance at Señor LaGrange told her he was in the same desperate straits.

They had walked perhaps a mile up what they named the Rio Blanco, the river of white sand, studying both banks for signs of habitation. They saw nothing. The towering saltbush formed a veil that was as good as a solid wall.

The heat oppressed her and squeezed moisture out of her until she felt parched. What madness had brought her to this? Believing they were near the place where the lost mine might be? He was right: She should head at once for the City of Mexico and plead for mercy from the dictator Diaz.

"We could walk along one bank going this way, and the other bank returning," he said. "We can't see a thing this way."

"I would like some shade," she replied.

They headed for the south bank, where the brush grew higher and the sun seemed less likely to penetrate. In most places the brush was so thick there was no place even to exit from the flat white sand, but at last they found an animal trail that plunged into the overarching brush.

He headed that way.

"Be careful," she said, following. This man La-Grange knew little of the desert and its dangers.

He nodded. The air didn't seem much cooler in this place of gray light, but at least the direct sun no longer hammered them. The brush was aromatic, releasing an acrid but not unpleasant scent, redolent of heat and aridity. She knew this belt of brush didn't extend far beyond the banks of the river of sand, but it formed a barrier to the passage of most animals.

He did find, at last, a bower with some ancient logs offering seats. It was like a ramada. He set down the wicker basket, uncorked the canteen, and handed it to her. She drank the tepid water gratefully. If only there was enough for her to wash her face, but they had to be careful. They were perhaps seven miles from Rio Blanco, a three-hour walk, but they could easily get lost.

He drank, and then opened the wicker. She had packed hastily this day, some bread, no cheese, and some wine. The stamp of last night's desolation still governed this day.

He ate. "This is madness," he said. "We invented a name for a sandy gulch and think we're close."

"I am thinking the same thing," she said. "If you would, *mañana*, would you see about a trip to the City of Mexico?"

"I will find out. I don't even know how."

"We would have to go to Albuquerque and then south. There is nothing from Silver City. Or we could go west to Tucson and south to Hermosillo, in Sonora, and find a way from there. Or maybe the ocean, New Orleans to Vera Cruz."

"It will be up to you," he said. But then he gazed contemplatively at her. "But we're here now. Maybe God's led us to this place. Maybe everything will change. Just for this hour, this hot day, let's keep the faith."

She reached across and took his hand. "Just when I am ready to give up, there you are, Elwood."

They ate the coarse bread and sipped the rough red wine and sat quietly, dreading to face the noonday sun. But they could not stay here, slowly dehydrating.

"Forgive me, Señor, if I go freshen myself," she said.

"Of course. If you lose your way, yell. If we don't hear one another, head for the white sand where we can see."

She nodded. She didn't know how far she needed to travel for privacy, but she would walk all of the needed distance and then some. She took off, fighting brush, her direction parallel to the white sand river, and in a few yards Señor LaGrange was invisible. But she kept on another ten yards.

There before her was an adobe wall, weathered down to three or four feet, and another perpendicular, making a square, with saltbush rising from within. She stopped, stared, scarcely believing. Even from a few feet away, it had not been visible. She stepped carefully around the walls, studying the interior. Nothing, nothing but sticks and vegetation and what once had been a beehive fireplace in a corner.

A lone *placita*. It was nothing. *Nada*. She peered around fearfully, took care of her needs, and found her way back to Elwood, who had repacked the wicker basket and was waiting.

"Come," she said. "I show you something."

She led him to the ruin.

"Good Lord," he said. He paced its perimeter, and then they both headed on a course paralleling the white sands, and struck another ruin, equally concealed by brush, and a third, and fourth. Maybe these were more than an isolated settlement. If anything, the brush grew thicker within the ruins than outside of them, but Elwood found a ruin that was more accessible and entered it. She followed. There in a corner were the remains of a simple bed or cot, and on the ground was a jumble of bones, yellow and dessicated. And mortal. There was no mistaking the skull. Scraps of ancient fabric still survived.

She intuitively made the sign of the cross, blessing herself against this.

"The plague!" she whispered.

"It might be. This person was never buried."

"We must look!"

They plunged through thickets of brush, fighting their way through the clawing and spiny foliage, feeling the prick of thorns. Water could not be far below, to have yielded a chaparral like this. There were more ruins everywhere, the walls caved in or eroded, though some stood as high as six feet. And more remains. An infant, the bones largely intact for some reason. Small adults, bones scattered crazily. Bones covering whole floors, bones with brush growing through them. The unburied dead left behind by those who fled in terror.

Something slithered away, startling her. A lizard perhaps. The sun was too hot even for lizards. She hated this place of death and terror. It was Rio Blanco, the town that had died of the plague. Once they pushed through the brush, they had found scores of ruins. Maybe a hundred. It could be no other! The whole of the town could not be seen from twenty feet away by someone walking up that river of white sand. It could not be seen from the hills because the brush hid it.

"It is true, what the *viejos* said, that the black plague came and the town was no more," she whispered. "And if that is true . . ."

"The mine must be true as well."

She gazed at him with eyes so yearning, so desperate for what she needed, that he was touched.

"Let's find it," he said. "Let's free Ricardo!"

"But where?"

They needed no answer. Beyond the town rose low

cliffs. These had few outcrops and were largely covered with soil, which made them the last place on earth to harbor a mine of any sort. She struggled inland, past the ruins of casas, each with its tragedy to tell her. In one, a mummified woman sat against a wall, a dessicated infant clutched close.

Guadalupe touched a finger to her breast, sideways, up and down, her hand forming a cross.

The saltbush thinned and gave way to other plants, an occasional mesquite, some juniper. When they reached open air, they realized they had climbed a hundred feet into the rising slope. The midday sun pummeled them murderously. It occurred to her they were lost; how could they ever find their way back to the present Rio Blanco, and water and safety?

It was not hard to find the mine. She and Elwood scanned the slope above, their gaze settling at last on a rectangular dark opening, a small flat carved out of the slope at its foot, the opening mostly concealed by juniper so that most hours it would not be apparent to an observer. But now the sun was high, near zenith, and no shadows of dark green junipers fell across the opening. In an hour, it would be entirely hidden in shadow. An hour before noon, it would have been hidden as well.

"Madre de Dios," she whispered.

"We will save Ricardo," he said.

She turned to him filled with a radiant thanksgiving, and hugged him hard. He held her for a long moment.

The trip upslope was oddly fearsome. What if this was nothing at all? Not the Lost Doubloon? And maybe this was not even the first Rio Blanco! But she knew she was entertaining foolish thoughts. The slope was steep here, slippery with loose earth, hot and pungent. Something sinister caught her senses, some odor she couldn't quite fathom, something that was sending alarms through her, like the sting of needles.

By the time they reached the mine head, two hundred or so feet higher than the saltbush plateau below, they were winded. But there it was, stretching darkly into some gloom deep within, its contents unknown and fabulous.

"I will see," she said, and stepped toward the opening.

She heard the shout, and felt his body slam over her, tumbling her to the ground.

"No, no!" he cried.

She heard the angry buzzing, buzzing everywhere, as if the world had become unhinged.

"Get up quick!"

He yanked her brutally, yanked her up as something slithered by. He stepped up on a boulder and drew her up beside him. Now the world buzzed, the world rattled like snare drums.

They peered in, and what had seemed to be the quietness of an old mine writhed and slithered. Ancient lagging kept back the earth to either side, but the lagging was desiccated and falling apart, and had become the home of a thousand snakes, all of them disturbed now, their tails humming, their bodies slowly coiling, their bodies flowing like water over a dam. She had never seen so many snakes. She did not know so many snakes existed in all the world. They hung from the lagging. They draped over the planks that supported the roof of the tunnel, their viper heads and dark eyes hunting for targets.

They wrapped and unwrapped themselves, so many that they carpeted the floor of the mine as far as she could see. They were a horror, the guardians of the gates, the fatal wall that anyone seeking gold must pass. And the last person to try to pass through had failed, and died.

Chapter 29

Elwood stared helplessly at the mine head, and at Guadalupe. Once again, he had not taken life seriously. They had hunted for a mine and he hadn't even bothered to prepare. He lacked so much as a prospector's pick hammer.

They were almost afraid to move, for fear of stepping on a rattler, but in fact the space in front of the bore was clear of them.

He ached to enter, to chip away the rich ore, the prize that the whole world, it seemed, sought. But he could not, and certain death awaited anyone who tried.

"How did that prospector get in and get some gold?" she asked, echoing his own questions.

"At night, I imagine. In the deep dark, when the snakes were quiet and couldn't see. He couldn't wait. He had to try, and it killed him."

"How do we get gold then, Elwood?"

"I don't know. Fire maybe. Burn out the rattlers."

"Maybe it is so," she said. "I will get sticks."

He sighed. "I didn't bring any lucifers." Then he thought to make a fuller confession. "I didn't bring a pick hammer. We have nothing to chip out some ore. I didn't prepare. I am sorry."

"This is an evil place!" she cried.

"I don't know that fire would do it, unless it burns

for many hours and is very hot, and if we do that, the timbers will burn, and so will those planks that hold back the dirt, and it will all cave in."

She nodded. This was beyond two people with an empty wicker picnic basket.

"Elwood, how do I claim this mine?"

He was struck once again by his failures, this above all. There was nothing to do but confess. "I read it in the prospectors' manual. You prepare a claim written in a certain way, and put it in a waterproof container, and put that in a cairn or safe place at the discovery. Then you need to measure your claim. The law says it must be six hundred by fifteen hundred feet for an underground mine. So you build cairns at the corners. The discovery should be right at the center."

"Well, we can do that, *sí*?"

He shook his head. "Guadalupe, I have no pencil and paper, and no measuring tape, and no watertight container, and no shovel."

She laughed, surprising him. "Well, I didn't have much hope either. We will go get these things and come back tomorrow. Then what?"

"We have to register it as your claim."

"Where do we do that?"

"At a courthouse or a federal land office, or if it's a new mining district, there will be a recorder, agreed on by the miners themselves, whose records will become the government's. Then it will no longer be a secret. And the next day, a thousand people will come and scheme and stake out claims next to yours and . . . maybe use guns."

They stared again into the orifice in the hillside, aware that the rattlers had quieted. Somewhere, just beyond that deadly opening, lay the richest ore ever discovered in this area.

"I wonder if we'll ever see what's there," she said. "Or even keep this. How do we keep it? Will men with guns steal it? This place. . . . It makes me shudder. It's evil. Can't you smell it? Smell the devil?"

"We'll have to defend it, Guadalupe. No doubt about it."

The fear in her face was transparent. "How do we keep the wolves away?"

"I don't know. You could share the mine with a well-armed partner maybe."

"Will the law, the sheriff, will he help?"

He shook his head. The nearest law was in Silver City.

"I don't know what to do," she said.

"Neither do I."

She wandered around the little flat in front of that sinister hole, and then stooped.

"Ah, see what I have found!"

She held up a fragment of quartz ore, milky white with visible specks of gold running solidly through it all. She handled it gingerly, as if it were something sacred, and then handed it to him. He licked it, making the gold even more visible.

"You wanted proof. There's your proof. Now you have a valid claim," he said.

She nodded, her face drawn. Something in her eyes pleaded with him to help her.

Suddenly, he wasn't so sure a gold mine was a blessing.

"I guess we'd better head back to town," he said. "There's nothing we can do here."

"How are we going to find it again?" she asked.

It was a good question. Down in that river of white sand, the walls of brush were unchanging and anonymous for miles, and there was nothing in the surrounding features to provide a landmark or a reference point.

"We'll need a marker," she said. "Several markers. But what?"

"We can build a cairn of logs and rock at the turnoff."

"What if we lose it again, after finding it?"

"We won't be the first," he said.

She rubbed her ore and slid it into a small pouch she wore at her waist. "At least I have this! If it all seems like a dream, or if we lose this place, I will have this!"

"Guadalupe, you're going to claim this mine. We're going to do this right, and carefully, and you'll have your gold. We'll do it together."

She smiled and clasped his hand. Hers felt warm and tender.

They slid downslope and into the brushy forest, reluctant to leave, and yet they had to. They faced a seven-mile hike. The day would be waning by the time they reached town.

They worked past the ruins, the mute evidence of plague long ago, and finally reached the white sand. The spot where they burst out was no different from all the rest of the brushy walls of this arroyo, and they knew they would need to mark it.

"The towel in the basket," she said.

They ripped the white cotton into strips, and tied several strips to the brush. The white strips were, alas, invisible. They stood the empty brown wine bottle in the sand, buried its bottom so it would stand upright. That helped a little.

Gingerly, wary of snakes now, he dragged dead brush, limbs, debris out of the bankside saltbush, and heaped a mound of it on the sand. That would be visible until the next flood washed it away. They could think of nothing else to do.

It was so painful to leave the bonanza behind them, to walk away, knowing they had seen the face of fortune and could not touch it. Not yet.

They found their own footsteps in the white sand,

and retraced their route for a mile or so. Elwood was feeling more and more confident about finding his way back to town, simply because their passage had been recorded in the sand.

But then, ahead, they spotted the one thing they dreaded most. Heading their way was a bushy-bearded man leading two laden mules.

"Oh, no," Elwood said, thinking of the trail in the sand, leading directly back to their markers.

The prospector, for he was unmistakably one, bore down on them at a great pace, and halted suddenly, his gaze hidden from under the huge slouch hat that shaded his face.

"Out on a picnic, are ya?" he said. "Hot day for a picnic, ain't it?"

Elwood vaguely knew this one. He was one of the bunch that hung around the Tia Juana Café when he was in Rio Blanco.

"A hot day," Elwood agreed.

"Looking for the lost mine, I suppose. It takes all kinds when there's a rush," he said.

"How far is it to town?" Elwood asked.

"Well, now, I reckon you pretty well know that," the miner said. "You and the widow, all you have to do is follow your tracks."

"You are mistaken," Guadalupe said. "My husband will return."

The prospector grinned. "I imagine so," he said. "Where've you been enjoying yourselves? This ain't mineral country, that's for sure. But looking for a mine is a pretty good way to spend a day by yourselves."

Elwood didn't like the tone of that.

But Guadalupe had her own response. She stepped up to that cheery man and slapped him hard.

"Oh, ho!" he bawled, wiping his face. He began

laughing. "Well, Rosie," he said, "I guess I insulted the lady."

He plunged past them, and they watched him go. He was following their tracks.

Guadalupe stood stock still, her lips drawn tight, watching the swine diminish and then disappear around a bend.

She glared at him and at Elwood, and then stalked silently toward town, her pace so determined that she was leading the way. They found the place where they had struck the white arroyo, and turned up it. From now on they could work through some hills toward town without trouble. From every hilltop he could see the distant mountain to the north with which he had oriented himself earlier.

But his thoughts were hardly on getting back safely. They were focused on one thing: his fear that the prospector would find the lost mine and claim it. He could not shake the fear, even when he told himself that it was wildly improbable. They weren't even in mineral country.

"Let him think it," she said suddenly, and he had to guess on what had been flooding through her mind.

"What?"

"I will not say what. I will only say that his mind will be far from gold, and that is what we want."

"I hope so. He studied us, studied the basket, examined our clothing. He didn't see a prospector's hammer or a pick because I didn't think to bring one. So let him think what he will think. Maybe it's all to the good."

She laughed suddenly. The same worry had been gnawing at both of them.

"I will throw away my reputation if that is what it takes to hide the mine!" she cried.

They both laughed, but he didn't much feel like laughing.

Chapter 30

Artie Quill laughed.

"Rosie," he said, "this is a great day. I shot a Injun and I got slapped by a spitfire."

Rosie yawned.

"Don't hardly get good days like this very often," he said. "Maybe it'll get even better."

On that optimistic note he set off, up the white-sand arroyo, past the walls of saltbush guarding the banks.

Slapped him! That was pretty good. She thinks she's royalty, living in that mansion on the hill like that. As if she had a reputation to protect.

He cackled. The thought of her and that fool from the East tickled his rib. Not that the man looked like a fop anymore. She had wrestled him into jeans and a blue shirt and a big old slouch hat. And come to think of it, he had shaved the mustache. Too bad. Artie had rather liked those waxed mustache points drooping over the man's cheeks.

Pretty good stuff. He hiked up the arroyo, following the tracks of the lovebirds, curious about where this little rendezvous had occurred. That was entertaining in its own right.

They were probably near Rio Blanco now, with only a couple of hours of daylight left, remembering their little picnic.

A few minutes later, the tracks in the sand grew complex and headed for a bank. And there, beside the bank, some brush had been heaped in the white sand.

He headed that way, and found not only brush, but some white strips of cloth dangling from limbs, and the shiny brown bottle poking upward. Well, they must have found quite a boudoir if they went to such extremes to mark it.

Artie enjoyed that.

"All right, Rosie, we'll just dodge in hyar and have us a peek."

He steered his two mules along a narrow game trail that penetrated the dense brush, and soon located a bower.

"Guess this is pretty private," he said, enjoying this all the more, having found out a few things. "Only, I wouldn't want to camp in here. Too many crawly things and bugs."

He was about to head for the white sand when he spotted the weathered adobe wall, dim and veiled off to one side.

"Well, now," he said, leaving his mules in the bower. He soon was examining a roofless square of adobe, with saltbush crowded its interior.

"Some Mex place, I imagine," he said, and remembered Rosie was thirty yards away.

Mex place indeed. Within a half hour he had discovered dozens of weathered, roofless adobe buildings overgrown with the brush. And human bones. And fragments of leather and cloth, so ancient they crumbled to his touch.

A whole damned city in there. And a man could walk up that arroyo a hundred times and never have a clue.

Or a man could stand on any ridge and look down in and never see the place.

Something was tickling his mind, something out of the past, something he had heard while sucking suds in the Tia Juana Café, while other sourdoughs were spinning yarns. But darned if he could remember what it was.

So the lovebirds found an ancient city while they were toying with each other. Ho, ho, no wonder they were piling brush in the arroyo. No one would ever find it again, that's for sure.

Something had sure wiped out that town. Half the dead weren't even buried. For that matter, he never found a cemetery. Something had swept through there and killed the lot. Maybe Apaches. Probably so. Apaches could have swept down and wiped out a whole town. Pretty good-sized village too. And now it had been lost to memory for a century.

But he hadn't seen any arrows. Maybe the Apaches had retrieved them. Arrows were hard to make, and a warrior got them back if he could.

Done with his wandering, he headed back to the bower, where Rosie nibbled coarse grasses and his pack mule stood stolidly. He collected Rosie's lead line and headed back to the white arroyo, and out onto that sand. Even at that late hour, the sand blinded him with its whiteness, and he squinted. Damned river of white sand.

Rio Blanco.

He stood there, paralyzed. The legend was that Rio Blanco had been wiped out by the Black Plague. And after that the mine had been lost.

Artie Quill sucked air, chilled at how nearly he had missed it all. Jaysas, he had come close enough to the mine to throw a rock into it, and would have walked away.

No wonder the señora and the dude had left markers. You could look up and down this river of sand at that wall of brush and never figure out where the place was.

"Oh, ho, ho, Rosie! We're so rich we'll own all the whorehouses in California!"

He plunged back into the saltbush, threaded his way through the ancient city, fighting limbs and leaves, bulling his way, breaking sticks, jamming his mules through openings hardly wide enough for a snake. . . .

Which reminded him to be careful. Very careful.

He stepped gingerly after that, heading straight up a slope until suddenly the brush gave way to dense juniper ground cover, and he could see an escarpment ahead of him, mostly soil-covered, the unlikeliest place he had ever seen for a gold mine. But gold was where you found it. He threaded through juniper, well aware that rattlers would be napping in the shade, climbed upslope until suddenly he was standing right in front of the thing, which was half hidden by the juniper.

"Well, well, Stud Malone, now I know where you been!"

The Lost Doubloon, timbered and battened against the loose soil around it. Dark and forbidding.

Artie laughed. He sure as hell wasn't going to let Nast know about this. He sure as hell wasn't going to register it with the claims office and let the world in on this one! This one was his little secret and would stay that way!

He parked his mules and crept forward, watching out for snakes, and finally reached the rectangular orifice. It took a moment for his eyes to adjust, and when they did, he gasped. Snakes. More than he had ever seen. Snakes coiled and piled and hanging. Snakes slowly undulating, like the waves of an ocean. Snakes with rattle tails and diamond backs and viper heads.

He stared in wonder, not believing what he was looking at.

How the hell did Stud get in? How did Stud chip out a sack full of ore? He got nailed coming out, not going in. Maybe he went in at night, pitch dark, with a candle, the snakes blind and slow. Yeah, probably that was it. But the racket he made, knocking out some ore, stirred them up and he bought his ticket going out. Yeah.

But maybe not. Artie eyed the cliff above. Juniper slope, steep. He decided to risk it. He eyed the distant ridges carefully. He didn't want to be seen. Up there he would be in the open. But no one was within miles of here, so why worry? He clawed his way upward, hanging on to juniper, scared of snakes, the soft earth crumbling and caving under his boots, but in time he topped out on a hilltop plateau, and there he hunted and hunted and hunted for another opening, a back door to the mine. Nothing. He poked under every cedar and juniper, studied tiny game trails, and finally concluded the Doubloon had no back door. Spaniards never cut one.

He studied the surrounding ridges, looking for someone to shoot, but all he saw was a great rosy cloudless sunset.

"Hell of a day," he said, his heart bursting with delicious pleasure.

He skidded and slid slowly to the mine head, wondering whether to risk going in for ore after dark.

"The hell with that, Rosie. We're going to blast them snakes outa there first."

But how?

That was a sobering thought. Build a fire? It would set the timbers and the lagging ablaze until they all caved in, and probably wouldn't kill all the snakes anyway. Giant powder? Blow the snakes to hell and back, and then dig a new bore? That sounded better. Blow those serpents out of the county. But that was no guarantee either. Percussion was funny; it would smack one place, miss another. Worse, it might cave in the shaft and the drifts. Old timbers like these, full of dry rot. Bury the gold under a hundred feet of rubble. If he did that, he'd have to raise capital to dig it all out, and he was damned if he'd do that. Nast would claim his half. Poison? Hell, he could dump pails of strychnine or arsenic over those reptiles and their scaly hides would protect them.

It was making him crazy. He was fifty feet from a bonanza, from a fortune, from a lifetime of dreams, from the thing he'd been stalking all his life, the Big Bonanza, the circus parade. And he couldn't even go near it. But crazy as he was, he was less crazy than Stud Malone.

"Ain't it so, Rosie? You like it here? No wonder you're so happy. Lotsa grass around this juniper. But don't get bit!"

Rosie gnawed at some forage.

Night was catching up with him and he was damned if he would bed down in the center of a rattlesnake city, so he retreated. He didn't like the old town either, with ghosts and bones and brush. There was nowhere to go but out to the white river, where he would be safe. Hell, even in the light of a new moon he could see any dark thing coming across that white sand, and if he saw anything moving, he would shoot it.

Which reminded him that his secret was shared by two others, and might be shared by even more, depending on what they said or did in Rio Blanco. Chances were, though, that they would keep it to themselves. Which suited Artie fine. When that Juliet and her Romeo returned, he would add their bones to the others in old Rio Blanco, and no one would ever know.

Chapter 31

The Indian, Soto Begay, had not returned. He was to report faithfully at sundown. Malachi Cromwell-Nast would have preferred that he report at ten P.M. each evening, in full dark, but what Indian could keep time? Sunset had to do. Begay, The Shadow, had been sent after Artie just to keep tabs on the man. The Shadow could trot for amazing distances, and could spend a day far from Rio Blanco and still trot in by sundown, having covered eight or ten miles in an hour or hour and a half.

But now it was midnight, and Begay had not knocked softly on the office door or slipped in with news. Begay always had news, and that was why Nast paid him well. He had given Begay a new red flannel shirt, a bowie knife, and soon would give him a quart of red-eye. If Begay still lived. Nast doubted it. He suspected that sometime this day Artie had pumped a bullet into The Shadow, and now Artie was roaming somewhere that Nast didn't know about, which annoyed him.

If Begay didn't report soon, Nast would be giving his other spy, the new one, Arnold Schwartz, the task of keeping tabs on Artie.

Nast organized in his mind what he had learned this day from his tipsters, whose ears funneled every whisper uttered in Rio Bravo into Nast's own. He had informants in the saloons, in the hardware and dry-goods stores, in the cafés, in the bank and livery barn and harness maker's shop. An apprentice blacksmith apprised him as to who was getting what mule or burro or horse shod. A certain clerk in the law offices of Bixby and Crown let it be known what clients had shown up and what sort of legal work was under way. Nast also paid a certain gent in the land office where local mining claims were filed. Nast wanted to know within ten minutes who filed what, where the claim was located, what sort of mineral was being claimed, and the exact wording of the claim.

This army of tipsters wasn't cheap, but Nast paid only for good information, and never twice for the same news. So most of the tips he received earned the tipster nothing at all. Some malefactors had invented false tips, and these Nast had dealt with his own way, usually with a warning to leave Rio Blanco or face a broken kneecap or worse. The new man, Schwartz, the former foundryman, would be a handy one to administer justice in that fashion. Nast liked to think he had his own private justice system operating, with appropriate rewards and punishments.

This day he had assorted tips to consider: Mrs. O'Rourke and the Estern dude, LaGrange, had returned from their daily amble, separated at the foot of her manse, as usual, and gone their own ways. If they adhered to their pattern, they would be off at dawn, looking for a mine as if they were going on a picnic. In fact, that was the key to it all. Let La-Grange start equipping himself with some mining or prospecting gear, and Nast would take immediate interest. The hardware clerk was told he would receive double compensation, two bits, for any tip about Guadalupe O'Rourke or her peculiar friend who fashioned himself a lexicographer. The very hour, some days previous, that LaGrange had bought jeans and a chambray shirt and a slouch hat, Nast had heard about it, and counted the information valuable.

Now, in the quiet of his study, well toward midnight, he waited for his snitches to report. He let them in one at a time, and they exited through the back door, down a rickety stair into the alley. At the end of each day he organized his tips on a yellow legal pad, then drew a line through the worthless ones, and pondered the valuable ones.

He heard a familiar unmistakable step, and was pleased. Even before Lame Willy knocked, Nast opened to him, and let the little swamper in. Lame Willy could barely walk, wounded from his very birth, and Nast felt a great tenderness toward him and rewarded him well. Lame Willy's information was always valuable.

"Hey, hey," Willy said gruffly. The man spoke in the rudest vernacular, but Nast didn't mind. "I got the stuff, eh?"

Nast nodded.

"That dude, LaGrange, he comes in, hour ago. He orders some red-eye, sputters it down his throat, then begins asking all about what's what with mining claims. He's asking how you file a claim. I get interested, and I'm swamping right there, getting an earful. You know. How do you record it with the guv'mint. Mark it. Fix them boundaries. Ah, them sourdoughs in there enjoyed that, fed him a bunch of horsepucky. Poor dumb dude. Then LeGrange wants to know all about giant powder, fuses, caps, blowing everything in the county to hell, so the sourdoughs tell him all sorts of stuff, all of which is gonna get himself blowed up. Then LaGrange, he asks about pick hammers, stuff like that, like the picnic's over and he's gonna dig."

"That's it?"

"Yeah, hey, hey."

"He say anything about Guadalupe O'Rourke?"

"Hey, hey, naw."

"Did he say he's going to buy some giant powder?"

"Hey, hey, I don't know. But he asks where to get it, and they tell him about the vault back of the hardware, where they've got the DuPont safe underground."

"Very good, Willy. That's valuable. Here's a small token of my esteem."

He handed Lame Willy a brass token good for one hour at Minnie's Parlor House.

"Hey, hey, I'm dancing," Willy said.

Dancing, for Lame Willy, was paradise.

Nast let Willy out the front door for a change, and listened while the wretch clumped down the wooden stair. Lame Willy was pure gold.

Was it possible that the picnicking twosome had found something? If not a mine, at least something that looked to them like one? Something to register? Something to pick at with a prospector's hammer? Something to blow open with Dupont Hercules dynamite?

That would be the best joke ever to befall the sourdough fraternity of Rio Blanco. Nast cherished the very thought, and cackled happily. The innocents had found the mine; the savvy old coots had never gotten close. Gawd, that was choice. Maybe the Doubloon would show up now, in which case Nast would be even richer, very soon.

He studied his pocket watch, and slid it back into its marsupial pouch in his buttoned-up vest. No matter how fierce the sun, he always wore his waistcoat, which he esteemed as a mark of dignity and social caste.

He was about to fold up operations for the night when he heard a clamor on the wooden stairs, and opened to that hunk of beef, Arnold Schwartz, who looked like he could terminate the existence of any living thing in ten seconds.

Nast was delighted. He had not heard from his newest minion since sending him out days earlier.

"Ah! You! Come in!" Nast said, waving the foundry-man into his shadowy lair.

Schwartz settled into the wooden chair, which groaned and creaked so loudly that Nast thought the chair might disintegrate under the monster.

"I ain't got much," Schwartz began. "Nobody's found nothing but a couple of ledges, a little gold they took out in a few hours. Me, I wander all over the damned country, talking with everyone. I never caught up with this Quill, except maybe when I was just heading out and this Quill was heading into town."

"That's the one. He did come to town."

"Yeah? I thought maybe so."

"Well, that wasn't very profitable. You'll need to do better. There's nothing I can use. Normally, I don't pay for anything if it's not something I can use, but you're new and I have future plans for you, so take this."

He handed Schwartz a brass whorehouse token.

Schwartz read it and broke into a toothy grin. "I can sell it," he said.

"Tomorrow, you're going after Artie Quill. He's south of town somewhere; that's all I know. Leave at dawn. That's barren country, nothing much by way of minerals, but who knows? If you should see a dead Indian, let me know how he died and how long he's been dead."

"How should I know that stuff, eh?"

"Learn it."

"Well, I ain't dumb, so I will."

"If you do find Quill, don't provoke him. I want to know where he is, mostly. Just steer clear and report back to me. That's your most important task. Find the man. You've got a tintype, so you can recognize him. Find him and get back here as fast as your big flat feet will carry you. If you can't avoid trouble, hammer him senseless and bring what's left of him to me."

"Yeah, I'll do it."

"Find Quill and I'll give you two tokens."

"I prefer cash," Schwartz said. He turned to leave.

"I'm not done with you. Don't leave until I dismiss you."

Schwartz didn't like that, but absorbed it. Nast made sure all his snitches knew who was the boss.

"I have something even more important for you to do. Tomorrow at dawn, a woman and a man will walk out of town. They will have a picnic basket. Follow them, but not closely. Stay way back. Make no contact at all. When you know where they are going, come back and report to me. If they are going to the same place as Artie Quill, I want to know it. And fast."

"Where will I find them?"

"The woman lives in the mansion on the hill, overlooking Rio Blanco. She meets her friend right here at the bank at dawn's earliest light. If you make a mistake, you won't ever work for me again. You will not let yourself be seen, but you will know exactly where they are going. Don't harm them."

"How do I do that?"

"If you are too dumb to figure out a way, find work somewhere else. You are new here, and I don't put much stock in your skills."

Schwartz smiled toothily. "I will work for you for a long time," he said. "And I want more money. Much more."

The effrontery of it amazed Nast. He would give the man a lesson later, when the moment was ripe.

Chapter 32

Sergei Gudonov suddenly enjoyed one of those bursts of prickly intelligence for which he justly prided himself. Truly, this was the ferment of the world's largest brain, and was a concept quite beyond those with lesser mental capacity.

Namely, Ricardo O'Rourke was not a revolutionary at all. He was a gunrunner, an arms merchant, in spite of what his wife said about him. Arms merchants were in it for the money, not for the cause. In time, Gudonov himself would be dealing with arms merchants on behalf of his own revolution. Greedy men like O'Rourke.

Yes! Ricardo O'Rourke lived to make a fortune, to live high and mighty in a mansion on a hill, surrounded by servants, with a beautiful Desdemona, lording over all of creation. He cared nothing about the very poor, the serfs, the bondsmen, the slaves of the world.

Therefore, he had money. Lots of money! To his wife he might be a revolutionary, but to Sergei Gudonov, who had a truer eye, he was a death merchant, and death merchants needed capital to buy and sell arms, and therefore O'Rourke had money hidden somewhere, even if Guadalupe didn't know of it. And therefore, Sergei would find it. He had no compunction about stealing from an arms merchant in order to foster a true revolution. Or from an arms merchant's widow, he reminded himself.

It was also plain the money was not in the house. Nor in the Cimarron Bank. Some quiet inquiries had determined that. Nor in the stable or sheds. Therefore, it was hidden somewhere else on O'Rourke's estate. And Gudonov would find it, for there was no scheme or strategy known to lesser mortals that a man of his intelligence could not penetrate. The estate encompassed eight or ten acres on a plateau overlooking Rio Blanco, and before the next sunset, he would examine every inch of it.

It would be simple. As soon as the widow and her lover departed on their daily picnic, he would ascend the hill dressed as a yardman, and begin the hunt, and this time he would find O'Rourke's fortune and smuggle it out without a soul knowing of it. This would be the perfect revolutionary crime: He would find a fortune unknown to the gunrunner's survivors, steal it, and disappear from Rio Blanco. The woman would never know! Oh, ho, what fun!

He could hardly wait for dawn. An hour before sunrise, he was dressed, this time in the rags of a gardener, a shovel and hoe in hand. He slouched along Casa Grande Street, the town so silent that his own shuffling gait was the loudest noise reaching his ears.

He settled in the deep dark of a store and waited for the lovebirds. He felt grand, knowing how his splendid mind had at last served him perfectly, with impeccable logic. It amused him, the turtledoves Guadalupe and Elwood, off hunting a lost mine, picnic basket in hand.

It took a while, but eventually, in the dimmest light, he spotted the two of them meeting at their usual spot at the bank. He plucked her wicker basket from her, and added a thing or two to the contents. Sergei wished he know what Elwood was adding. Whatever it was, it was fairly heavy and the basket weighed more. Then the pair strolled away, toward the Mexican precincts off to the south, and into the barren lands beyond. Sergei watched them go, waiting easily for the right moment, and then slid quietly up the hill, unobserved, until the mansion loomed darkly over him and its grounds stretched in all directions. This marvelous day, he would find O'Rourke's fortune and liberate it so that it might liberate the oppressed.

He decided to focus on the rear of the place. That was only logical. O'Rourke would not hide his fortune anywhere in full view of the town below, where hundreds of people might stare up the slope and see him.

Speaking of prying eyes, Gudonov studied the gloomy light of predawn, using his Cossack skills to spot observers. He saw no one, but that didn't mean anything. He used his hoe to pluck up weeds along the drive, gradually working toward the back of the property. Ah, he was no one's fool!

Gudonov hoed and weeded his way around the mansion and found himself in an open level area. The turned soil of a garden attracted him at once. No servants remained to plant and cultivate and weed it, so the whole garden consisted of desiccated cornstalks, dried leaves, brown tomato vines, fragile runners of squash plants, and debris. A perfect place to hide wealth, he thought. A man could seem to weed and plant and hoe, and no one would see his true occupation, the hiding of cash.

He began poking here and there, working systematically along the long-harvested rows, hoping his hoe would strike something hard. But all he achieved was to turn over yellow soil. He hoed irritably for an hour, and finally surrendered. It was nothing but an abandoned garden that had supplied the household with greens and squash. But there was money nearby; he felt it, as if some uncanny sense unknown to lesser mortals were steering him closer and closer to the prize.

Even as the sun rose, he furtively watched the hills, the gravelly road up to the mansion, the surrounding canyons, and the town far below. He felt only the silence and the heat. Stupidly, he had brought no water, but he thought he could remedy that and hunted for a well. He found a spring that burbled out of the far cliff. A tile pipe carried fresh cold springwater into the manse. He drank lustily, admiring this private oasis, a rich man's treasure in an arid land. Water, he thought, was the greatest of all forms of wealth. Give a wise man water for his land, his gardens, his cities, and a man could perform miracles.

But it wouldn't buy a revolution. At least not unless he could sell water for gold or rifles.

A great stillness lay over the whole area as the midday heat exploded over it, and even the birds took refuge until the blast of the sun had waned. But no amount of heat would allay Sergei Gudonov, dedicated as he was to changing the world.

A rage filled him. He alone, among all those searching for gold in Rio Blanco, was doing so selflessly. Not one penny of it would he keep. Every ounce of the precious metal would be spent on making the world a better place. How different he was from all those squalid prospectors, gouging the earth for wealth! Did they care about the world's poor? The serfs trapped on land that wasn't theirs? Did they care about the sick, the ones so poor they couldn't find food? About infants starving to death? Ach! They were all swine.

Of course, it might be argued that he was robbing wealth from a penniless widow, but he set that aside. She could sell the mansion and get along. And who knows? Maybe she wasn't a widow at all. One couldn't trust a word issuing from Nast's pursed lips.

But it troubled him.

He set aside his hoe and began a careful tour of the rest of the grounds. Apart from a few juniper bushes, much of the estate was barren, with yellow clay that supported little more than cactus and greasewood. The next logical place to hunt was the spring, which fell into a green bower, a small and sweet heaven in an arid land. There he refreshed himself, drinking heartily and washing his face. In the shade of the over-arching cottonwoods he found comfort and peace. And also a way to study the surrounding area, looking for spies and intruders. But there was nothing. Sleepy Rio Blanco, far below, snoozed in the midday heat.

If he left one widow poorer in order to benefit hundreds of thousands in Mother Russia, would that not be a fair and just exchange? Yes, of course. His motto was the greatest good for the greatest numbers. One woman made poorer, deprived of gold she didn't know she had and would never have found all by herself, against a swift well-armed strike against the corrupt monarchs and nobility. A devil's bargain.

The spring interested him. It poured out of a fissure where a fault separated two distinct types of rock, one igneous, the other sedentary. Where would one look for gold? Maybe in the pool itself; gold was impervious to everything, and would endure the water flowing over it. And so Sergei Gudonov unlaced his boots and pulled away his britches and plunged in, finding the water numbing to his feet and calves. Slowly, he waded the mucky pond, his feet hunting for treasure. Once he stumbled on something hard, and his heart raced with anticipation. But it proved to be only a boulder that had careened down the cliff some long while ago.

Disappointed, he abandoned the pool and began

studying the majestic trees, looking for a secret compartment, a trapdoor, a nest. He actually spent most of the afternoon at it, chiding himself for it, because it was easier to hunt for gold in the shade of a spring-fed bower than to brave the brutal afternoon sun. He found nothing.

He grew angry. In fact, he fell into a towering rage. How dare O'Rourke defeat him? O'Rourke had no great mind; *he* did. It was a temptation to stalk down the hill and into town and order a quart of vodka and make his rage go away. But rage had its uses. He could stay angry for days, thinking about the time the Cossacks trampled a village in the Ukraine, driving the screaming women and children away, torching the wheat fields, butchering the men. The village had harbored a nest of revolutionaries and anarchists, and the Czar was making sure the village was stomped from the face of the earth. That made him angry. He had been with the Cossacks that bright bloody day, and the day had changed him forever.

There was little left to look at on the O'Rourke grounds except the cemetery, so he wandered over there, and discovered half-a-dozen graves, each surrounded by an iron fence, the mounds ancient and weathered. He read the names carved into wooden markers, and recognized none of them. Servants then. Peons who had worked until they died, and were buried there, with a slab of wood carved with a cross, a name, and some dates, to memorialize a life. But there was one with a small granite headstone, and that one interested him. The name chiseled into it was Ricardo O'Rourke and it bore a birth date, and that was all.

Chapter 33

Guadalupe looked tired this dawn. Elwood marveled at her courage and strength. There were black pits under her eyes, but she seemed ready to face whatever they would find at the lost mine. The more he knew her, the more he marveled at the fire burning within her, the passion that had led to the mine, and would soon lead to restoring her beloved to her arms. Elwood felt a sharp pain at the thought. He knew he was nothing but a handy helper, and that her dreams were only of Ricardo.

"I have some things," he said. "A gallon of coal oil, a hundred-foot tape, a pencil and a pad of paper, three empty watertight baking powder tins for the claim notices, and a geologist's pick hammer."

She smiled and touched his arm. In that touch was all the reward he would ever receive for this, but it sufficed.

He took the wicker picnic basket from her, and slipped his equipment into it and covered it with the checkered cloth she had provided. This time it was heavy. The gallon of coal oil would soon start his arms to aching. But he didn't mind. The oil, combined with sticks and brush and set afire, might drive away the snakes. If not, he would need to learn a lot more about dynamite than he knew.

They walked quietly through the predawn gray, past

dozing burros in pens, and up the lonely grade leading south from Rio Blanco, while the city still
slumbered. This would be an exciting day! With luck,
they might penetrate the Lost Doubloon, chip out
some of its rich gold quartz, write a claim, build corner cairns, and come away with the gold and the
ownership. He hoped she would give him some of the
quartz, but this mine would be hers. She needed it; he
would do his utmost to help her claim it.

How odd it was. Just a few days earlier he was lan-
guorously listening for new words and keeping them
in a journal and finding little else to occupy him or fill
up a life. Now . . . he was in the service not of himself,
but of a determined Mexican woman whose steely resolve was a marvel to him. He didn't really care about
words anyway.

As they topped the ridge to the south, the sun rose
over the rim of the world, shooting long golden rays
across the emptiness. It would be another hot day. He
didn't care. They had a mine, if they could keep it.
They were alone again, walking through a hush that
seemed to embrace the whole world. There was little
to say to each other; they were companions on a great
quest, trusting in one another.

Ahead, a circling column of vultures wheeled slowly
in the horizontal sunlight, slowly soaring round and
round.

Guadalupe instinctively crossed herself.

"Something died," he said.

"It is far away," she replied.

Indeed, whatever died was off to the east, far from
where they were heading.

"We had better have a look," he said, surprising
himself. A few days ago, he would carefully have ignored or circumvented that wheeling column of
scavengers.

She nodded. They left their familiar trail and cut

over dry slopes until they topped a low ridge and peered into a broad valley. A hundred yards distant a swarm of creatures were tearing at something. Birds, small animals, maybe larger ones.

Elwood strode bravely forward, while Guadalupe hung back a little. At twenty yards, they exploded, the whole mass of creatures. Black birds burst heavily upward, flapping slowly. Creatures retreated, snarling. The flap of wings pulsed the quiet air. A rank sweet odor reached his nostrils, and he instinctively yanked a handkerchief from his jeans and pressed it over his nose. Not that it helped.

The remains were mortal. And beyond identification. And there was nothing they could do. He could say only that it was a man, and his hair was black, and he wore jeans and a green shirt.

He sighed. "I will report it to Silver City," he said, uncertain that he should say anything at all to anyone.

"Can we bury him?"

"With what?"

She acknowledged their helplessness with a shrug.

The carrion-eaters waited just beyond striking distance. Above, the red-headed vultures circled in the hot air, and bided their time. He thought he saw a coyote, or maybe a fox, sitting on its haunches, ready to dine. A raven crabbed forward on the ground, bolder than the rest.

Guadalupe knelt, and he saw she was praying for the soul of this unfortunate, giving the gift of prayer to whoever lay there. Guadalupe had a great and good heart, he thought. He never would have thought to give a blessing to that terrible corpse.

She rose. They fled. Neither spoke. They hadn't the slightest idea what had felled that man in that place. And Elwood didn't want to think about that. They reached the river of white sand an hour later, and headed up the dry watercourse, following the dimples of their previous passage. The wicker basket grew heavy, and Elwood shifted it from hand to hand. Seven miles was a long way.

The walls of gray saltbush rose silently to either side, veiling what lay beyond the banks. About where the turnoff should be, Elwood watched sharply, hunting for the pile of brush out in the sand, the brown bottle, the strips of cloth tied to limbs. But he saw nothing. At least there was the mark of passage in the sand, the dimples in the brilliant white that recorded the tread of man and beast. Silently, they toiled up the broad arroyo, and Elwood grew itchy. Surely they had gone too far. He didn't remember coming this far. Yet the dimples continued, and even some brown manure, suggesting that they had walked farther than either realized.

"We have gone too far," she said suddenly.

"We'd better go on; we have this trail in the sand."

She stared at the dimples, and at him.

"Bastante!" she said. "We have been fooled."

He remembered that wily prospector, whose eyes surveyed them coldly even while he smiled. A dread filled him.

"He found it," Elwood said.

They turned. He guessed they had gone two miles too far, but who could say? The walls of brush guarding the white river looked the same, mile after mile.

It was already noon and the heat was brutal, hammering the moisture from them.

"Lunch," he said.

She nodded. He found a game trail, and they took it, and soon found a bower, cool and shaded. They studied it sharply for rattlesnakes and then settled down. She spread the checkered cloth over the ground debris, but discovered they had chosen a place where fire ants swarmed, so wearily they packed up and headed down the arroyo once again. At the next game trail, they did better. Elwood found a glade shaded by lush and tall gambel oak, spacious and cool. This time, they could eat peacefully. She had packed the usual bread and cheese and wine.

"He has stolen it from us," she said.

"We don't know that."

"I have the inner eye."

"We need to find it before we can come to conclusions."

"He brushed away the tracks. He led his mules up there. He would not do that if he hadn't found it."

It was hard to disagree with her logic. He tried to remember the bearded man. One thing he did remember was the shining butt of a rifle poking from a saddle sheath on one of his mules. The sourdough was armed. It tormented him to think of finding the Lost Doubloon only to have it stolen. It was unbearable, wrong, terrible.

"We need to spy on him first," she said.

It was she who was formulating plans, not giving an inch. She ate lustily, breaking off chunks of sweet moist bread, and washing it with red wine, flashes of anger lighting her face like lightning bolts.

"We will go close to the bank of the arroyo. He couldn't have hidden everything," she said. "We will see something."

"He's armed, Guadalupe."

So am I," she retorted, and he wondered how, and whether she would use whatever weapon she possessed.

Now he noticed the weight, the bulge, in a pocket in her skirt. This was a different skirt from any she had worn before, more utilitarian, plain gray cotton.

They packed the basket and headed down the white sand, hugging the south bank, their gazes alert to the smallest disorder. They worked slowly, through the blast of midday heat, until at last Guadalupe pointed triumphantly. Several saltbush branches had been recently broken off. A little more hunting revealed a place in the white sand that had been brushed with a branch.

Her black eyes glowed, and she smiled triumphantly at Elwood.

"Be careful," he whispered.

Her glare was disdainful, and he felt himself to be the timorous one, while she was the fiercer. They slid silently inland, finding the trail familiar and showing signs of passage. Soon they reached their bower. They were greeted only with silence. Minutes later, they wandered past the adobe ruins of the first Rio Blanco, under a canopy of saltbush, and finally made it out of the river flat and onto the juniper-covered slope. Up above was the mine, dark and barely visible.

It seemed too silent.

They looked at each other, seeing no one anywhere, and began the ascent, watching for rattlers, rounding clumps of juniper, until at last they topped the flat in front of the mine.

"Been expecting you," said the prospector, who had been sitting with his back to the cliff, watching them the whole time. He held a shining revolver in his fist and its bore was aimed straight at Elwood.

"Did you bring me some giant powder?" the man asked. "That's the way to do it."

Elwood didn't respond.

"Put the basket down and back away," the man snapped. "After that, walk in there."

He waved the barrel toward that black rectangle that was guarded by vipers.

Chapter 34

The sourdough waved them toward the portals of death. Guadalupe froze, her eyes upon the huge bore of that revolver.

"Let her go," Elwood said. "She's a lady."

"If I let her go, I'd just have to sell her someplace," the man replied.

"Who are you?" Elwood asked.

"Why ask? I could tell you, but it wouldn't be worth a damn to you, now would it? I'm the man who's got me the Lost Doubloon."

Guadalupe couldn't see far into that hole; the blinding sun kept her from knowing what lay beyond or how far back the rattlers nested. But at least at the front of it, no rattlers were coiled. They stretched, entwined, enervated by the heat and light. She thought she and Elwood might manage to light-step past them before they could coil and strike. And then die slowly within their prison.

She thought of her little five-shot revolver and slid her had into the pocket in her skirt, only to be stopped.

"Hands in sight! Whatcha got in there, little spitfire?"

"Wouldn't you like to know," she retorted.

"Move!"

"Mind if we take the picnic basket?" Elwood asked.

The bearded man cackled. For an answer, he kicked the basket and spilled its contents. Pick hammer, a gallon of coal oil in a tin, paper and pencils, empty baking soda tins, half a bottle of wine.

"I guess you ain't gonna be writing no claims after all," the prospector said. "Move."

Guadalupe decided she wouldn't. A bullet would be faster than the agony of dying from a few rattler bites.

"Move!"

She sat down, very slowly, sweeping her skirts about her and drawing her legs under them.

He fired, the shot searing past her and plowing ground. The crack shocked the quiet. That awakened the rattlers. She was startled, saw a vast undulation at the front of the mine, and realized that now there were scores of snakes coiling, writhing into striking position, ready to sink fangs into anything approaching.

Elwood took a tentative step and stopped. He too realized that a bullet was a mercy.

"Move!"

He joined her, settling quietly on the ground. She expected a crash, a blinding pain, and nothingness.

"You killed the man we saw this morning," she said.

"What of it?"

"It tells me what you are."

"Lot of good that'll do ya."

She resigned herself, pulled her white rebozo about her, and bent her head. "Lord have mercy on my soul," she mumbled.

Several rattlers unloosed themselves from the nest and wound toward them, fat, slithering death creeping closer and closer. Swiftly she rose. Elwood did too.

The prospector shot the snakes, one bullet into each, with an expert skill that astonished her. One's head was blown off. Another was severed from its undulating body at the neck. The third took a bullet a foot back, and writhed, snapping at air. A fourth paused, frozen, and the bullet pinioned it to the ground until it broke in two.

"A man can't even stand around here without them snakes coming at him," the prospector snapped.

He grabbed the gallon of coal oil, unscrewed the cap, and splashed it furiously into the opening, enraging all the rattlers that were soaked in the kerosene. Now the sound of rattles made an unholy din, a murderous whine like the snare drums proclaiming an execution. Snare drums, those were the rattles of human beings. She shuddered, somehow suddenly seeing Ricardo, her Ricardo, being led by blue-clad troops to a stake before an earthen wall pocked by a thousand bullets, her Ricardo, hands tied behind the post, his eyes pleading, snare drums. . . . Seeing him with her inner eye! Whoom. Fire!

A lit lucifer sailed into the writhing, rattling mass, igniting the kerosene. Yellow flame boiled outward from the entrance, a ball of fire. She swore she could hear the shrieking of animals within, but snakes didn't cry. A thunderous crackle accompanied the flame as the timbers and planks caught fire. The kerosene burnt out in a few minutes, but flames raged in the timbering.

Several rattlers slithered toward them. The prospector, cursing, jammed his revolver into a holster, drew an ax from his gear, and bashed them or sliced them with a wild frenzy, a man berserk. When he was done, he found himself staring into the bore of her small revolver.

"Put that thing down," he snapped, and reached for his own.

She squeezed. Her shot missed. His did not. It smashed the revolver from her hand, and shot numbing pain through her arm. Droplets of blood oozed from her fingers and wrist.

"Damned spitfire," he said. "Serves you right." He plucked up the little revolver, saw that it was ruined, its cylinder cocked oddly, and pitched it aside.

The fire crackled, sending a column of black smoke upward into the sky. Scarcely a breeze stirred and nothing pushed the smoke away. She hoped it would signal others. Succor us! She drew her rebozo over her hand, which still stung. Shattering lead had gouged a dozen little cuts in her hand and arm, but none of them mattered. Her hand was red. But she had endured ten times as much pain before.

The prospector cursed softly. The smoke had become a beacon, rising a hundred feet, two hundred, before dissipating. There was nothing to do but watch as the yellow flame licked the timbering. Not all the snakes had died in the initial inferno, and now writhing snakes, twisting and turning, dropped from the planking above, their flesh fried, bubbling and leaking yellow fluids. It was only a matter of time before the timbering collapsed, perhaps with the earth and rock that the timbers held at bay.

"I would have preferred a shot of giant powder," the man said. "Now I'll have to dig my way in, and it'll take a week to cool down before I can try, and there still might be live serpents in there."

Her hand ached. Dots of red speckled her white rebozo.

"We will go now," she said.

"Who says? You'll do what I say."

"Then it is better to die now."

She turned to leave. Elwood stood, paralyzed. The prospector fired, the shot searing past her, and she knew she had won. A man who could kill a racing snake with one bullet could have killed her more easily.

"Elwood, come."

He stared at that revolver pointed his way, flinched,

and followed. They walked ten, twenty feet. They entered the juniper brush on the slope. She heard a sharp click behind her, and cursing. The hammer of his revolver had landed on an empty cartridge. The bullet intended for her or for Elwood didn't come. The man had fired his last bullet.

"Dios," she whispered, trembling.

The prospector didn't follow. She saw him racing toward his packsaddle, where the rifle rested in its sheath. But Elwood reached the man's ax and grabbed it, swinging wildly. One blow glanced off the prospector, the handle cracking into his left shoulder. Elwood swung again and missed, and then the prospector closed, ducking the wild swing, and tackling Elwood, knocking him back. The prospector slammed one hard fist into Elwood, each blow sending shocks through him. Elwood bucked and struggled, but he was no match for the hardened old sourdough, even though the man's left arm was hanging useless. She watched, horrified, and realized suddenly that Elwood was giving her life, and that was his entire purpose. Flee!

She raced downslope, through the green juniper, dodging around the bushy obstacles. Just as she plunged into the saltbush, she turned, catching sight of the prospector sitting up and on top now, hammering on Elwood's prone body.

"Elwood!" she cried.

But Elwood wasn't moving.

Her new friend, a man little used to hard living, had sacrificed himself for her. She plowed deeper and deeper into the thickets of brush until she burst into the ancient village, hidden under its canopy of brush.

She found shelter behind an ancient wall, its eroded adobe chest-high, and there she studied her back trail as her heart slowed and she recovered her senses. She heard or saw nothing. So dense was the brush that she could not see someone twenty feet away. She scarcely knew where she was or where to go next.

Surely Elwood would die. Or was dead.

She was alone in the deep silence and without the slightest means of defending herself. She wrapped the rebozo tight about her bloodstained hand, trying to ignore the pain. She must be careful not to leave a trail of blood.

Ricardo. Dios! She had seen it all in her mind's eye. Her beloved Ricardo, marched to the wall, shot, his body spasming and slumping as death crashed through him. She stood, stunned by the vision. One moment she had been staring at that nest of vipers, the next moment she was transported to the City of Mexico, seeing the murder of her husband by that swine Diaz.

She clung to the adobe, and then slowly slid to the ground, unable to stand.

She sat that way a while, her mind lost to the real world, and yet her senses alert for the slightest movement. She needed to rescue Elwood if she could. Not leave, not flee, but linger here in this impenetrable thicket, until she could free him. If Elwood still lived.

At last her mind returned from a far place, and she began weighing her chances. She dared not walk out upon the white sands of the arroyo, making herself an easy target. She dared not move at all by daylight. She needed water and would soon need food, and she had neither. She could make it back to Rio Blanco if she escaped now.

But she knew she had a larger task, larger than any gold mine, larger than saving her own life, and that was to rescue the man who had given her the chance to escape. If he was alive.

Chapter 35

Elwood LaGrange sat up slowly, hurting where he never knew he could hurt. It hadn't taken long for the iron-fisted sourdough to flatten the Eastern man. La-Grange thought he had a black eye. Blood dripped from his nostrils. His ribs hurt so much he could barely breathe. His knee had scraped something and smarted. His shoulders had taken so many blows he had trouble lifting his arms.

He peered about and found the prospector studying him. The man held his reloaded revolver in right hand, a shovel in the other. He was favoring his left arm, which had taken the flat of the ax Elwood had swung.

"Start digging. Clear out that mine head. That fire dropped a ton of earth in there. Only reason I didn't kill you, I need a slave for a while. You wrecked my arm."

Elwood furtively examined the brush and the slope, not seeing Guadalupe.

"She's gone, but I'm gonna fetch her. She's not going far. You start digging. You won't see me in that brush, but I'll see you, and I'll have my Sharps with me. You quit digging, you try to run, and you'll get a buffalo ball through you."

Elwood tried to stand, but had trouble doing it.

"Dig, damn you," the prospector said. He kicked the shovel toward LaGrange.

"It's still burning."

"Just smoke."

"I can't even get close. The heat."

"Then die."

The old sourdough seemed to be enjoying himself. He leered at LaGrange, a smile lighting his face. "Thought you had a mine, did you? Thought you could pound on an old man and win?"

Elwood picked up the shovel and wondered whether he could swing it to good effect. The old man laughed. "Go ahead, try it. Just remember, dude, I can read your mind."

"Got some water?"

"Dig."

He punctuated his command with a shot that plowed the slope inches from Elwood's boots.

Elwood jumped sideways and the man laughed.

"You'll remember Artie, won't you now?"

"I saw you a few times in the saloons."

"Did you now? And what was I doing?"

"Listening. And so am I."

LaGrange walked as close to the mine head as he could without being roasted. The cooked remains of snakes littered the whole area. An incredible heat smacked him, and he didn't know how he could dig at the soft earth and charred timbers blocking the entrance for more than a minute at a time.

The mine was not completely plugged; he could see over the top of the heap into the gloomy interior. But it would take a day of digging to open it up enough for a man to move easily into the Doubloon. And there probably still were vipers on hand.

Tentatively, he scraped a little of the soft earth away, while Artie watched.

"I'm on my way, dude, and if you stay lazy or try anything tricky, you won't live to see the sun set. Work, and I might let you off."

Elwood watched the man trot down the hill, his Sharps in his right hand, the revolver in its holster, and plunge into the saltbush. Within seconds, the prospector had vanished. Elwood leaned on his shovel, not eager to deal with that heat.

A shot startled birds out of the brush, and a bullet thumped into charred timber inches from him.

"You never know, do ya?" Artie yelled.

Gingerly, Elwood tackled the huge cave-in at the mouth of the mine, moving slowly, well aware that the soil might be loaded with snakes. But the work proceeded quietly, and in a half hour he had cleared a cubic yard or so of blackened wood and earth. He did not encounter any live snake.

He thought about escaping, just walking off. The saltbush was thirty or forty yards downslope, and once into it he had a good chance. Maybe not. He would make a lot of noise pushing through it. The white sand arroyo below would turn him into a target. Maybe it would be best to dig, and plot some way to run after Artie got inside the mine and started chipping samples of the quartz ore.

He hoped Guadalupe was lying low somewhere. If she moved, Artie would catch her. If she raced for her home in Rio Blanco, she would soon be lying in a pool of her own blood in that white sand arroyo that gave this place its name.

He rested after a while, leaning on his shovel, when a shot racketed out of the brush, whanging into the charred wood.

Artie didn't even yell. The shot was message enough. Elwood dug some more, weary as he was from the desert heat and the pent-up heat at the mine head. At least Artie hadn't reappeared with Guadalupe.

LaGrange dug steadily until he could no longer stand up, and then sat down, half-expecting a bullet. In spite of hours of shoveling, he had cleared only a small part of the blockage. Then, as he sat, he saw someone working through the last of the brush, and a stranger emerged, a man Elwood LaGrange had never before seen. So the pillar of black smoke had drawn someone after all. This man was a giant, broad and muscular, with a bull neck and an easy way of traveling. His gear rested on the back of a little white burro that followed him around like a dog.

A thousand thoughts flooded Elwood's mind. What should he tell this man? He hardly had time to think when the man climbed the last yards to the mine head, studied it and Elwood, and smiled.

Elwood didn't waste a breath. "Mister, I don't know who you are but you're in mortal danger. The man who stole this from me and my partner—he's in that saltbush looking for her, and ready to shoot us both. I need help, fast. The man—only know his first name, Artie, is a killer and a thief. If you'd help me—"

"Artie Quill."

"I don't know. I need help. He could put a bullet through us both any moment. He can see us; we can't see him."

The stranger seemed unafraid. He didn't appear to be a prospector, but he certainly was massive and powerful. "I didn't catch your name," he said.

"Elwood LaGrange, and my partner's Guadalupe O'Rourke, and we found the Lost Doubloon yesterday. This is it. It was full of rattlers, and Quill tried to burn them, and that's why there's a lot of smoke. You saw the smoke, and headed this way."

"Ah, so you have the mine. You got proof?"

"No," Elwood said, as honestly as he could. "We found it. We went for the things we needed to write the claim. It's ours. Now for God's sake, man, help us."

"Just call me the bulldog."

By this time, Elwood was certain it was already too late. Artie would emerge from the brush, dragging Guadalupe, and shoot this bulldog on sight.

But the seconds ticked by and that didn't happen.

"You get some ore?" the man asked.

"No. Rattlers in there. Unless you hide, fast, you're going to get yourself shot."

The bulldog laughed easily. "I don't shoot easy," he said, which struck Elwood as madness. Maybe this man was a lunatic. "Maybe if I help you, I get half of the mine, yes?"

"Half! No."

The bulldog was grinning again, even white teeth all in a row.

"I'll just hunt for Artie Quill. I know what he looks like. I seen some tintypes of him. Maybe we'll parley a bit, yes? Maybe I'll get my half of the mine from him. Maybe he owns it."

"Maybe I do," said Quill, who emerged suddenly from juniper brush, from barely ten yards away. His revolver pointed straight at the new man. He held it in his right hand, the rifle in his left, and Elwood wondered whether the prospector had gotten back the use of that arm.

"A man gets too nosy, a man dies," Quill said. "But first, you're gonna dig out that mine, just like this Eastern dude here. I need some sweat-labor, and all of a sudden I'm rich. I got slaves. Now, how do you know my name?"

"I heard it," said the bulldog.

"You heard it. Maybe from Malachi Nast?"

The man went silent.

"I thought so." Quill grinned. "Nast keeps sending poor devils after me, and I'm forced to reduce the world's population. He grubstaked me, but what he wants is everything I find. He's not going to get it, and his spies won't help him. You aren't gonna take a bit of news back to Nast now, are ya?"

The man who called himself bulldog sat down. "No sense in working then, Quill."

"Get to work!" Quill raged.

The bulldog smiled. Elwood marveled that a doomed man would defy Quill, and Quill's revolver.

"It's him and me and you," the bulldog said. "Looks like we each got a third of the Doubloon."

Quill laughed.

"Looks to me like that arm of yours ain't working, Quill, so you need us worse than you're admitting. You don't even know if there's gold in there, or whether it's just another hole in the ground full of nothing. So, it looks like you got two partners, like it or not."

"Three partners," Elwood said. "My friend, Mrs. O'Rourke, has the best claim."

Quill did an odd thing: He retreated. "All right, I got partners," he said. "You dig, I'll find the woman, and we'll all have a piece of the mine."

LaGrange thought that Quill's sudden cooperation hid his true intentions, which was to butcher all of them the moment the last of the debris was cleared from the mine head.

But for now, it bought time, and maybe life itself.

"One shovel. We'll switch off," LaGrange said to the newcomer.

The bulldog took the shovel and grinned.

Quill drifted back into the saltbush, revolver in hand, the rifle loose in the crook of his wounded arm.

Chapter 36

Twice she heard him. Once, a sharp crack when his foot snapped a dry branch, followed by a faint rustle only a few yards away. Another time, even as she froze in place, some wild creatures burst away and she heard him curse. So he was stalking her, closing in, hunting as a man hunts game. And her gender would not protect her, not from this one who had death in his eye.

She slid into the ancient village, now so overgrown with saltbush, greasewood, mesquite, and a canopy of willow. But as she slipped down brush-choked streets, past half-eroded adobe walls, in the deep lavender shadow of dense foliage, she knew the ancients had called this place home, had lived and died here, in bright sun, under bold blue skies.

He was coming, listening for her, waiting to pounce. She had the disadvantage of her skirts, which caught in every barbed limb and tugged and dragged her every time she tried to move. And yet, somehow, she slipped farther and farther away, going she knew not where except that she was parallel to the great white arroyo on her right, and the steep hillside on her left.

The town had been elongated, occupying the flat between the brilliant white arroyo and the hillside, and now it was so jammed with foliage that she couldn't see ten feet ahead.

She came to a place where the brush was thicker

and different, a lush green wall, and she sensed safety in it, a place so densely overgrown that her pursuer would recoil from it and try to find his way around. She stooped, for only on her hands and knees could she make her way, and slowly worked her way into a deep and cool forest. Then, suddenly, she was thwarted by a wall, which rose over her head. A stone wall, not adobe, carefully laid up with dressed rock. The adobe mortar was long gone, but the rock wall stood. She worked her way around the building, and discovered rock steps, a tiny plaza, and beyond the building, more brush.

The steps were broad and made of stone set in the earth, and there were three, rising to a massive doorway, hidden in the fierce brush that crowded every corner and had fought its way into the wall, dislodging stones here and there.

It was a church! A mission chapel, a place that had seen a mass probably once or twice a year, when an itinerant priest had wandered into the old Rio Blanco. She stared upward, marveling that an entire church could be enveloped in the brush and hidden from the world.

Beyond was a flat, densely overgrown, and issuing from it was the music of running water. Curious, almost oblivious of her pursuer, she fought her way through this lush green growth and found herself, suddenly, at a pool fed by a spring issuing from the hillside rock, and surrounded by cottonwood trees that drew their sustenance from the water. Here, beside the church, was Rio Blanco's water supply, collecting in a small pool that overflowed and vanished into the sandy flat beyond, never reaching the white sand arroyo at all.

She hesitated, unsure of the water, but the silvery flash of minnows assured her. So did the little game trails radiating from this heavenly place. She unwrapped her bloody hand and washed it gently. The cold water felt marvelous, cleaning it and numbing the sting. Then she cupped her hands in the icy water and drank with joy, feeling that sweet water slide down her throat, cooling her, quieting a raging need, calming her whole body and her soul as well. She had found a tiny paradise. She marveled at the minnows, wondering how they had ever reached there.

Comforted, she stood, brushed by limbs that crowded her at every side. God had sent her here to spare her. She turned toward the ancient stone steps, which had effectively shut out growth at the front of the church, and stepped upward into a dark, shadowy sanctuary, the roof intact but the windows broken out and jammed with foliage pushing its way in.

Strange odors assaulted her, animal feces heaped in a corner. But what caught her eye was not the altar or its ornate black and silver and gold retable hung behind the altar, but a carved *santa* in a niche at one side, the most beautiful image of Nuestra Señora de Guadalupe, her patroness and Mexico's, she had ever seen, the sunburst behind her done in rich gold, the glossy enamel of her serene face and the sky-blue of her robe perfectly preserved by stone and a canopy of trees and dry air.

"Ah, Mother of God!" she cried, and fell to her knees.

She was seeing what no mortal eyes had seen in over a century, when this place had succumbed to the plague and was soon engulfed. She was feeling the succor that refreshes heart and soul and mind. The quietness that stole through her, calmed her heart, and brought her peace was more precious than gold. She was safe here. Her pursuer would not pierce the walls of brush that guarded this fortress, walls barely negotiable even crawling on one's hands and knees.

She had water, she had coolness even in this scorching afternoon.

But she could not stay. The man who had befriended her, who had wrestled with the demon long enough for her to escape, was in mortal peril. And she hadn't any idea what to do. She knew only she must save him if she could. It would have to be at night, using the cloak of darkness—if he lived that long. She thought she might have a way. This mission was set close to the slope, and so was the spring. If she climbed that slope, from behind the church, surely she would find herself escaping the brush maybe a few hundred yards from the mine. If she could free Elwood in the depths of the night and lead him back to this safe place . . .

Surely finding this image of her patroness, the Virgin of Guadalupe, was a sign from heaven. And that was all she needed.

Her thoughts turned to her husband, Ricardo, but now she was not seeing the handsome, sculptured face with its bold eyes and even row of white teeth and wry smile and knowing nod. No, she was seeing something darker, shadowy, sadder, and the feeling again reached her that her lover, the only one she had ever taken in her arms, would never return to her arms or gladden her heart again. She stared up at the image, and swore she saw a tear there on that sweet face.

Eee! Every ounce of gold from this mine she would spend on rifles to arm the guerrillas seeking to overthrow the dictator! She would continue Ricardo's work! She would herself take rifles into Mexico! She would hand them out, black engines of liberty, one by one, to the barefoot ones, along with shiny copper cartridges! Someday they would call her the Guadalupe of Sorrows, for she would make widows out of wives of the soldiers and lieutenants of Porfirio Diaz! Eee! And someday the snare drums would snarl, and El Presidente would meet his fate! To the wall, you who betrayed the humble of Mexico!

She thought of Sergei Gudonov, himself a revolutionary careening about New Mexico in search of the loot that buys armies. She felt an odd empathy, even though he had tried to pillage her house, steal whatever he might find for his cause. But his cause was the peasants and serfs of another land, and this she could understand. She hoped he would find some gold, enough for his own revolution.

Soft on the air, she heard someone calling, a man's voice so muffled by foliage she wasn't sure. But yes, someone was calling. It was not the voice of La-Grange. "Señora, Señora, Señora, all is settled. We will share the mine, work together." This she heard until the man's voice grew hoarse and she heard him curse. He was luring her, enticing her. How close had he come? She didn't know. She felt violated. His voice had carried to this sanctuary.

"*Bastante!*" she muttered.

He would get nowhere with her.

She sat quietly in the ancient mission chapel, worrying about Elwood LaGrange. Was he alive? Would this prospector shoot him? She had not heard a shot, but what did that mean? Nothing. Maybe, in the darkness, she should flee to her home in the new Rio Blanco. Surely, if there was no moon, she could slip along one of the banks of the sandy arroyo unobserved. But to think it was to reject it. Elwood LaGrange had given her life; she would try to give him life, if he still lived.

She whiled away the slow afternoon, growing hungry, but that didn't trouble her. So long as she could drink that clear water, she would be strong.

Evening brought insects humming around her, swarms of gnats that maddened her. Full darkness brought a sliver of moon, and she was glad. The darker, the better. At last, when night had lowered, she slipped outside, stumbling through the mesh of foliage, bumping constantly into trees and limbs and thorns. A nightmare! All she had to go on was that she needed to find the slope, and soon she found it, and worked her way upward through brush so terrible it scraped her clothing and face and hands. As before, the brush ended suddenly and she found herself in dense juniper that barred her path and made her wander her way up the slope. When at last she reached the ridge and could see stars, and the dark mass of brush below her, she realized she would have a bad time finding that sanctuary or that spring. Maybe it would be best to free Elwood and head for Rio Blanco, while that swine of a prospector slept.

She ghosted along the brow of the hill toward the mine, wondering what she would find and what she could do. She lacked even a knife to cut a rope if Elwood was bound, as she thought he might be. It was hard to see. She couldn't find the mine head. She wondered whether she had gone too far along that ridge. Whether she would need to clamber downslope halfway, until she was level with the mine, and start hunting it. The night confused her and blotted out detail. All she knew for sure was that she was walking along the south ridge and the white sand arroyo was north of her.

Sure she had gone too far, she turned back, hunting for the mine in the mysterious and opaque night. Three times she worked back and forth, once through the juniper halfway down the slope, and yet she found nothing. She was lost. She had no idea where the ancient village lay, with its water and succor. She stumbled down the slope, intending to push through that wall of brush and make it to the white arroyo. Until a hand suddenly clamped her and a strong arm pinioned her, and another hand muffled her scream.

Chapter 37

The little red granite headstone intrigued Sergei Gudonov. There it was, stuck in undisturbed ground, awaiting a future grave. He could find not the slightest evidence that the yellow clay had ever been opened to receive a coffin. He circled the grave, his great brain industriously pondering this unique grave, his instincts shouting at him that he was close to something important.

Why would Ricardo O'Rourke plant this unimposing headstone in this plot reserved for his servants? Why would he not be buried in a family plot reserved for himself and his wife? Was it a grave at all? Feverishly, Gudonov hoed away the hard clay surrounding the stone, first on the grave side, then on the rear, chiseling deeper and deeper into the undisturbed earth. But he found nothing. It was simply a small arched stone set in the ground.

Maybe his wife was right: Ricardo O'Rourke was not so much a gunrunner as a revolutionary, betting his last chip on the jackpot. Yet Gudonov was not satisfied, and he hated to be wrong. He, above all mortals, had received the gift of intelligence, and now he must employ his gift.

He peered about, but he was utterly alone on a hot afternoon in a deserted corner of the O'Rourke grounds. He studied the birth date carved in the granite, March 12, 1860, hoping to cipher something from it, but nothing came to mind.

A small black iron cross had been attached to the top of the monument, and this he wiggled, finding it solidly anchored. But when he twisted it, the cross rotated, as if on a threaded rod. Curious, Gudonov continued to rotate the iron cross until it came off its anchor, a rod rising through the stone. Now the monument was loose; he could wiggle it. He found he could lift it easily; it was not solid rock at all, and in moments he had lifted it out of its hole. Ah! There, below the monument, was an iron-walled chamber containing a small black box, which he yanked out, his fingers fumbling.

It opened easily, a simple latch, and within lay green currency, neatly banded. United States bank bills, Mexican peso notes. So! Ricardo O'Rourke had a stash after all! And Sergei Gudonov alone had the intelligence to figure it out. Now he could begin a revolution! He squinted about, seeing no one in that sleepy heat, and then began a quiet count. Each banded packet contained fifty one-hundred-dollar United States banknotes. There were ten packets. Fifty thousand dollars, a fortune. There was also a thick packet of Mexican notes, worth less because inflation had eroded the peso, but still of great value. Who knows? Maybe worth another ten thousand in dollars.

He reared back on his legs and howled. Sergei Gudonov would make history! This was, well, not as good as a gold mine, which might yield a million, but faster, much faster. He had cash; he could return to Russia and begin. He could topple Romanovs! He could scourge Mother Russia of its oppressors! And someday, every humble, worn peasant in his beloved land would speak his name with gentleness, and chip in a few rubles toward erecting a statue of him in the Kremlin.

Triumphantly, Gudonov restored the gravestone to its niche, screwed down the cross on top to the rod, thus pinning the stone to the ground, and carted his fortune off. Aha! Here was enough to launch a small army! To bribe the Czar's officers, who were already corrupt. To arm peasants. Ah, he would not keep one ruble. He would not even buy a bottle of vodka. He would not buy a shirt, though he needed two. Every bit of it would be spent upon the task at hand.

The iron box felt heavy and required both arms to carry it, and he grew concerned that he might be discovered lugging this case down that hill, then along Casa Grande Street, and straight through town to his adobe quarters. He was abashed. Here he had a fortune in his arms, yet he must for the moment hide it and bring a burro or a mule here and carry the fortune away in a saddlebag. Or perhaps he should just get a burlap sack and abandon the iron box. He liked that idea better.

In fact, until he could get some feed bags, the iron box was better where he had found it, so he returned to the odd grave, unscrewed the ornate iron cross from its rod, lifted the hollow stone, inserted the box in its usual nest below it, and reassembled the marker, taking time to dust away any footprints he might have left in the gritty clay. He hated to leave a fortune sitting there, and yet it was perfectly safe. So safe not even O'Rourke's wife knew of it. And it was all his!

The thought of her triggered pity in him. She had yet to learn she was a widow. Clearly, she loved O'Rourke and her life would shatter. Love! Gudonov knew what to think of sentiment and foolishness. He didn't believe in love. He believed in justice, and perhaps mercy on certain occasions, but not love, which was a trap to ensnare people of low intelligence and weak ambition.

He plucked up his hoe and meandered down the road, elaborately pretending to be unoccupied with anything but chopping away a weed or two. It was a new role for him, being someone else. All his life he had been himself, a surgeon's assistant in a Cossack company. But he would do whatever must be done, and so he assumed the role of a hapless gardener or groundsman, braving the blistering sun.

He reached his spartan casita unobserved, headed to the small stable at the rear, and found a heap of burlap bags that had once contained oats for his mules. Two would suffice, one inside the other to keep his treasure secure. The whole of his fortune wouldn't weigh ten pounds, he thought. A little paper! He checked the ancient bags for holes, not wishing to bleed away a fortune through some ripped seam or hole. And being farsighted and extraordinarily bright, he inspected his small quarters for a hiding place. He found nothing suitable for a fifty-thousand-dollar bonanza. But maybe he didn't heed to hide his loot. He could pack it all into his portmanteau, catch the next coach to Silver City, and away. He could be buying arms in Europe within the month.

Yes, that was it. Why stay? He was done with Rio Blanco. It had not yielded a gold mine, but a good enough facsimile of one.

"Aha, O'Rourke, I salute you!" he said. "You were a gunrunner after all! You kept your capital safe, and never risked all of it! If you were alive, I'd employ you to arm the peasants!"

He eyed the sun, worrying that the day was waning and Mrs. O'Rourke and her foolish friend might soon return. But there still was time enough, if he acted swiftly. He took his burlap feed sacks and headed once again through the sleepy town, up the hill, and into the grounds. He was less careful this time; he would be in and out in half an hour. He reached the gravestone, swiftly unscrewed the ornate cross, lifted the stone, plucked the banknotes from the box, and reassembled it all. The cash lay in his bags; the stone stood where it had been, and no one would ever know, least of all Guadalupe O'Rourke. What crime was it to take money from someone who never dreamed it existed?

He glanced about, seeing not a soul, and walked boldly into town carrying his sacks. No one stopped him. No one even asked what he might be carrying. The sacks weighed nothing at all. He could scarcely imagine how a heavy fortune could weigh so little.

He reached his adobe room, pulled his portmanteau from under his bed, and swiftly transferred the notes to his bag, putting them into good order. But then he stopped. He wanted to gaze upon this fortune. He unpacked the notes and laid them across his kitchen table, packet upon packet, in military order, a sea of green. Thousands and thousands. The peso notes he tossed elsewhere. He would dispose of those for whatever he could get for them. The United States banknotes mesmerized him. Enough to support him for a lifetime.

Yes, here was enough to permit him to do research and write books. He could head for London, invest his fortune in gold-plated bonds, and do the theoretical work that was necessary to justify the revolution. He had the brain for it!

He remembered how it was, when he was a youth and wanting to attend the university. He was the son of an Orenberg shopkeeper, without the social status to obtain an education. Racially, he was a Russian, not a Cossack. There he was, with the biggest brain known, a skull that mushroomed over his eyes and ears to make room for his great brain, his uncanny intelligence, but he could do nothing. The universities were for the very rich and privileged. He chose the only avenue of social advancement open to a boy in his circumstance, the Czarist army, and soon distinguished himself as a surgeon's mate. But all the while his mind was fevered with the need to put his brain to use.

In the army he was attached to the Czar's imperial Cossacks, an entire warrior class drawn from several clans, or *voisko*, who congregated in their own *stanitza*, or towns, such as the Don, Terek, and Kuben. These lifelong warriors handed down weapons from fathers to sons, and were always at the service of the state, running roughshod over the poor peasants, the dissidents, the rural Jews. He saw armed force used to oppress farmers and confiscate their crops. The revolutionary was born there in the army, and someday Sergei Gudonov would lead the great uprising.

Now, before him was a fortune, exactly what he needed to write a great treatise against the Russian imperial state that would justify the forthcoming revolution. He could live modestly, yet as a man of means and substance, even while pursuing his great quest. For he knew the source of all discontent was land. The nobles possessed most of it and the Czar the rest, and no humble person could be anything more than a tenant or crop-sharing serf. The land must be divided.

He gazed fondly at his fortune, realizing that he could put it to the best use, not in buying arms and starting a premature revolution, but by a life devoted to scholarship and writing tracts. London appealed to him. He had mastered English; the city's liberties and intellectual ferment would suit him. He could, year after year, live with a private income suitable for a man of his intelligence. The euphoria of wealth and living the life he had dreamed of stole through him. This, truly, was a great moment in his life.

That decided, he swiftly packed his fortune in his portmanteau and slid it under his bed. It wasn't secure, but who would imagine a penniless Russian emigre would possess such a thing? He studied the mound of Mexican notes, most of them well-worn and even torn, but cash nonetheless. How might he exchange them for gold? Should he take them to England too?

The Cimarron Bank perhaps, but only a few at a time. Maybe, he thought, he could work a deal with Malachi Nast, the one man capable of buying and selling pesos on such a scale.

Yes, he would do that. Nast always liked to profit, and he would gladly buy pesos on the cheap.

Chapter 38

Artie Quill clamped hard on the witch, gradually subduing her, though she had scratched him in a few spots and jammed an elbow where it hurt. But Artie didn't mind. He had her. She was his only worry. The chance that she'd get away and spill a lot of beans in Rio Blanco was all that kept him from finishing up around there.

He would stuff her in with the others and decide what to do in the morning. The mine made a fine prison. It stank of dead snake and foul smoke, and that was all the better. He had forced in Romeo, whatever his name was, and then the big dumb brute too, and both were plenty nervous about it. They'd had to crawl over earth and rock that was still hot and loaded with crushed snakes, and then through a two-foot gap at the top, and into the stinking mine. Romeo—his name was Elwood, my Gawd what a name—Romeo had asked for water, but Artie had just laughed.

That big galoot had all his possessions on the burro, which Artie now added to his growing stable. The big one's name was Arnold Schwartz, and he probably was one of Nast's bloodhounds, which made this little triumph all the sweeter.

He wrestled the Mexican lady toward the mine, though she never quit struggling, and once she bit his ear. He laughed and boffed her on the noggin, and then she fell silent.

"In there," he said. "Git."

"There's snakes."

"You bet there is, and I hope a few hundred are still alive."

She glared at him. A slender moon had risen, lighting the way. He manhandled her to the heap of rubble at the mine head. "Go on," he said.

"You'll have to drag me."

He booted her behind. Without a working left arm, he couldn't toss her in there.

She scratched, this time tearing his old shirt.

"Whee!" he said. "I could use you when I buy my whorehouse in San Francisco."

She kicked too, but her shoe bounced off his thick boot.

"You shouldn't have come back," he said. "I was waiting. Now I got everyone, I can do what I want."

"Which is?"

"I hate decisions, but maybe the snakes will make my decisions for me."

She struggled again, but he lifted her and deposited her halfway up the rubble.

She immediately slumped in a supine position.

"Git in there," he yelled, his patience wearing thin. But she was not moving.

"Guadalupe, don't come in. There's still some snakes."

That was Elwood's voice, just inside the rubble.

"Elwood!"

"Make him carry you in."

For an answer to that, Artie pulled his hog-leg out of its holster and shot through the hole. She screamed.

Elwood laughed. "I can see you, but you can't see me, Quill."

Quill fired a couple of rounds into that black hole. The noise shattered the quiet night.

Elwood laughed. Then someone else laughed, a strange, abrupt, and unexpected guffaw.

"Who's that?" she asked.

"A friend of ours," Elwood said.

"How many more?"

"Two of us."

"Quit talking. One more word and I'll throw a stick of DuPont in there. Now crawl in."

But she didn't move. He realized that if he tried to carry her into that hole with one arm, he'd be jumped. He was in a pickle, but not much of one. He had the revolver, and he'd use it. He eyed the spitfire, huddled on that smoky, hot rubble, the stink of fried snake hanging everywhere, and came to a hard decision.

"All right," he said to her, "get back. Get down off that rubble and stand there." He pointed at a place below. She did as she was told, glaring at him.

"All right, you two in there, come out."

No one moved, but he'd expected that.

"Come out."

Plainly, his captives had discovered they were occupying a fortress, and had achieved a standoff.

He grabbed the Mexican woman. She screamed, but could do nothing to free herself from his iron grip. Then he let go and pointed his revolver at her head.

"Come out fast, or she buys a bullet," he said calmly.

"You wouldn't," LaGrange shouted.

For a response, Artie lifted the revolver slightly and pulled the trigger. A crack racketed through the night.

"You have about ten seconds," he said.

LaGrange crawled out. The other one, Nast's big bloodhound, followed him.

Now at last he had them. They stank. That hole must have been fouled beyond anything that Quill could imagine. But in a few moments, he alone would possess the Lost Doubloon and no one would have the faintest idea how he got it, nor would they even know he had it. This would be the best-kept secret in New Mexico.

The moon was higher and brighter now. He waved them away from the mine head, toward the cliff near the mine. It would all be over in moments. All he wanted was to get them away from the rubble, which he would have to dig out himself when his arm healed up.

The men were ahead; he was dragging the woman by her arm, using his bruised left arm for that while his right held his revolver. He lifted the revolver. The big galoot was the only one who worried him. Romeo and Juliet he could take care of. But just as he aimed at the man's back, she slammed into him with all of her 110 pounds, and the shot went wild.

"Damn you!" he snarled, and began clawing free of her. She was in a frenzy. Romeo landed on Quill, but Quill shook him off and wrestled the revolver around until it aimed at LaGrange's head. But just as he fired, something massive slammed into him and shook him. Nast's bloodhound. Two sledgehammer hands began pulping him, each blow shocking through him. He let go of the screaming woman and tried to shield himself from these hammers, but he could no more stop them than he could stop a freight train. Then one blow landed on his right arm and he felt the bone snap. It hung useless, the revolver sliding into the dirt. The woman snatched it.

The hammering didn't stop. This brute was exterminating him.

"Stop!" Quill screamed. "I quit."

The wild pain in his arm shot through his whole body, paralyzing him. The monster let up, and Quill lay on the ground, groaning and sobbing, his arms tormenting him along with every other inch of hammered flesh. He wished he would faint; what he was enduring was not for mortals to endure.

When he finally quieted and his lungs stopped heaving so violently, he stared up at the moonlit apparitions. All three of them were staring down at him. LaGrange was somewhat injured, the woman had a bloody hand, and the brute of a boilermaker from somewhere in the East wasn't scratched.

"You kill that man I saw back a way toward Rio Blanco?" the brute asked.

"Splint my arm, damn you."

"You kill anyone else?"

"I wouldn't harm a fly."

"I heard you killed someone in a quicksilver mine."

"What mine?" he said.

LaGrange turned to the others. "What should we do with him?"

"He tried to kill us all," she said.

The big one turned to Quill. "How many you kill in all?"

"Go to hell."

"That's about the right place for you," LaGrange said.

"Into the Doubloon?" Schwartz asked.

"Good as any."

"But my arm's broken."

"Maybe we should break your leg too," Schwartz said.

"How are we going to stuff him in?" LaGrange asked.

"Get a blanket. We'll carry him up there and heave."

"Don't move me! Just leave me be."

If they tossed him in there, he'd never climb out. One arm broken, the other bruised and weak. He'd have to endure that stink, dead flesh, smoke, charred wood.

But LaGrange and Schwartz took off, hunting for Quill's gear, while the woman held the revolver on him.

"Give me that and let me shoot myself," he said.

"Bastante!"

The pain let up a little in the night air. The slim white moon cast ghostly white light over the cliff, illuminating the mine head, the rubble that mostly plugged it, the black juniper and the dark brush below that concealed an entire town.

The men returned with a blanket, spread it, and dragged Quill onto it. He screamed. Any movement at all tortured his arm.

"Set the bone, dammit, don't just leave me like this. Splint it and bind it."

The big boilermaker lifted the corners of one side, while LaGrange and the girl lifted the opposite corners, and together they hauled Quill up the rubble, taking their time in the treacherous footing. When they reached the narrow aperture, they let the blanket down. The rubble stabbed at Quill's back.

"How do we do this?" LaGrange asked.

"We swing him, and heave."

"No, no, don't! I can't stand it."

"Neither could we," Schwartz said.

"There's snakes."

"That's right. A few are still alive. I killed one with a rock," LaGrange replied.

"But I don't have an arm."

"That's right."

"You ready?" Schwartz said.

They lifted the corners of the blanket and began swinging it, back and forth, tossing Quill.

"One, two, three!" Schwartz said, and they let loose. Quill felt himself projected through that hole, and then he tumbled down a slope of sharp rubble into blackness. He shrieked. His arm howled. Then he landed, sobbing, at the foot of the rubble, and sucked in air that was so foul he could hardly imagine anything so offensive.

He writhed, trying to make himself comfortable, and then stared upward at that patch of moonlit sky. He could see some stars. Around him was gross, foul darkness.

Then he heard the rattle, the angry chatter, and he thought he knew where the snake was, close to his head, close, so close.

The fangs struck him in the neck, sharp, cruel, a swift jerk, then heat and pain, radiating pain, horrible paralyzing pain that rose into his head and sank into his chest, and he knew that those stars, in the sweet clear heaven outside the Doubloon Mine, were the last things he would ever see.

Chapter 39

Sergei Gudonov pulled a venerable black leather trunk from a corner of his quarters and opened it. It was cedar-lined and kept the contents fragrant. He gently lifted his uniform out of the chest and spread it on his bed.

A good seamstress had removed all the red and green Czarist insignia from it, leaving a deep blue suit of thick and luxurious wool, serviceable in all weather. It would be too hot to wear here, but he was going to wear it anyway. Now he was a gentleman of independent means and he would dress as one.

The suit coat had a blue silk lining, and that would suffice. He had not been a surgeon's mate for nothing. He carefully cut and fit a duck-cloth inner lining that would fit between the silk and the wool. This he sewed to the silk along the bottom, and then sewed vertical seams, making compartments. He used a strong thread and a coarse needle, because he wanted no accidents. Then he added a second seam along the bottom for insurance and safety. The whole of the new money compartments hung from the silk, and was not attached to the suit coat except at the yoke and collar. Then, cheerfully, he slid a packet of hundred-dollar bills into each compartment, until the fifty thousand dollars nested comfortably between the silk lining and the wool. From now on, the money would remain next to his body. Not a cent would be carried in the valises in the boot of the stagecoach or even in a portfolio in his grip. Never say that Sergei Gudonov didn't use his splendid brain.

Satisfied at last, he headed into the hot morning, intending to dicker with Malachi Cromwell-Nast. He had stuffed into his pocket the thousands of peso notes he wished to unload. He would let Nast drive a hard bargain, but would complain bitterly about it, though in fact he didn't much care. He would do whatever his instincts suggested. The pesos would supply some travel cash.

Thus did the former Russian imperial army man and new-minted revolutionary walk quietly down Casa Grande Street in the cool of early morning and climb the creaky stairs to Nast's chambers. He doubted that the suit he now wore would make the slightest difference to anyone, so why not wear it? Nast himself had never been seen in shirtsleeves, and always wore a black broadcloth suit.

Nast greeted him coolly, looked him up and down, plainly curious about the sudden change in dress.

"You seem to think this won't be a hot day, Gudonov, but it will be."

"Oh, certainly, Mr. Nast, but I am leaving. Today I vill catch the stage for Silver City, and tomorrow I vill be heading south for the Southern Pacific and after zat I shall return to Russia. I've failed here; I came looking for a mine, and found I lacked the skills."

"Well, bon voyage then."

"That's what I came to see you about. I lack travel money, except for a few Mexican peso notes. I am hoping you will exchange them for dollars."

"What would I want with pesos?"

"That's for you to decide. If you don't want them, I vill try the bank."

Nast stared. He kept on staring, his gaze studying

Gudonov until the Russian was disconcerted. "Is there something about me that bothers you, Mr. Nast?"

"No, I was just wondering. It's a preoccupation of mine. Why do people do what they do."

"And what do you make of me?"

"You have turned into a gentleman. Yesterday you were a revolutionary, ready to throw bombs."

Gudonov laughed. "Oh! This makes me a gentleman? Look closely. I had a seamstress remove the insignia, here, here, green and red, all gone. What you see is my ancient uniform, suitable for travel and that's all. It is good for the road."

Nast smiled, a strange alligator smile. "Very well. I suppose a Russian won't wear anything less than his best suit when on the road."

It was a question.

"We're like the British," Gudonov replied. "Starchy. I would not dream of traveling in shabby clothes if I could prevent it."

"In hundred-degree heat?"

"Sir, in hundred-degree humidity if need be."

"It's rather sudden, seems to me. One day, you're looking for a way to start a revolution. The next day, you want to trade some pesos for dollars and are leaving."

Gudonov didn't like the probing and shrugged it off. "It doesn't matter. I'll see what the bank vill do."

"No, wait, let's just see here."

So Nast was hooked after all. Gudonov pulled a handful of pesos from his pocket, making sure it was a small fraction of the total. "Few thousand pesos at eight to the dollar, yes?"

He pitched some loose notes at Nast.

The American stacked them neatly and began counting, his spidery fingers fondling each note. "There's two thousand three hundred. I have no use for them," Nast said.

"That's more than I thought. Almost three hundred dollars," Gudonov said. "I haff been gathering them ever since I arrived in New Mexico. I suppose I can exchange them in Albuquerque. A little place like this, well . . . there is no need."

"All I could offer is fifty cents on the dollar. Sixteen pesos on the dollar."

Gudonov stiffened. "I am not so poor as all that!" he said, and gathered the notes from the desk.

"Twelve pesos for a dollar?"

"That's beneath what I will accept."

Nast shrugged. "Very well. I don't want the pesos, so we can't bargain."

"I vill surrender ten pesos for each dollar."

"No profit in it for me."

Gudonov was tired of bargaining and scraped up the pesos. Nast stared, catching every motion, his gaze disconcerting. "I am not here to give away my money," Gudonov said. "I vill keep the pesos."

Nast shrugged. "I prefer it. You catching the noon stage?"

"What else takes me to rails?"

"That's been robbed a few times."

Gudonov shrugged. "By the time I spend the pesos on tickets and luggage, I vill not have enough to excite bandits."

Nast stared again, disconcerting, immobile, and in the end Gudonov blinked.

"Where is Mrs. O'Rourke and her friend?" Nast asked.

"How should I know?"

"They did not return last night from their, shall we say, picnic."

"I do not follow the lives of those two."

Nast stared again, his focus steady, and finally smiled. "Maybe they had good reason to stay away," he said.

"It is of no consequence. I am going to Europe. This exotic interlude is over."

"Certainly sudden," Nast said.

But Gudonov had enough of Nast's curious probing. "Good-bye then."

Nast stared, sadly, and nodded.

Gudonov's flesh crawled. He hated the man. He stalked back to his casa in rising heat, quieted himself, finished packing, paid off his landlord, which was the Cimarron Bank, hired a drayman to carry his trunk to the Butterfield Stage Company line on Casa Grande Street, and then waited impatiently for the four-mule mud wagon, open on the sides, to haul him along the lonely twisting mountain road to Silver City, and from there to the rails.

At noon promptly, he was allowed to board, and settled in a window seat along with two other passengers, both male. He was sweating in his thick woolen suit, but no one but himself knew it. He peered about one last time while the jehu loaded goods on top of the wagon, cursed the mules, and swilled something that was probably spirits. No one in this sorry little burg had come to see him off. Had he not one friend? No prospector, no woman, no miner, no liveryman, not even a whore. And not Nast either, though he could see the miserable man standing in his upstairs window, watching, watching. Well, someday, the world would know who Sergei Gudonov was, the great theoretician of revolution and land reform. And then they would be sorry they had not befriended him.

The Butterfield coach started for Silver City promptly at twelve-thirty, on schedule. The jehu, unlike others of his breed, did not curse or whip the mules, but let them amble along. Gudonov realized the heat had much to do with that. The oppressive, furnace heat of a midday in June would draw the starch out of any mule, and the driver was letting them set their own pace. Gudonov was in a hurry, but there was nothing he could do about it. The road snaked into high country, a little cooler and occasionally shady under the brow of yellow cliffs. Then, at the brow of a steep hill that had slowed the coach, he heard a commotion, some shouts. The coach stopped, creaking gently on its leathers.

Two masked men, each with a red bandanna covering their faces, appeared.

"You," they said to Gudonov. "Out."

One had a Navy Colt; the other a huge hog-leg of some sort with a bore the size of a cannon.

"What do you want of me?" Gudonov asked. "I am a simple traveler. I suppose you want my purse."

He reached into his pocket to extract a small leather purse, and tossed it to the ground.

"Out," one of the ruffians said, scooping up the purse.

The other leveled the hog-leg at him. "You really want to croak?" he said. "Because you'll croak in about ten seconds."

Gudonov sighed. It would be a foolish death, wasting the world's largest and finest brain. So they would extract his pocket Waltham and his gold ring. They would not discover the cache under the blue silk lining.

He clambered to the ground.

"Off with your suit. Drop the coat right there," one said.

Gudonov froze. No, not that. So brazen. Nast . . . "But why? It is my old uniform."

The answer was a cocking of the single-action Navy. A long silence followed. Gudonov glanced at the coach. The driver sat with his hands up. There was no shotgun messenger; this coach wasn't carrying money, so it wasn't protected. The other bandit trained his hog-leg on the passengers and drivers, who sat very still.

"The coat," said the bandit with the Navy.

Sadly, thinking maybe death might be better, he shed his coat.

"The pants."

"But I am traveling!"

"The pants."

Gudonov sighed, undid his belt, unbuttoned his trousers, and let them slide to the ground.

"Take them off."

Gudonov slid them over his polished travel boots, and finally stood in his linen drawers.

The bandit snatched up the blue suit coat and pants and backed off.

"Get on," he said. "Don't come back. If you come back you'll be hunted down and shot."

Gudonov slowly clambered inside, and only then did a great tremor rattle through him.

"Go," the bandit yelled at the jehu.

The Butterfield man cracked his whip, and the mules lolled forward, snorting and rested.

It had been Nast. And brazen too. The bandits had not even camouflaged the act by robbing the others or pawing through the luggage in the boot.

"Sorry, friend," said the drummer across from him. "I hope you have a change of clothes in your valise. Mighty strange affair, I'd say. They must have known something."

Gudonov nodded, trying hard to formulate a plan. He had next to nothing; a few items he might pawn. But in the space of a few minutes, he had been transformed from a gentleman back to being a revolutionary, and his first incendiary act would be to liquidate his oppressor.

"Driver," he yelled. "Let me off, and my trunk and valise."

"But we're nowhere," the driver called back.

"Exactly," Gudonov replied.

Chapter 40

A silence shrouded the night. They had all heard the muffled sounds issuing from that narrow opening: a buzz, a scream, a sob, soft cursing of God, and then quiet. They all knew what it meant.

Elwood LaGrange thanked God that he and Guadalupe and Schwartz were safe. There were still a few live vipers in that chamber of hell, yet he and Schwartz had not perished in there. The slit-mouth of that mine, a sinister black slot atop the rubble that blocked the entrance to the Doubloon, exuded evil. The mine was a fitting tomb for a man who had tried to murder them all, and had murdered others. Elwood might have grieved over the man's death, but there was no grief in him.

This was truly a place of sorrows. Even as they stood in the sweet cool night, staring at that death-hole, Elwood was aware that a hidden town lay only yards away, a town that had perished from the plague, a town that could not even bury its dead in the end, but let them lie in their adobe homes until they were bones and scraps of cloth.

But the night breeze bathed them in fresh air, and the stars were an assurance of eternity. He stood, his hand firmly clasping Guadalupe's hand, thankful that they were alive, drawing the clean air into their lungs.

The giant stranger turned to Guadalupe. "You saved my life," he said.

"You saved ours," she replied. "He was too much for us."

The man turned to Elwood. "You wrestled with him long enough to spare me a bullet."

"I was no match for him," Elwood said. "He had that revolver and was forcing it toward my head when you landed on him."

"We have all helped each other."

That was true, but Elwood didn't like the drift of this conversation.

"This is the Lost Doubloon Mine?" the man asked.

"Yes," Elwood said.

"Whose mine is it?"

"We found it," Elwood replied in terms that brooked no argument.

Except from Guadalupe. "It belongs to no one."

"Guadalupe! It's ours. We were the first."

"This is a cursed mine. Who owns it must die. That is the old legend, still whispered among my people."

"That's just a legend. We'll kill the snakes. There must be millions of dollars of rich gold ore in there."

"It killed a whole town. It killed that man who rode into Rio Blanco with its ore. It killed this man Quill. It almost killed us. It will kill anyone who claims it."

This was a Guadalupe he had never seen. Was this the same woman who so strenuously had tried to find this very mine, employing every wile and skill she possessed? What had turned that Guadalupe into this new one? Superstition?

"You saying you don't want it, that anyone can claim it?" the Easterner asked.

"It is yours if you wish to die."

"I know mines. I come from West Virginia. My people were all coal miners."

"Guadalupe, what are you saying? We need money

fast. Your husband! We have to sell ore, take the cash to Diaz."

"Ricardo is dead."

"How do you know that? My God, what are you saying?"

"I have the inner eye. I saw it. I saw it when Quill poured the coal oil on the vipers and lit it, and in the great flame I saw it. I was transported to the City of Mexico, and I saw them shooting Ricardo. I know it is so."

She clenched and unclenched her small hands, and then stood rigidly, awaiting his protests. But he had the sense not to object. It was all superstition, this business of seeing things, this inner eye. But now she stood, a widow in grief, fierce in the darkness.

"Ricardo? Who is that? This is not your husband?" the stranger asked.

"This is my friend, Elwood LaGrange. Ricardo O'Rourke, my *esposo*, was a citizen of Mexico, a rebel with fire in his eye, and a man filled with justice and passion. He came here, a quiet and safe corner of this nation, so he could run rifles to the rebels. Ricardo, he despised the dictator Diaz who trampled on the humble and favored the rich! Ricardo bought good rifles and sold them to the rebels, taking them by pack train deep into Sonora and exchanging them for gold or pesos. Yes! He was himself a rebel! Two years ago he never came back. I was beside myself. He vanished. And the long wait began, every hour, every day, every season, in the middle of the nights, in the heat of noons. But he never returned."

"He sounds like a great patriot," the stranger said.

"He was a patriot of Mexico. Then, not long ago, word came. He was in Diaz's dungeon, his life in danger. Diaz, never a man to refuse money, wanted to ransom him. One hundred thousand pesos! I must raise the money swiftly or Ricardo would perish! I was desperate. Ricardo left nothing in the banks or in our casa; his business forbade it. He always handed me what I needed to run our household. And for a while I survived by selling off good things, even most of the furniture. And then suddenly I have word of him. A ransom, and I have no money!"

"How did the word come?" asked the stranger.

"A letter, mysteriously to Señor Nast. From an attorney in the City of Mexico. And enclosed was a small Maltese cross, the very cross I had given Ricardo. I must raise the money swiftly, or my husband . . ."

"Do you trust Nast?"

"Of course not! Maybe Diaz wants fifty thousand pesos and Nast makes it one hundred thousand, intending to profit from my distress. Look in your house, he says, because money must be hidden there. He even planned on looking himself. But I knew there was nothing. And so I despaired. I lacked even the money to go to the City of Mexico and plead with the dictator Diaz."

The massive stranger stared into the bright skies. "I was working for the wrong man," he said.

"Nast?" said Elwood, frozen.

"The same. I was a foundryman until the foundry closed, and unemployed since then. My family mined coal until my father and two brothers died. It's a long story, coming out here. I knew I could mine, I know mines. I could manage a mine. And I have a sick mother, consumption, and she has no way of supporting herself. But I won't trouble you with all that.

"I came here looking for honest work. I thought mebbe I found it. Nast hired me to hunt for someone he thought was cheating him. Then he asked me to follow youse. That is why I am here. I followed Quill, and ended up finding youse."

Elwood eyed this emissary of Nast's uneasily. What next?

"There's something about Nast I don't trust. Now I know why. But a job was a job, enough to stay afloat until I found a position. I came hoping to become a mining supervisor. I know that stuff. And you, pal?"

The question caught Elwood by surprise. "I came here without design, wondering how to squander a life." He stopped abruptly. Why should he bare his soul to a man he had never met, a man who might be luring him and Guadalupe into some sort of new disaster?

Guadalupe took his arm. "He has helped me," she said.

"Then you are lucky to have his help," Schwartz said.

Elwood was restless. "Guadalupe, I don't think you should be making momentous decisions at night. When the sun shines, you'll change your mind, see things differently. The Doubloon's a rich mine. You have no money. Here's a dream come true."

"*Mañana,* I will show you things I found in the village, Elwood. And you too, Mr. Schwartz, if you care to look. If you want the mine, sir, file your claim and post your notices."

Schwartz sighed. "Why am I hesitating?" he asked. "It's a dream. You are handing me a fortune."

"Well. I'm not hesitating," Elwood said. "I'll file for Guadalupe. I'll write notices right now."

He felt that tender pressure on his arm. "I would like you to preserve your one life on earth," she said gravely, and Elwood knew she meant it, straight down to her soul.

A rich mine, and she didn't want it. He could hardly fathom it. And not even the massive foundry-man seemed in a hurry. Never in history had people turned away from a bonanza!

"Come," she said. "We have things to do. The animals need water. We need a safe place. I know where we can go if the moon will give me enough light."

Elwood could barely stand to leave the mine, the bonanza, that could make them all rich. But this was no place to spend a night. The foul smell alone was enough to drive him off.

They collected Quill's mules and Schwartz's burro, and she led them on a mysterious route along the hillside and halfway up it in the pale white light. Then, mysteriously, she turned right, straight downslope, through the usual juniper and into the dense thickets. Soon they were tearing their way through walls of brush. Mesquite thorns stabbed at them. Ironwood blocked the way. Then, suddenly, before them was a lip of rock, and beyond it a lovely pool, shimmering in the ghostly light. They could hear the steady gurgle of a spring.

Arching above were cottonwoods.

"Yes, I found it! Come this way, and let the animals drink. The water is good!"

They followed her around to one side and let the animals drink. Elwood marveled. How had she found such a place?

"This spring gave Rio Blanco its life," she said. She led them all to a small patch of grass. Amazingly, they found themselves before a high stone facade, clearly the front of a small mission church, a building so hidden that no one observing the brush from the hills above would ever see it.

"Leave the animals," she said, and beckoned. She and Elwood and Schwartz mounted the steps, she pushed aside a creaking door, and they found themselves in a sanctuary.

"We will be safe here," she said, "in the presence of God. In the morning, you each may decide what to do. I know what I must do, which is go to my home, light a candle, and remember my beloved."

In the soft white light pouring through glassless windows, Elwood discovered an ancient rope dropping through a hole in the ceiling, and guessed it led to the belfry. He pulled gently. A sonorous gong resulted, a sweet throaty gong that rolled out upon the moonlight and out upon the hills, sweetly tender music in the desolate light.

It reminded him of Donne: For whom does the bell toll? It tolls for thee.

Chapter 41

The men graciously left her to the ancient sanctuary and bedded outside in what had once been a small plaza before the church, but now was choked by trees. Between Quill's and Schwartz's equipment, there were blankets for all, and there would be hardtack enough in the morning.

The interior of the mission seemed oddly clean apart from dust and a few bird droppings. A deep silence pervaded this hidden place. White moonlight had rotated across the dusty floor of paving blocks, and had reached the niche where the Virgen de Guadalupe stood before her sunburst of gold leaf.

Guadalupe thanked the blessed Madre for life and for her friends and for understanding, and soon drifted into a dreamless sleep. She had feared the night would be alive with painful memories of Ricardo, her beloved, with his swift bright smile, those even teeth, and eyes that revealed joy and tenderness and fire.

But next she knew, she was hearing birdsong, and pale dawn light was filtering into the sanctuary. She rose, wrapped her rebozo about her shoulders, and peered out a narrow window upon the spring and the pool just beyond. Wild creatures were greeting the dawn. Birds hopped from limb to limb, robust in their joy at the awakening day. There was a vermillion fly-

catcher, and beyond, a yellow-headed verdin, and on
the other side, just above the water, a gilded flicker
preened itself on a twig. She quietly stepped outside.
Elwood was still asleep, looking innocent and vulnerable, but Schwartz, the big one from the East, was
sitting up. He smiled.

She washed herself at the pool, feeling the cold
water quicken her pulse and drive away the shreds of
sleep. By the time she had completed her toilet and
had paid homage to her patroness in the sanctuary,
both men were up. No one spoke. Whatever else this
might be, this was a small oasis of tranquility.

They chewed some miserable hardtack, content
with that for now, and braved the cool morning.

"Come," she said to Arnold Schwartz, "I want to
show you the first Rio Blanco—and what happened
to it."

She took them both on a tour, wrestling through saltbush and ironwood and in some places mesquite. The
roofs of these old adobe houses had vanished, and the
walls had eroded down. But within was mute testimony
of the tragedy that had beset and finally destroyed Rio
Blanco. She did not have to point; the man's gaze took
in the ancient beds, the bones, the scraps of cloth, the
grinning skulls. The plague had swept through so
swiftly that most were never buried; indeed, the men
who would have buried all these people, children,
women, ancient ones, perished first of all.

It had been a goodly town, Rio Blanco, supported
by the great mine on the hillside. They found the
brush-choked cemetery at last, far beyond the limits
of town, and found few graves, each protected by iron-
work fences, their wooden crosses or headboards long
gone. And they also found the shallow pits of hasty
burials everywhere, and she did not want to dig into
them or know what lay down there. Now the cemetery
was shaded by overarching brush so thick that each

grave seemed to be lost in some private bower. It was a miracle they had found the old graveyard at all.

These were her people, the brown-fleshed people of Mexico, lying in their eternal beds. She felt ancient bonds of kinship, feelings she could not reduce to words. But at last she turned back to the secluded mission church, where the animals snapped up what little grass they could find in a place so choked over with brush.

"We should go up to the Doubloon now," she said to Schwartz. "You have a decision to make. I have made mine."

He seemed puzzled.

They struggled uphill, out into the juniper, and finally across the hillside to the glowering old mine, whose mouth was almost choked with rock and dirt. A fat diamondback rattler sunned on top of the rubble that choked the mine head. The Doubloon was still owned by the vipers, no matter that fire and slide had reduced their numbers.

A strange foulness filled the air, driving off the fragrance of desert flowers that permeated Rio Blanco. It was a malevolent breath from some dank place far below the earth. This place was scarcely a half a mile from the quiet spring surrounded by birdsong, but everything had changed.

She turned to Arnold Schwartz. "The mine is yours if you want it. I will not object, except to sorrow for you."

"Not LaGrange's?"

"He agreed to help me. We agreed that he would not take a share. It is mine to surrender if I wish."

She watched the massive man, whose gaze fell upon that mine head that was exuding foul odors. By turns he seemed bewildered, unsure, and finally he shook his head. "I don't know. It's a fortune."

"Yes, and death."

"How do you know that?"

"The story of my people, the people who lived in Rio Blanco, the new town, before the Anglos came. I learned it from them. Whether it is literally true I could not say, but there are other truths."

"Tell us."

"According to the legend, here in old **Rio** Blanco, the miners, most of them Indians who received the smallest pittance for hard work, struck a giant cavern one day, and terrible gasses boiled up, sickening them all. It was the roof of Hell. They had dug into the Devil's own caverns. Once the hole was cut through the Devil's roof, he came out, his foul breath murdering everything. That's when the whole town took sick and died, save for a handful who fled. In time, this place was forgotten, and no one could even say where it was, but the stories lived on, the stories of how the Devil was released from Hell and murdered a whole town. And to this day, his breath rises from the mine, killing all it touches."

Schwartz stared at that sinister opening. "Hard to believe that," he said. "Hard not to believe it."

"It was hard for me to believe it," she said. "Until yesterday. Until then, it was just a story, like so many country stories, a way of looking at the world."

She looked at Elwood. "What do you believe?" she asked.

He looked sheepish, but summoned courage. "A while ago I would have dismissed all of it. Here's a strange answer. Easy wealth almost destroyed me. Now I believe there is virtue in hard work, and that a man gains favor in this world by doing something productive."

"Gold is productive," she said.

"I have no answers. But my life depends on doing something worthy of reward, not something easy like finding a gold mine. I . . . don't want this easy road. It would kill me."

She loved him then. Elwood LaGrange had come home.

Still, their imaginations worked on them. Within that stinking hole lay the richest gold ore in the region, by all accounts barely tapped, barely scraped out of the hole and reduced to fine, yellow, pure gold. Within that hole lay a life of comfort, money for emergencies, fashion and friends, travel and delight.

And death.

"I guess I'm crazy," Schwartz said. "I came all the way out here to make my fortune, and now I don't want it."

Elwood smiled.

"Let us seal the Devil in his hole," she said. "Let us hide this from the world, so the demons inside of it never see sunlight again."

"You mean shovel dirt into that hole and fill it up and block the entrance?" Elwood asked.

She turned to Schwartz. "You're the mining man."

He stared at that leering hole, the hole that was mocking them, the hole with vipers for teeth between its lips.

"That mine's braced against several feet of overburden, earth that's been kept out by lagging. Planks, you'd say. Maybe I could do something. . . ."

It was Elwood who turned to Quill's pack and started removing things one by one. Then, close to the middle and well shielded from shock, he found three sticks of DuPont Hercules. In the pannier on the other side, he found two fulminate-of-mercury copper caps, and a small roll of Bickford fuse. He knew these things only from his studies, but he knew them, and pulled them out.

"I will shut the Devil's hole," said Schwartz. "You

stand far back. If this giant powder is old, it's unstable, and it might blow up."

"Then we should find another way," she said, her voice edged.

The foundryman lithely picked up the dynamite and examined it slowly, rotating the sticks slowly. "It is old," he said. "Quill was a fool. This stick is leaking."

"Then don't use it!"

Schwartz ignored her, studied the mine. "I will need all three," he said.

He eyed LaGrange. "Go up above the mine head, and watch for snakes. Take Quill's shovel. Dig down, maybe three or four feet back from the mine head, through that loose soil. If you are lucky your shovel will strike the lagging, the planks holding the surface soil out of the mine."

Elwood nodded, and walked gingerly up the slope and over rubble. At one point she heard the buzz of a snake, and he danced sideways. But soon he was above the mine and quietly chipping away the hard clay, working down and down.

"You, Guadalupe, you get away. Clear down to there," Schwartz said, pointing to the place where the dense brush gave way to juniper. "Be careful."

She retreated, fearful that something terrible would happen. She watched him work. He was slitting open one of the waxy red sticks. He inserted a copper cap into the slit, and was binding the cap to the stick with wire or string, she couldn't tell which. A long piece of fuse dangled from the cap. Then he bound the other two sticks to the capped one, making a sinister triangle of red.

Above, Elwood worked quietly, and then struck something hard. A resonant thump echoed down the slope.

"Got it," he said.

"All right, go down and join her, and watch for

snakes, and when I light the fuse, both of youse get
down to the ground and cover your faces and heads."

Elwood did as directed, slipping swiftly down the
steep grade, past the mine head, through the barriers
of juniper, and joined Guadalupe. She had chosen a
bare area well clear of debris—and snakes.

They watched the Easterner, still virtually a stranger,
a man who was setting his dreams aside, clamber
slowly up the slope. Once he slipped, and miracu-
lously held the charged dynamite up and free as he
fell to one knee. A rattler buzzed. But soon he had
lowered the dynamite into the hole, and gently, handful by handful, poured soft earth over the sticks until
at last only the fuse stuck out.

Schwartz pulled a candle from his pocket and lit it
with a lucifer. The air was so dead the flame did not
waver.

"Cover your heads," he yelled, and held the candle
to the fuse for what seemed a long, long time. But
then it spit white sparks, hissing angrily as it ate itself
up. Schwartz watched for a moment, and then walked
swiftly sideways along the side of the hill, a path less
strewn with juniper. He was still walking when a violent whump raised the earth and shattered the peace.
A blast of heat slapped her, knocked her backward. A
yellow column erupted into the sky and fell gradually,
small rocks sailing in all directions. She didn't see
Schwartz for a moment, but then he appeared out of
the yellow haze, standing quietly a hundred yards off,
farther than she had imagined he would get. The
overburden above the mine slid, caved, rolled down,
an eerie thunder, and when the dust settled, there was
a raw smooth scar, as if a landslide had rolled tons of
yellow clay downhill. Even as she watched for the next
minutes, small streams of clay and sand and dirt slid
down and settled into a long smooth slope.

A strange pressure in her breast diminished. It was

as if whatever was biting her with fox teeth had released. She looked about her. The column of dust was floating over the ancient city, catching the sun's rays, lacquering Rio Blanco with gold. All the ghosts haunting the brush-choked town would sleep quietly now and evermore.

Something had happened. It was as if the evils of the whole world had been driven back. She knew she must return to the mission church and take the image of the Virgen de Guadalupe with her. It belonged in the humble little mission church of the present Rio Blanco. Now this old town would sleep in peace.

And now there was not the slightest sign of a mine.

Chapter 42

Malachi Cromwell-Nast waited impatiently in his second-story lair, the yellow light of the coal-oil lamp casting a glow into dark corners. Everything was coming to a head! Everything would work out! The snitches he employed had reported that Mrs. O'Rourke and her friend, the absurd LaGrange, had returned, along with Arnold Schwartz, plus one laden burro and two laden mules, believed to belong to Artie Quill. Oh, ho!

Mrs. O'Rourke was carrying a carved image probably snatched from some church somewhere, which was puzzling. It was the Virgin of Guadalupe, or so three snitches said, and she cradled it in her arms as if it were a child. Maybe she was a thief! Oh, ho!

She had found nothing, no gold mine, obviously, and that meant that Nast would soon wind up his business with her. She hadn't a thin dime and wasn't worth bothering with. Tomorrow he would show her the other letter from Mexico, carefully drafted by Otero for a price, hand her a handkerchief, and then offer her two hundred dollars for the handsome mansion and grounds. That was actually a fair price, he thought, given the amount of restoration he would undertake. That would suffice to pay her way back to Hermosillo where she belonged. She might remarry, settling on some wretch down there.

He would soon own the O'Rourke mansion, and

then he would decorate it with lovely statues of women. He preferred women in stone to women in the flesh. Some elegant Grecian statues of women in diaphanous gowns would grace the grounds, and some discreet white-marble nudes in his parlor would perfect the mansion. He hadn't decided yet whether to employ women as cooks and housemaids; if they were fat and old, he might.

Everything was working out well enough except that no one had found the Lost Doubloon. Nast doubted that the mine existed. A thousand prospectors combing the district had not found it. That was a pity. He fancied that the mine belonged to him. Anyone who found it would soon surrender it to him, because he had his ways and means, and strings to pull, and ways to make a mine unprofitable as well as profitable.

He would consider it unfinished business. That unknown prospector had ridden into Rio Blanco with a sack of fabulous ore and word that he had found the mine—before he inconveniently died of snakebite.

The dying man was obviously a romancer and liar. He had plucked some rich quartz off some ledge somewhere, and built it up in his fevered head until it was the legendary lost mine, setting off the wildest and stupidest gold rush in New Mexico. But all that was history. The gold rush was almost over. Rio Blanco would soon be a sleepy little burg again. The prospectors were leaving, having found nothing but a few ledges. Nast now had ample investment capital, which he would employ to buy up existing and fruitful mines all over the Southwest.

Schwartz did not come up the stairs. The black lacquered Seth Thomas seven-day clock continued to tick the minutes away on the mantel. Where was that big oaf? Too dumb to know where his bread was buttered? Nast decided to cut the man's pay to a dollar and one bawdy-house token. That would show him that Malachi Cromwell-Nast was not a man to be toyed with.

There were things Nast needed to know at once. What was the fate of Artie Quill? Where did Romeo and Juliet go with their new pick hammer and tape measure? Drat that Eastern oaf.

He rose, headed for the window overlooking Casa Grande Street, seeing dark figures slip in and out of lamplit doors. For a change, the sleepy town was alive with people, most of them frustrated prospectors giving up on the Lost Doubloon.

Then, finally, he heard footsteps on the creaking stairs, and opened the door to . . . Sergei Godonov, dressed in his field attire. The Russian pushed in without waiting for permission. This wasn't in the cards, and Nast hastened around to his desk, where his small revolver would be handy. But Gudonov stopped him, a powerful hand clutching Nast's black coat.

"Unhand me, you lout," Nast said. "What do you think you're doing?"

"Open that safe. I haff a revolver aimed at your gizzard, and if you don't, you won't have any gizzard left."

"And what is the cause of this?"

"You know as well as I do."

"The last I knew, Gudonov, you were dressed to the nines and departing New Mexico, having failed in your quest to fund your little revolution."

"Open the safe."

"I really can't manage it under this sort of duress. I suppose you intend to rob me."

Gudonov laughed nastily.

Nast saw how it would go. This mad Russian meant business. Irritably, he approached the five-foot-high black-lacquered safe, his pride and joy. There was none so fine in all of New Mexico. This one had three inches of plate steel on all sides, and was bolted to the floor. It featured Cupids and yellow roses climbing the door, along with the Holy Grail. Not even the Cimarron Bank had a safe so fine as this one.

"Stand back; I won't have you memorizing the combination so you can rob me again."

Gudonov laughed. Nast truly did not like that laugh, which sounded like a cackle, or maybe it was merely the man's obvious dementia. But all Russians were mad. It was a truism. If you were born Russian, you were mad.

Nast shielded the work of his waxy fingers from Gudonov's eyes, and eventually the combination lock clicked, and Nast swung open the great door, which whispered silently on well-polished hinges.

"All right. There's my entire fortune," Nast said. It consisted of some legal papers, and a small pile of ten-dollar banknotes, handy for purchasing loyalties.

"Stand back. Away from your desk," Gudonov said. "If you approach a wall or a desk or a chair, you vill find a bullet going in one side of you and out the other."

The man was serious. Nast positioned himself carefully, but just one lunge from the lamp. If he could reach the lamp . . .

But Gudonov was pillaging the safe with one hand, ejecting papers in disorderly heaps that curdled Nast's orderly soul.

Furiously, the Russian tore open folders, kicked open files, rattled pasteboard boxes, and never found what he was looking for. Nast would never have put his proceeds from the robbery in his own safe. He was not a fool. His boodle was back in O'Rourke's cache, which had been described to him by a snitch who had watched Gudonov one recent afternoon. It was the perfect place; shortly, he would own the mansion and continue to use the gravestone box.

Gudonov whirled, and again that mean black bore pointed straight at Nast, raising his pulse.

"Where?"

"Where what?"

"Your share."

"Of what?"

Suddenly, Nast knew that Gudonov was defeated. "Leave here at once. I'll report you to the deputy."

Gudonov laughed, and then slapped Nast. The blow was utterly unexpected. It jerked his head back, stung his cheek, right through his well-curried beard. "You think I'm through, do you? That you're clear of me?"

The second slap staggered Nast.

"Take me to it," Gudonov snapped.

"I truly don't know what you're talking about."

Gudonov studied the room, then smiled darkly. He strode to the lacquered safe and yanked out the three shelves. They fell with a clatter.

"In there," he said, his revolver leveled at Nast.

"No!"

"Crawl in and be quick about it."

The horror stunned Nast. "I'll suffocate!"

"That's the idea."

"And you don't know the combination."

"That's exactly right."

The thought of suffocating to death in that black cramped safe terrified Nast. "No one could open it," he whispered.

"I'm glad your limited mind has figured it out. You'll be there a year or so. You have no friends who might inquire about your absence. And the safe would truly be the last place. . . . Why, they'll ship it to Denver to get it opened. In a year or two."

"Please, please don't." Nast didn't mean to whimper.

Gudonov collared him and jammed him into the safe. Nast refused to pull his legs in, so Gudonov yanked them and stuffed them in and swung the door almost shut.

The dark, cramped safe terrified Nast. He was a quarter inch from suffocation in an inky tomb. A tiny

rim of lamplight around the edge of the door was all
that remained of the whole world.

"All right! I'll tell."

The door opened a few inches.

"It's where you found it," he whispered.

"What is where I found what?"

"O'Rourke's money. The fifty-dollar bills."

"And where is that?"

"Under the gravestone in the cemetery, the gravestone with O'Rourke's name on it."

A long silence ensued. "You have more snoops than
I gave you credit for," Gudonov said. "All right, climb
out. I'm going to tie you tight and go get it. Who
robbed the coach?"

"Joe Goddard and Will Pilgrim."

"And where are they?"

"I don't know."

The door swung almost shut.

"For God's sake, I don't know."

Let Gudonov think it. Actually, the robbers were in
the Silver City jail.

Gudonov sighed. "I should kill you and be done
with it."

He motioned to Nast, who crawled out onto the
floor and then stood shakily. The nightmare of suffocation still terrified him.

"Sit," Gudonov said, pointing to the wooden desk
chair.

Gudonov extracted a roll of cord from his field
jacket and brutally tied Nast's hands behind the back
of the chair. Which hurt. When Gudonov was done,
Nast was bound hand and foot, and gagged. The
bindings were so tight he feared no blood was reaching his hands and feet.

"If the money's not there, you vill end up in your
safe," he said. "Pitch dark, no air."

Nast nodded wildly.

Chapter 43

Arnold Schwartz unpacked in his cubicle in a cheap rooming house on Avenida Bravo and returned Nast's burro to the livery barn. He was not the same man. One Schwartz had hiked out of town to do Nast's bidding; quite a different mortal had returned.

His hardworking Hessian forebear Otto had settled in America at the time of the Revolution, soon purchased the passage of a bride from the old country, and the Schwartzes had lived quietly in Virginia and then West Virginia, farming and mining coal. Arnold was the first of them to venture westward, or catch that strange fever that took men out of the settled East and plunged them into a wild land without the spiritual or ethical cornerstones that governed lives in settled country.

Nast had told him that he would be tracking down thieves and those prospectors who were violating the terms of their grubstake agreements with the financier. And yet Schwartz had sensed, even then, that maybe Nast was the one who would be doing the stealing. It was paid work, and Schwartz needed work until he could find something more suited to his skills as a miner and foundryman. And he had to earn something swiftly; grief and illness haunted what was left of his family. The need to help his mother warred with his wild itch to sample all of the rough and fierce West.

But now, thanks to the strange spiritual powers of

Guadalupe O'Rourke and the odd, brave courage of the out-of-place Elwood LaGrange, Schwartz had experienced his bath of fire and his redemption. And in his soul he knew it.

He pondered whether even to report to Nast, but finally decided that he must, if only to sever the employment. Nast usually welcomed his snoops after dark, when his paid informants could slide up to his office and impart their news and receive coinage for it. That was Schwartz's unfinished business, so he decided to see Nast, even though he was worn and ready for bed. He avoided the saloons, at least for the moment, and hiked to Nast's Casa Grande Street lair, climbed the creaky stairs in deep darkness, and knocked. Lamplight shone through the pebbled glass door.

No one answered. Schwartz knocked softly again, and this time he heard an odd thumping, a clattering, as if a chair were being rocked back and forth. He decided to leave, come some other time, but the thumping persisted. He paused, turned the knob, and opened the door a crack hesitantly. The sight that greeted him was the last one he could imagine. There was Malachi Cromwell-Nast bound hand and foot to his wooden desk chair, white cord wrapped copiously around his black-clad ankles. A gag tied tightly about the man's face kept him silent. But his wild eyes begged for help, and the muffled muttering from under that gag told Schwartz to free the man.

Arnold Schwartz found himself enjoying the sight, and then he felt ashamed of himself. The man was in desperate straits. Whether he deserved help or not, he was suffering.

"I'll free you. I need to find a knife," he said.

The response was a wild flood of noise, none of which he could interpret. He hunted for something to cut those tight knots, and finally settled on a letter opener on the desk. But he didn't need it. He was able to pull the gag free.

"It took you long enough," Nast snapped, after gulping air.

Schwartz stared.

"Free me and be quick about it."

"Where's a knife?"

"Don't go digging into my desk. It's private. Now get these ropes off me before my hands and feet die."

Schwartz tugged at those brutal little knots, getting nowhere. Finally he began sawing with the letter opener.

"Hurry up, damn you," Nast said.

Schwartz stopped. He wasn't going to listen to that sort of abuse.

"I came to quit," he said.

"Quit! That's what I get for entrusting you with a crucially important task. Did you find Quill? You have his mules."

"You have quite a bunch of spies, don't you?"

"Nothing escapes me."

"I was gone two days. Do I get my dollar a day?"

"I don't know what good it did. Now cut me free."

But Schwartz was in no mood to cut the man loose and worked desultorily with the letter opener to saw through strand after strand.

"If you don't hurry up, you won't get anything."

"All right," Schwartz said.

"What do you mean, all right?"

"I've wasted two days. Why are you tied up?"

"I've been robbed, you idiot."

"Who robbed you?"

Nast paused a moment. "The Russian."

"The Russian? He's a good man, fighting for a cause."

"That's it. He has no scruples. I'll have him hanged."

Schwartz sawed listlessly, deliberately getting nowhere.

"My hands have fallen asleep. Free me before they perish."

Schwartz smiled. This was more entertaining than he expected.

"He may come back here. When he does, Schwartz, you grab him. You could flatten him with one fist, man like you. I'll make sure you are well rewarded."

"Come back? Why would a robber come back?"

"Just do as I say. What did you find out? Where's Quill?"

"Dead."

"Ah! You do it?"

"The Devil got him."

"The Devil! What are you talking about?"

"A viper."

"Oh, he got bit then. Did he kill my Indian helper?"

"There was a body, yes, beyond identifying. The vultures had feasted."

"Hurry up, you oaf. What's taking you so long?"

"These are tight cords and clever knots. You wouldn't want me to stab you with the letter opener, would you?"

A long pause. "Did you find Romeo and Juliet?"

"Yes, they and Quill were at the Doubloon Mine."

"The mine! The lost mine?"

"That's right."

Nast struggled, half-berserk, writhing in his chair. Schwartz was inclined to let him writhe.

"Let me go, you imbecile."

Instead, Schwartz stood back. "I can't saw the cords with this letter opener until you quiet down. I wouldn't want to stab you."

It was obviously an act of sheer will, but Nast settled down. Schwartz serenely sawed away, and finally unloosed the cords binding Nast's feet. Nast stood up, the chair humped behind his back.

"My hands, my hands!"

"Sit down."

"Damn you, Schwartz." But he did sit down awkwardly.

"Where is the mine?" Nast demanded.

"It no longer exists."

"Doesn't exist? Of course it exists!"

"It is buried under a mountain of rubble and will never again be found. The Devil was driven back into his hole."

"I will give you a thousand dollars if you will take me to this place."

"That's a cheap price for a mine that might have hundreds of thousands of gold in it."

"Two thousand!"

Schwartz sawed listlessly, knowing that when Nast's hands were freed, the man would leap to his desk for a revolver or some sort of weapon.

"Maybe Guadalupe O'Rourke or Elwood LaGrange will take you there," he said.

"Yes indeed. Between the three of you, I'll find out!"

At last, the cord popped and Schwartz unwound it from Nast's wrists. The financier leaped up, but Schwartz was ready for him, collaring him by his black suit coat.

"My fingers! They don't work," he said, waving his flapping hands.

"They will in a few minutes. You going to pay me? Lots of banknotes in front of the safe."

"My hands don't work."

"I'll help myself. What did I earn?"

"One bawdy-house token. That's all you're worth to me. I sent you out on a mission and I get only half an answer."

Schwartz laughed, loosened his grip on the coat, and let Nast dance around his office, flapping his hands and useless fingers.

"Quill's buried inside the Lost Doubloon, in case you're wondering."

Nast stopped his prancing. "Well, he got what he deserved. He was cheating me. I grubstaked him several times and all I got for it was betrayal. There's two thousand dollars on the floor. Take it and tell me. Or take me there. Just you and me. We'll go to this place and you can show me."

"Ah, why didn't the Russian take it?"

"Russian? Russian?"

"You said the Russian robbed you and tied you up. Some robber, eh? I can see he made you open the safe, but why did he ignore the money lying all over here?"

"Careless of him. Now tell me, Schwartz, did Romeo and Juliet claim the mine? Stake it and file on it?"

"No. No one has claimed it. I didn't. It doesn't belong to a single human being. It belongs to the Devil."

"Oh, the Devil again!"

"Evil then. Something evil owns it."

Nast settled into a quiet glare. "Here's an offer, blast you. One fourth of the Lost Doubloon. I'll develop it, bring in the equipment, hire the supervisor. You'd like to be supervisor, wouldn't you? One fourth of the profits, a supervisor position, and the two thousand lying around here. We'll put it in writing, a contract, signed by both of us."

Time slid by. Schwartz grew aware of the tick of a black enameled mantel clock. It hands pointed to eleven forty-five. Fifteen minutes to midnight. And a new day.

"No," he said, and walked out.

Chapter 44

Sergei Gudonov worked swiftly in the deep dark. He needed no light. His fingers twisted off the iron cross on O'Rourke's fake grave; he lifted the headstone, pulled out the iron box, opened it, and discovered the cash there. Swiftly, he counted ten packets, none of them opened. That surprised him. He had expected no more than five, half the loot, but he had underestimated Nast's genius for treachery. The robbers were probably in the Silver City jail, betrayed by the man who tipped them off. He found as well a handful of loose peso notes, also taken from his blue suit. Here was the entire fortune, minus some minor spending for a coach ticket.

He restored the iron box, replaced the headstone, and screwed the black iron cross onto the rod that had supported it. He stuffed the fortune into a burlap sack and then sat on the clay, staring at the heavens. A meteor streaked across the sky, delighting him. But black masses of clouds blocked most of the heavens, and he sensed from the whipping zephyrs that a spring storm would soon sweep through western New Mexico. Even as he watched, he saw lightning whiten a huge thunderhead to the west.

He had a decision to make, and sat quietly on the hard clay ground. A few hundred yards away, the widow slept in her darkened mansion. A widow, yes.

No doubt about it. Nast had concealed from her the fact that her husband had perished long ago, shot by Diaz's executioners. It profited Nast to extract money from her, if he could, with his schemes. Nast had failed. She had nothing to give him to buy off Diaz.

Nast was the very sort of mortal Gudonov loathed most in this world, so devoid of decency that he would rob a helpless widow if he could. And that was what stuck in his craw just now, for he, the reformer and revolutionary, was doing the same thing: All of this struggle was merely between thieves. And what did it matter that he was bent upon improving the lot of the humble in his mother country? He had stolen from her; Nast had tried to steal from her. What did it matter that she didn't know what she possessed? It was still theft, and he could not quiet his conscience over it. He and Nast were brothers in the evil they did.

He eyed that dark forbidding mansion, hating what he had to do, but knowing he must do it, for there could be no just revolution funded by money robbed from a widow who believed she was penniless. For that was what she was, so long as she knew nothing of this fortune now lying in the burlap sack in his hand. Very well then. He was an idealist, a man of principle. Maybe he had too many principles and someday someone harsher and meaner and less ethical would succeed where he would fail. But his huge brain, and his superior intelligence, told him that nothing built on sand would last. Only reform that was built on bedrock, a solid foundation, would ever improve the world.

He arose, knowing that this could well prove to be his biggest folly. Indeed, he might get shot. The woman was not shy about defending herself. He felt the freshets of wind whip him as he hiked toward the mansion. The storm was bearing down on him. At last he reached the darkened veranda, hesitated, and finally knocked. No one responded. The wind whipped the burlap bag and rustled through his hair. He knocked again and waited. It would take her some time; he knew that.

He was about to give up when he heard a voice. "Who is this?" she asked.

"Sergei Gudonov."

"I will not open to you."

"I haff good news for you."

"There is no good news that could come from you."

"I found your husband's money."

"Ha! You try to fool a woman."

"If you don't take it, Malachi Nast probably will."

"Why would you give me this money? You are a revolutionary!"

He was growing impatient. "I will leave it in front of your door in a bag. If the wind blows it away, that's your bad luck. From a window, you will see me a little distance away. Wait for the lightning to see me standing there."

He set the bag down and walked to one side. The rising wind toyed with his clothing. After a moment, lightning lit the western sky.

He heard the door creak, saw it open in the gloom. She stood there in a dark wrapper, then picked up the sack. The door thudded shut. He watched a lamp flare in the windows, and heard a strange wail, like a woman seeing the corpse of her beloved, and saw the door open again; she was silhouetted by the lamplight.

"Mr. Gudonov. Come."

She stared at him. Her honeyed face, framed by a tangle of jet hair, showed signs of utter exhaustion. She held the blue cotton wrapper tight about her, a thin inviolate wall. He walked quietly into her parlor and she followed with the wobbling lamp, which heaved light and shadows every which way. She gazed at him from a face filled with questions, her mouth trying to form words.

"How much is this?"

"Fifty thousand United States dollars and some Mexican pesos, maybe worth several thousand more. Maybe sixty thousand in dollars and pesos."

"Madre de Dios! Is it mine?"

"I found the money in Ricardo O'Rourke's grave. Under the stone."

She stared. "There? There? It cannot be so." She though about that a moment. "Why, why do you return it?"

"I ask myself the same question. It would buy me all that I ever wished."

She stared at the heap of banknotes on a polished table. "I did not know. I thought Ricardo. . . . Ah, what difference does it make?"

"Now you can pay the ransom."

She shook her head, and then lifted her chin. "He is dead, Señor. I saw this. I have the inner eye."

"How could you know?"

"I know."

"But . . ." He wanted to say that a hunch or intuition could not possibly be the same as real information, but he stayed himself. He was smart. Smart enough to know there were things beyond human understanding. He nodded, a quiet affirmation.

"Tell me why you find this and knock on my door in the night, scaring me to death?"

"I had to get it before Nast did. He knew where it was. That is a long story. Just take my word: He almost got it. Why do I return it to you? That is not so easy. I dream of a better world, one without cruel men who rob the poor. Then, with all that money in my hands, my dream changed. Ah, yes, I am afraid so. I am a man of few principles. No, I thought, I will not start a revolution. No, I won't buy guns and bribe corrupt generals. No, I will take it and write. I will produce powerful tracts and essays and compelling books that will shock the world and awaken consciences and enrage the just, and these will tell why there must be reform, or maybe a revolution. And while I write all of this, I will live comfortably in London. It is enough to live on for many years."

He stared at her and shook his head. "And then I knew that I could not begin a revolution for the good of mankind with money stolen from a widow, even if she never knew of it. Nor could I go to London and write, living off stolen money, bitter about my fortune because my conscience would trouble me every time I bought a lunch. And so I am damned. Damned! I am a man of honor, when a thief is what I should be."

He stopped suddenly. A crack of thunder rattled the lamplit parlor. The curtains swayed.

She stared kindly at him, and finally walked to him, stared into his face, lifted his hand, and kissed it. "You are a great man," she said. "This will help me. But there is something I must do."

She divided the greenbacks into two piles, five packs in each. Then she counted out the pesos, and divided them also. He watched, understanding her intent, and utterly melted. He loved her. He had loved two other women, but always the revolution had interceded; the revolution had always been his imperative, and there was no room for love, no room for a home and children.

She took half and handed it to him. "Ricardo would be pleased that you will write about the injustices of the world, and that you inflame the consciences of people everywhere. That was his passion, you know. Justice! He would be pleased and proud to give you this."

"Señora . . ."

This was too much, too profound. He accepted the

money, tucked it into the pocket of his field jacket. So light, just a few packs of paper, yet money enough for him to live without need for many years and write many tracts, and enjoy a good lamb chop and some Guinness now and then. London, with its ancient liberties, would be a good place to live and write. But now he could only stare into her liquid dark eyes and nod.

And then he wept. He didn't want to; this was an unmanly thing, but the tears rose to his eyes.

"Señora O'Rourke, I will dedicate every dollar, every peso here to making the world a better place, and I shall dedicate my greatest work to you, who made it possible."

"Oh . . . to me?"

He saw her reluctance and responded at once, thanking his great intelligence for the insight. "Then to Ricardo O'Rourke, who gave his life to change the world."

She smiled. She seemed breathtaking. He wished . . . and then set aside his wish.

"And what of you?" she asked. "It is dangerous to carry so much money."

"I have found that out," he said. "I have already surrendered my house here. All I need is a horse and tack and I'll be on my way. I will wake up the hostler. He always has a few horses to sell. I will head for London this very hour."

"It is a long way. *Vaya con Dios,*" she said.

"*Vaya con Dios,*" he replied. He kissed her gently on the cheek, and walked into the night. It had started to rain.

Chapter 45

Guadalupe awakened to a rain-washed world. She threw back the curtains and beheld one of those bold blue skies that only New Mexico could produce. The thunderstorm had washed the dust out of the heavens. Soon there would be carpets of wildflowers, yellow and magenta washing the slopes. From her window she could see Rio Blanco below, and off in the distance, the sharp edges of the horizons. She liked it here.

The morning was well spent, and no one had disturbed her. She had devoted much of the night to thinking about Ricardo. He had meant for her to find that cache of money, and had told her where it might be without ever saying it.

"My darling, if something should happen to me sometime, bury me in our graveyard if you can. I have prepared a place. The stone is there. Under the stone is a lockbox with some of my hair in it. Add some of yours, so that our hair may be together there."

Now she remembered. She had protested, told him surely he would always be with her, but he had only kissed her and smiled and whispered in her ear, "Remember the keepsake box."

She had, but she'd never imagined what it held. So now he was looking after her from beyond the grave. She thought of him, of his hug, of his wild laughter, his face the face of a young eagle, and she sorrowed. She had been loved. Had any woman been so loved?

Now, thanks to the genius and honor of the Russian, she had a fortune. Sergei had left in the night, and she had watched from her window, watched him walk down the hill, his steps lit by bold charges of lightning. And then he was gone. He had started out a revolutionary and ended up a reformer and pamphleteer. She didn't doubt that his passions would soon be known throughout Europe.

She faced a long journey. The City of Mexico would be months away. Sea would be best; overland travel almost impossible. She would need to travel to New Orleans by *ferrocarril,* and sail south to Vera Cruz, and then take the *ferrocarril* to the city, and then . . . find her beloved and arrange for him to be borne to Rio Blanco. She would lay him to rest in the very place he had prepared. She knew Elwood LaGrange would accompany her; he'd offered to do so, and she had accepted.

She found the Maltese cross taken from Ricardo's body. *Sí,* that is what had happened. He was dead when they took it. She didn't know the details, but she knew some swine of a Mexican lawyer, along with Malachi Nast, had schemed to get money out of her with that emblem that had graced the neck of her dead husband. She hoped they would both rot in Hell.

She dressed slowly, a stiff and coarse white cotton this cool day, over a camisole and petticoat, to let the sweet clean air pour through her ensemble. No sooner had she completed her toilet than she spotted Nast himself, this time driving an ebony victoria drawn by a handsome trotter. Her first thought was about the safety of her money, but then she ceased worrying. He would never imagine that she had any; that Sergei Gudonov had given her everything.

Oddly, she enjoyed what was to come. She watched

him alight, tie the lines to the hitching post, and approach her door. He looked a little bedraggled; she was in much better fettle than he was. She met him at the door with a flash of a smile.

"Señor Nast, I have been looking forward to your visit."

"Ah, you have?"

"Oh, *sí*, it is good. Come into the parlor. May I serve some tea?"

"Oh, no, Señora. Tea is a stimulant and my faith forbids stimulants, tea and coffee." He stared at her, his spidery eyes seeing half through her gauzy attire. "Ah, you are ravishing this fine day. Quite a storm, yes?"

She nodded.

"Have you come to tell me that my husband is dead?"

His head bobbed upward. "Why, no, no, I've heard nothing. I am sure his condition is perilous, but soon you will have funds enough to pay the ransom."

"How would you know that?"

"You have found the Lost Doubloon Mine. Forgive me for saying it, but it has come to my attention."

"Did Arnold Schwartz tell you where it is?"

"I'm afraid he was most uncooperative, especially after I had employed him to look after my interests."

"The mine doesn't exist. It is buried."

"But Mrs. O'Rourke, if you hope to rescue your husband, every effort must be expended to reopen the mine. That's why I am here, to offer my assistance."

"My husband is dead."

"Why, how could you know that?"

"He was dead when you first approached me. Executed by Diaz. There never was a ransom."

She found bitter pleasure in his astonishment. She watched him absorb all that. For one moment, his eyes gave him away, and then the veils were drawn.

"I have no word. How could you know of this tragedy?" he asked.

"I have the inner eye. I saw it all. I saw them take the Maltese cross off his dead body. I saw all this."

"But you have no real knowledge."

"It is as real as your kind of knowledge."

"Well, I can't imagine believing something without the facts."

"I am going to the City of Mexico to find his remains and bring them here."

"But that costs money and you have none."

She smiled. "I will find a way."

"Of course, if you were to sell this great house, I might be able to help you finance your trip."

"Your help is not needed."

"Ah, I get it. LaGrange is paying. He's a smart fellow, getting on your good side."

"Is that how you view friendship?"

"Why, certainly. Now I'm going to be firm about this. You must tell me where the lost mine is. If you don't, I will get the information by other means. I will reopen it, develop it, and give you half."

She shook her head. "It will never be known. Even if I took you there, you would not find it. It was the Devil's mine, and when he roamed, all manner of evil befell Rio Blanco. Now he is back in his hole, in his eternal darkness."

She watched Nast. He listened with a smirk, then with a shake of the head, then with cunning.

"Everything I might take from the mine will be devoted to good works," he said.

She smiled.

"I assure you, I will never rest until you divulge the secret. The mine belongs to me. I employed Schwartz to find it and perform certain chores, and he betrayed me. He knows, but won't tell. He told me none of you claimed it. I financed him. I financed Quill, on

shares if he found it. He was to give me half. I have a
just claim. But Schwartz says no one will ever own it."

"That is so. It belongs only to the lord of evil."

Nast smiled gamely. He was obviously at wit's end.

She stood, dismissing him. "You wanted only to
cheat a widow," she said. "Diaz never asked for a ransom. Poor Ricardo, he was shot before you and your
henchmen ever dreamed up the ransom."

"Good day, Mrs. O'Rourke. I won't listen to such insults to my person."

He headed for the door. She followed.

"You want me to take you to the Lost Doubloon?"
she asked.

He paused.

"I might. I just might take you at night, and leave
you there."

"You would? I agree to it."

"I will think about it."

"Mrs. O'Rourke, I would gladly pay you a hundred
dollars to lead me there. All of Rio Blanco would benefit."

She laughed. "Come tonight, at sundown. My
friend and I will take you and leave you. It is a three-
or four-hour walk back here. Seven miles. If you can
find the way."

"You are a very strange woman, and I don't know
what you have in mind, but I will take the risk."

"*Bueno!* At sundown then."

Chapter 46

Elwood was ready with the three saddle horses from the livery barn, but he had doubts.

"Are you sure you want to do this?" he asked her.

"He makes his own fate."

Elwood nodded. Malachi Nast had been warned that he might not return alive, but that didn't deter the man. He wanted the Lost Doubloon.

She looked lovely in a split skirt of pearl gray and a red silk blouse and a flat-crowned black hat. He had not known she was an accomplished horsewoman.

It was he who had little experience in the saddle, and he suspected Nast would be even worse off.

Nast appeared promptly at sundown, still in his black suit and white shirt with the boiled and starched collar.

"Well, now are we ready?" the mining entrepreneur asked. He was as eager as a chipmunk.

"Before we go, let's review the terms. You understand we will take you to the Lost Doubloon and leave you there?" Elwood asked.

"Just leave me there. That's fine. It's a three- or four-hour walk back, correct?"

Elwood nodded. "All right then."

Nast clambered awkwardly into the saddle and held the horn.

They rode quietly through the dark town, up the

grade to the south, and were soon in a silent night world. The faintest glow of the dying day still lit the northwest. A half hour later, even that had vanished and the night was lit only by bold stars. The clean rain-washed air opened the limitless heavens to his eyes.

Guadalupe led, riding expertly. Elwood brought up the rear. No one spoke. Elwood didn't want to hear a word; didn't want Nast to open his mouth. Nast didn't. He was busy memorizing every detail he could see in the dim light.

She knew exactly where she was going, and after an hour they began their descent toward the white-sand arroyo, which was rain-dappled now. They crossed it and she pushed through the dense brush on the far side until they had traversed the chaparral-choked flats and rode into the open hills beyond. They were still miles from the old Rio Blanco up the arroyo. She turned right, and rode through open country dotted only by juniper and cactus, riding parallel to the great white wash but a mile or so south of it. Then, finally, she descended toward the wash. How she knew when to do that Elwood couldn't imagine, but she had senses and intuitions he could only marvel at. When she stopped, he vaguely recognized the area, though he couldn't say why.

Their horses were standing on top of the Lost Doubloon. Below, the loose soil of the landslide had been solidified and hardened and eroded by steady rain and then baked by the sun, and it looked like the adjacent naked clay.

"All right, Mr. Nast. You may get down."

Nast peered around. "Here? I don't see it."

"It is here."

"How could there be a mine here? Where's the rock? You're going to leave me here? Is that brush down there?"

"That's brush. That is old Rio Blanco, this is the Doubloon."

"I don't follow."

"You're standing on the mine."

"But I don't see it."

"We promised to bring you to the mine," Guadalupe said. "And we have. Now we will go."

"But wait! Where is it?"

"We told you it no longer exists; it is buried."

"Where is it buried?"

She pointed straight down. "Here."

"We're on top it? I'll find it, no thanks to you."

"It is yours if you want it," Elwood said.

"Is this the truth? Are you telling it the way it is?"

"A man who schemes to extract money from widows with lies about a ransom ought not to be asking such things," Elwood said.

Nast ignored that. "Which way is Rio Blanco?" he asked.

Elwood pointed exactly toward the new Rio Blanco. "It's about seven miles that way. I have a question and consider it carefully: Would you like us to take you back to Rio Blanco now? You have a choice. We'll put you on the horse and take you to our office. You can return when you're better prepared to do some prospecting."

"I didn't come all this way just to abandon what's mine," Nast said. "I claim it."

"Then that is your choice. You are at the mine. You are standing on it. Have we fulfilled our terms?" Elwood asked.

"How should I know? I suppose so. I'll find it."

"Señor Nast, do you wish to save your life? Come back with us. Don't give yourself to the Devil. He is here, waiting for you," Guadalupe said.

"I'll find it," he yelled. "I own it."

"Adios," she said.

They rode back with the spare horse, again by a roundabout route, and arrived in Rio Blanco in the small hours. Neither of them spoke.

They had seats on the noon stage to Silver City, the beginning of a long, sad journey to the capital of Mexico to reclaim a body. They boarded the stage that noon, having seen no sign of Malachi Cromwell-Nast. She wore black, but also a sweet smile. Their trunks were loaded into the boot, and two more passengers boarded, both with boozy breaths. She slipped her hand into his and held it as the coach jerked to life and they rolled away.